THE REGENT'S REIGN

ALEX MCGILVERY

The Regent's Reign

Copyright © 2018 by Alex McGilvery

This book is a work of fiction. Names, characters, businesses, organizations, places, events and incidents either are the product of the author's imagination or are used fictitiously. Any resemblance to actual persons, living or dead, events, or locales is entirely coincidental.

For information contact:
http://alexmcgilvery.com

ISBN: 978-1-989092-00-2

CHAPTER 1

The dress had looked beautiful in the morning when her maid dressed her, but now it weighed on Marriette like a heavy chain. She rested her hand on her husband's arm to maintain balance as she navigated the rough cobbles forming the street in this district of Bellopolis.

"I hadn't expected the simple act of opening a school to require such a circus." Marriette leaned a little more on Torrance's arm. As the King's Ward and Regent, she would not give in to exhaustion. She looked around at the people, both those protecting her and those who came to see her.

Marshal prowled ahead of her examining everything from the crowds to the windows overlooking the street. Men in the crowd watched too. Three more followed behind her. Torrance held her right arm, and at her left the secretary of the day walked with a disapproving look etched on his face. From the slippers he wore, the man rarely left the palace walls. A maid walked behind the soldiers and at the tail end of the parade, a carriage rumbled along in case the Regent became tired.

Marriette was far beyond tired, but not ready to give in and ride. Her people had turned out in hundreds and thousands to see her. Marshal wouldn't let her greet individuals, but she smiled and nodded to those who waved. One more block to the new school and at least she would be able to stand instead of walk. There might even be water.

Marshal stiffened and strode to the side of the road. A man quailed under the warrior's glare. With good reason, as Marshal loomed over everybody—the tallest and biggest man Marriette had ever seen. It appeared from where she stood as if another poor soul had forgotten the edict and carried a belt knife.

As the man wilted, three more men burst out of the crowd carrying knives which might as well have been swords. Marriette drew breath to warn Marshal, but the men behind her were faster.

"Attack!" one of them shouted. Marshal pushed the man he was talking to away and dashed toward the three. One turned to face him while the other two charged toward Marriette. The soldiers behind ran to place themselves between her and the threat. Torrance pulled her back toward the carriage holding his drawn sword in his other hand. Another three men with knives jumped out of the crowd at her. The first impaled himself on Torrance's sword. The second tangled in the body and he, the dead attacker, and Torrance went down in a heap.

The third man grinned and stalked toward Marriette. She backed up and tripped on a cobble. The dress made it impossible for her to find her footing again. Marriette landed hard on the pavement. A crack sounded from the hand she'd tried to catch herself with, and pain shot up into her shoulder. The attacker twirled his sword and let his grin widen.

Marriette's skirts were up past her waist, her right hand broken and trapped beneath her. Her left hand scrabbled uselessly at the mounds of fabric. The maid screamed and ran at the man with the knife. He swatted at her, but missed. She stabbed at him with a comb, but it bounced off leather armor under his clothes. He swore at her and swung again, but once more missed by a hair's breadth. The maid scratched his face with the comb and blood ran into his eye.

The attacker who had fallen with Torrance and the first man pushed himself to his feet and ran past his comrade. He kept trying to kill the maid yet inexplicably couldn't succeed. The secretary placed himself between Marriette and the man, but the attacker punched him with the hilt of the knife without missing a step. He threw himself at Marriette and plunged the knife toward her heart. She tried to roll out of the way, but the dress held her pinned.

White hot pain seared through her as the knife cut through the jewelled bodice. One gem turned the blade enough so it didn't find her heart. He raised his hand to try again but Torrance's sword skewered his knife hand and twisted the knife away. Her husband's boot connected soundly with the assassin's head and the man rolled away, his eyes already glazing over.

Torrance knelt beside her and tried to stop the bleeding. The secretary tore his shirt sleeve away and handed it to Torrance. A brave gesture, but not enough to save her. The pain moved from being white hot to ice cold. Marriette shivered on the street. She tried to lift her hand to touch Torrance's face, but even the comfort of touch lay beyond her strength.

An old woman pushed her way out of the crowd and knelt opposite from Torrance.

"Let me help her."

"Please!" Torrance's face crumpled with fear and hope.

She put her hands on Marriette's wound and sang notes that set Marriette's teeth on edge. She wanted to scream or cry, but no sound would come out. Her lungs held no air, and she couldn't draw any in. The old woman leaned down and blew into Marriette's mouth. Rank breath filled her and lifted her ribs.

She could breathe again.

Marshal loomed over the old woman.

"Stop." She put her hand out in command. The pain vanished with the word. Marshal frowned but stepped back.

"Rest," the old woman brushed her hand across Marriette's right wrist. "And you'll be fine." She pushed herself to her feet, curtseyed to Marriette, then disappeared into the crowd.

"We should have held her for questioning," Marshal looked after the old woman with a scowl on his face.

"She saved my life," Marriette said.

"We must get you back to the palace and out of this dress." The maid came over and arranged Marriette's skirts carefully.

Two men lifted Marriette and carried her to the carriage. They handed her up to others who laid her on one seat.

"Thank you," Torrance said, "we'll be fine now." The men nodded and closed the door after the maid climbed in.

"You are still holding your sword." Marriette tried to keep her words light.

"I will carry it until you are safe within the palace walls." He sat at Marriette's head and planted the tip of his sword between his feet.

"It's a shame about the dress. The colour is especially nice on you." The maid used a damp cloth to clean Marriette's face.

"You are brave," Marriette said to the girl. Though when she looked harder the maid appeared closer to her age.

"You are my Queen," the girl said, "I couldn't let that horrible man hurt you."

"But you could have been killed." Marriette touched the maid's cheek. "I would be terribly upset if you died because of me."

"You're a Queen." The maid frowned slightly. "People are supposed to die for you."

They arrived at the palace and servants came with a chair to take Marriette into her rooms.

More maids fussed over her while the maid who had ridden with her back from the attack broke down into tears and begged to be excused.

"Come back when you're ready," Marriette said. "I'm sure you saved my life." The maid curtseyed and ran off weeping. Strange she would show no upset until they were safe, but everyone was different.

The dress vanished and Marriette was placed in a bath with hot water. A young girl sponged the blood from Marriette's skin and looked with wide eyes at the scar marking the top of Marriette's breast.

"When?" the girl asked.

"Just a short time ago. I was dying. I knew it, then an old woman came and healed me before disappearing again." Marriette ran her finger along the scar and a faint echo of pain twinged her chest. "Apparently she healed my wrist as well."

"Maybe she was a saint!" The girl's eyes widened.

"Perhaps."

"The Doctor is here to see the Regent."

"Bring me my robe," Marriette said. "Let's get this over with."

The Doctor limped in, a man of indeterminate age who leaned on a cane. An assistant carried a large bag.

"Let's see now." The Doctor made opening motions with his hands. Marriette pulled her robe open far enough to show the scar. "Does it still hurt?"

"If I put pressure on it."

"Hmmm." The Doctor peered at the scar with his hands behind his back. "Not a complete healing then, but enough to stop the blood loss. Did you have trouble breathing?"

"Before she helped me," Marriette said.

"As I thought, the knife punctured your lung. You are fortunate, your Majesty, even I would have a hard time preserving your life in such circumstance." He stepped back from her and tilted his head. His sandy coloured eyes gazing into hers. "You must drink water to replace the blood you lost. I will speak to the kitchen about sending you plenty of red meat as well. Walk around if you must, but do not lift anything with your left arm for at least a week."

"I barely lift anything with either arm." Marriette let her exasperation at how everyone spoiled her tinge her words.

The Doctor put his hand over her right arm before nodding. "Your right arm is fine. You should have no problem." He nodded in satisfaction. "If the pain returns or you bleed, have me summoned at once. You will want to avoid more such adventures if you wish your child to be born healthy and whole." The Doctor reached back, and his assistant put a package in his hand. "For mild pain, make a tea of this and drink it with honey. Don't overdo it." He put the package on a table beside the chair, then bowed and left, followed by his assistant.

"Your Majesty!" The young girl who had helped her in the bath looked at her with a glowing smile. "An heir—your husband must be very pleased."

"I'm sure he will be once he knows," Marriette tugged her robe closed. The Doctor never touched her, or anyone else she'd ever seen. Yet he knew things about her that should be impossible. She'd only started to wonder this very week. She smiled and wrapped her arms around her. "Please go ask him to attend me here." The girl curtseyed and ran out of the room. The other maids helped her don a dress to make sure she was properly attired for her husband.

Torrance strode into the room and knelt at Marriette's feet.

"I should have been faster," he said. "I let them slow me down."

"You slowed them down as well." Marriette touched his face. "And you were there when I needed you."

"After you were wounded," Torrance clenched his fist in the fabric of her skirt. "I was sure I had lost you."

"We owe a debt to the old woman."

"Marshal is out of sorts because none of his men can find her."

"I will deal with Marshal in time." Marriette put her hand on her husband's shoulder and played with the hair that curled there. A few grey hairs hid among the dark.

"I have more momentous things to discuss." She couldn't keep the smile from her lips.

"More important than you almost dying on an assassin's blade?"

"Much more important," Marriette said. "It appears you are to have an heir."

If Torrance's head had snapped up much harder, he would have broken his neck. Tears he hadn't shed over her on the road sprang to his eyes. Marriette couldn't think of any more words she wanted to say. She pulled him to her as the maids discreetly left the room.

It didn't take Torrance nearly as long to get the dress off her as it had taken the maids to put it on.

CHAPTER 2

Marriette followed Marshal's stiff back down the hall toward the Council Chambers. The only words he'd spoken to her after the attack on the street were a request to retire. That was a week ago.

"Marshal." Marriette stopped and glared at him. "I will have words with you."

"Your Majesty." He stopped, but did not turn to face her.

"I must know what is bothering you." She made her words hard to break through the shell.

"I do my duty," he said. If it had been any one else she would have sworn he was forcing back tears.

"You do." Her voice softened. "Yet..."

"I failed you."

"How many men did you kill during the attack?"

"Eleven, Your Majesty,"

"I don't call that a failure." Marriette winced at how much those men must have hated her.

"The one that mattered..." Marshal turned. His face twisted with the effort of speaking. "I should have been at your side."

"Yes," Marriette said, "and yet I live, as King Harald lives. You are but one man; you must place yourself where you will do the most good. These men threw their lives away knowing you must join the fray. Then they were free to send others to attack with less interference. Some things you cannot predict, Marshal. You are destroying yourself trying to cover every eventuality. If you are destroyed, you will not be able to do the duty you have taken on yourself."

"Your Majesty." Marshal took a deep breath and visibly pushed his demons aside. "You are kind. I will think on what you have said."

"I repeat what King Harald told you," Marriette said. "The day you hand over the burden of being Marshal to another, you will be free to do whatever you wish."

Marshal turned and led the way to the Council Chamber. He opened the door and stepped through. Marriette imagined him glaring at the members of the Council and their aides. Unfortunately, while Marshal protected her from physical attack, the barbed words the Council threw at her were beyond his reach.

She took her own deep breath. Four months and no word from King Harald. It would take no less than six months for him to reach the Holy Father in Banstophe and return if he did nothing but travel and sleep.

She walked through the door and nodded at the men who rose at her entrance. She chose not to notice reTaggin's backside barely left his seat. The others stood and watched her with various expressions of anger and distrust.

Torrance smiled at her, but seGraine looked at a spot on the wall over her head. Raspin deLanguiers played with a coin and ignored her completely. He was, until she bore a male child, her heir to the deLanguiers estate. He must pray every night for her to have no such a child. ReTaggin thumped back on his seat as soon as she seated herself. Marshal's growl tickled her teeth, but she'd forbidden him from reacting to any but the most egregious breaches of conduct. As edifying as it had been to see Marshal thrash the young vonFrome boy for his rudeness, it didn't endear her to the Council.

"Gentlemen." She tried not to look at the Archbishop's seat. He hadn't been present in weeks. His health continued to fail rapidly, but he refused to let anyone take the seat without the Holy Father's approval.

"The dry summer was hard on my grape vines." SeGraine glared as if Marriette caused the weather. "With the amount of wine being imported from Vandelusia, I cannot sell my wine."

"So you would cut my throat to save your own?" ReTaggin didn't look at all old and frail as he glowered across the table.

"A tariff on Vandelusian wine would be ill advised at this time," Raspin sounded bored. "We cannot afford to trouble the Empire with the King away."

"I agree," Torrance grimaced at Raspin's raised eyebrow. "I know, we do not agree on much, but I agree a tariff is not a good idea. We still buy more from the Empire than we sell. If they were to decide to make it difficult for us to sell..."

"Spoken like a true lapdog," seGraine said. "You sell more to the Empire than the rest of us together. If they ever invade it will be on ships built with leBraun wood."

"Gentlemen," Marriette tapped her fan on the table. "I think we can agree few people will mistake seGraine vintages for the wine imported from Vandelusia. I am happy to let those with no taste drink imported wine. I see no shortage of thirsty throats."

10

"We were told you are carrying an heir," Raspin pursed his lips.

"That is true," Marriette said. *Which of my maids is in his pay?* "The Doctor confirmed it when he examined me after the attack by the assassins."

"That was a week ago, and you didn't inform the Council?" SeGraine scowled at her.

"If it is a boy, it might solve our succession problem," reTaggin steepled his fingers. "The girl could stay on as Regent until the boy reached maturity."

Marshal's growl rattled her teeth, but had no visible effect on the old man.

"We have no succession problem." Marriette rapped on the table to emphasize her words. "The King is on pilgrimage. When he returns, you will have your King."

"If he returns," seGraine said. "We have heard nothing from him since he left. We know many ships have gone down between Belandria and the Empire."

"His penance was to lay down being King. He can hardly do that if he is constantly writing to give you instruction."

SeGraine frowned as if the King's lack of correspondence were a personal affront.

The Council stumbled from one subject to the next, mostly wrangling with each other. Marriette had given up hope any one of them would give her useful advice. The actual ruling of the country went on without her interference as troops of scribes sent out edicts and bills and who knows what else. She wondered if these old men—well, mostly old men, she thought, looking at Torrance and vonFromme—knew how little difference their ranting made.

***

"They are so like children," Marriette complained to the Archbishop. She went to visit every evening. Torrance teased her that she had thrown him over for the old man.

"Indeed," the Archbishop said, "but very dangerous children. Prone to tantrums and odd fits of jealousy, but they have private armies and spies, and a word from them can kill."

"I will remind myself of this next time I feel a giggle trying to replace the solemn face I wear at the meetings."

"Please do." The old man smiled at her. "I do not wish to survive you."

"You do look better today."

"It helps that the young man poisoning me is in the cells."

"Poison!"

"Old fool that I am, I got complacent and stopped having all my meals tasted. I had a bottle of particularly pleasant vintage seGraine gave me. I was working my way through it. It took me a while to isolate where the poison came from. Once I knew that, it became easy to trap the poor young soul who was murdering me. He used my greed against me. I would trap the last drop out of the neck of the bottle with my finger and lick it off. He rubbed the poison on the outside of the bottle. The only person who knew of my habit was the noviate who brought me my evening meals. I fear he came from Reme and the Emperor; our local assassins are not so subtle."

"Might he have been used by someone else?"

"Probably, probably, Church politics are even more twisted than what you deal with. We are all so sure we are achieving God's will, and we need to look holy even while our hearts are as thick with sin as any."

Marriette shifted. What hope did any of them have if even the Church was filled with plotting and murder?

"Don't look so downcast, my dear," The Archbishop patted her hand. "God has been using the Church for centuries to do his work, flaws and all. Just keep in mind not to blindly trust everyone who wears the robes."

"You're getting better, so you'll keep things in line until Harald gets back."

"I pray so," the Archbishop said, "but it is not in my hands."

"I will add my prayers to yours," Marriette said. "I want to see you in your seat in the Council before too long."

"Ah, well," the Archbishop shook his head. "I will have to work on my self-control. It wouldn't do to have the Archbishop break into giggles during council."

***

Marriette bent over her needlework. Torrance went over to his own home while she visited the Archbishop. He needed to reassure the staff they weren't forgotten. As hard as she tried, Marriette hadn't made to her home twice in the months she'd been regent. Torrance often returned later than she to their rooms.

The knock on the paneling was the *long, short, long, short* Mastor Tiron used to announce his presence.

"Come." Marriette threaded another needle. The panel opened and Master Tiron slid into the room.

"I hear the Archbishop improves," he said, "and a young noviate answers questions in the cells beneath the cathedral."

"As always," Marriette stitched carefully, "your hearing is excellent." She looked up at him. "What else have you heard?"

"Your Marshal is trying to track down the people who hired the attempt on your life in the street last week. I suspect he will be disappointed. They appear to be a group of men who were disinclined to be ruled by a Queen. Hard to say as not one of them survived the fray. Your husband's boots are hard." He shrugged slightly. "Marshal is also trying to find the woman who so miraculously healed you."

"Why?" Marriette paused in her work.

"Someone who can heal a mortal wound is dangerous to leave wandering free. What if they start healing the wrong mortal wounds?"

"You are twisted."

"Why, thank you." Master Tiron nodded at her with no sign of sarcasm. "I brought you a gift. He pulled out a piece of leather and a bag. "This is a very old game. Kings play chess, spies play this game." The leather had been marked out into squares. The spymaster pulled a smaller bag out and placed two pieces diagonally in the center four squares. He showed her they were black on one side and white on the other. He put two more pieces with the white side up.

"At its most basic," he said. "you play with only one kind of piece. Later we will add other pieces to make it more complex. The idea is every piece can be turned." He flipped a piece over from black to white, then back. "With this level a piece on each side will turn a piece, or a row." He placed a black piece down and turned over one of the white pieces. Marriette took a turn and flipped a piece to white. They played for a while until most of the pieces on the board were black.

"You must be willing to sacrifice—sometimes the path to victory is to appear to lose." He stood up and gave her a brief bow. He'd vanished into the secret passage before Torrance came through the door.

"I see your secret admirer paid you a visit," Torrance said, waving a hand at the game, still mostly covered with black pieces.

"You realize he is undoubtedly listening?" Marriette gathered the pieces and put them back in the smaller bag. She pulled a few pieces out of the larger bag. They had symbols inscribed on them. Some on both sides, some on one.

"I hope so." Torrance sat down beside her. "So how do you play?"

Marriette taught him the game. He beat her three times in a row, but the last game she came close to winning. When Torrance slept beside her, possible moves ran through her head until she gave herself a shake and put all thought aside for the night.

CHAPTER 3

Harald struck his broken knife against the stone trying to get the spark to land on his last shred of dry tinder. It did and a tiny flame flared up. He put twigs on the fire, then larger sticks. He split sticks with his knife and put them split side against the flames. He added ever larger pieces until the fire grew strong enough to hold its own against the half rain, half fog soaking them to the skin.

"If I'd known you were expecting," he said, "I would have not been so insistent we walk the entire distance."

"If you hadn't decided to walk." Sarandia held her hands out to the heat. "We would not be alive to shiver in front of this marvelous fire."

"This penance has been nothing but bad luck," Harald picked up more wood to split, "with the ship sinking and all our gear being lost. I don't know how we will get an audience with the Holy Father without the letter from the Archbishop."

"You have your ring." Sarandia smiled at him. "Trust yourself, trust God."

His stomach growled before he could answer.

"We used to sneak out, my brother and I," Harald said, "and light fires in the woods to roast apples. I'm sure our guards were given strict instructions not to let on they were close by. It was as close as the heir and a prince could come to being alone. When he died of the fever, I never went out to the woods again. I never thought our struggles to light a fire would come in so useful."

"We are near a village," Sarandia rubbed her stomach. "We can work tomorrow in exchange for food. It is good luck to feed a pilgrim."

"How do you know we are near a village?"

"A haze hung over the trees; smoke from many chimneys."

She huddled close under his cloak. Her belly stretched the ragged clothes they wore, but not big enough yet to be an encumbrance.

Harald fed the fire, keeping it barely large enough to warm them. He had no desire to let bandits know they were here; though they looked poor enough, the signet ring he wore in a pouch around his neck was worth a kingdom's ransom.

All the years he'd been married to his princess, he never knew the strength of her determination. Days when he wanted to lie beside the road and give up, she dragged him up and along their way. By mutual consent they stayed away from the main highway. They travelled tiny paths winding across the country from village to village. All that mattered was each morning they walked toward the rising sun.

They rose with the sun and hiked into the village as the sun crested the trees. Harald took Sarandia's hand and led into the church where they knelt in prayer.

"Pilgrims?" An old priest nodded at them before he celebrated the Mass. After the liturgy, they drank weak tea and shared a slice of bread with him.

"Thank you, father, for the hospitality." Harald picked the last crumbs from the plate.

"There's not much work here," the priest said. "Farmer Creckan on the way out of the village felled a tree; he may trade some work with the ax for some bread."

Harald walked through the village holding Sarandia's hand. The warmth of her hand in his gave him confidence. Though he had been a king over a prosperous land, and God willing would be again, he needed confidence.

Farmer Creckan did indeed want some help with the ax. Sarandia helped the farmer's wife with the laundry as Harald chopped the tree into lengths then spit the logs to stack them in a shed beside the house. Three months ago, Harald's hands would have been covered with blisters. Now he picked out splinters between the callouses on his hands. The ache in his shoulders and arms warmed him. Such satisfaction had always eluded him as King.

The Farmer put them up in the barn with fresh straw. Harald and Sarandia nestled down to stay warm. It didn't get as cold as in Belandria, but winter was coming to the land and the nights could be chill.

They finished with the tree the next day. The last swing of the ax, the shaft vibrated and fell out of Harald's hands. The ax head sat jammed in a knot in the log.

"Eh." The farmer rolled his shoulders. "Tis a blessing it made it this long. Ye keep the handle. I'll whittle another one soon enough. The head is the precious thing. T'was my grandfather's, made with real iron."

They walked back to the house to eat a meal of bread and barley soup. In the morning, the farmer met them at sunup with a loaf of bread and sliver of cheese for the road. He handed Sarandia a stick with the bark whittled off and polished smooth.

"'Twill make your journey shorter." The farmer shook Harald's hand. "Light a candle for an old man in the great cathedral when you get there."

When they lit all the candles they had been asked to light, there would be a night sky's worth of light. Harald intended to light them all.

The path led them past other villages. Harold traded work for a sliver of steel pretending to be a knife. He used it to smooth the ax handle and when it was smooth to cover it with decorations.

"Don't go into the next village," a fellow pilgrim warned them. "They don't take kindly to pilgrims. You'll want to turn on the next path. It swings wide of the village. An old woman in a house where the path meets the road will give you a cup of water from her well in return for a blessing."

"Thanks," Harald said.

"Keep that stick of yours loose in your belt too," the pilgrim said, "there's waggoners about."

Harald found the path and they walked through a pleasant wood. Every so often sounds from the village would float across the fields to their ears.

"Why is it always the prosperous villages that don't like pilgrims?" Sarandia asked.

"Perhaps they wish to keep their prosperity." A dark man leaned against a tree beside the path. He smiled at them and showed them his open hands. "I am curious about your club," he said without moving from the tree. "If my eyes don't mistake me, those could be waggoner runes on it."

"I carved them from what I remember," Harald looked the club. "I didn't intend anything."

"They are powerful runes, for not being intended." The man shrugged. "but safe enough I imagine. I'm trying to imagine where you might have seen such runes. A palace or at least a rich house. They are for protection and strength. May I?" He put out his hand. Harald laid the ax handle in it. "My mother could tell you what each of these meant and what they meant all together. I see bits and pieces. Alas, I haven't seen her in many years. She went across the sea to find a place where we weren't feared and loathed for daring to breathe good air. That she hasn't returned suggests she has failed to find such a place." He flipped the handle in the air, then tossed it back to Harald. "May it bring you such fortune as it can."

"Thank you," Harald said, "and may you too find what you seek."

The man's eyes widened slightly and he gave a bow, still leaning against his tree. Harald nodded and they kept on their way. The old woman's water slid down his throat cool and refreshing and she was pleased with their blessing. A little further down the road they left the road to sleep under the shelter of a tree whose branches reached the ground.

Sounds of fighting woke Harald in the night. He crawled out from under the tree and crept to the road. The man from the path the day before fought against three opponents. Steel sang in the air. The man held his own, but it wouldn't last. Not if he refused to take openings to disable or kill those who were trying to kill him. Harald put his hand to the ax handle and ran his fingers across the runes. They were from the Shield of Binding. He suspected the Binding was waggoner magic, but no one talked about it. The man grunted. One of the opponents must have struck home.

Harald pushed himself to his feet and used the club to lay out one of the attackers on the road. The closest to him swung hard at his head but Harald knocked the blow away with the club and kicked at the man's knee. The other man chopped at Harald's leg. He tossed the club to his other hand while twisting away then dropped the man. The third backed away and ran into the night.

"I think I have discovered where you would have seen those runes," the man checked the two who lay on the road. "I thank you for not killing them. They are kin, though misguided." He went through their pockets efficiently, tossing a bag of coin to Harald. "I imagine you are as good with a sword as you are with a club."

"I'm a pilgrim; not supposed to carry a sword." Harald ran his fingers along the length of wood

"Of course," The man tossed the swords into the trees, pocketed a knife, then carefully used another knife to cut the men's clothes so they would fall to pieces when they stood. "Tis a shame to wander naked, but worse to shed a kin's blood. We may be even." He looked at Harald. "You may wish to wake your woman and leave this place. It will not be pleasant when they awake.

"I'm here, husband," Sarandia crawled out of the brush. Harald helped her to the road.

"I am Harald," he said to the man, "and my wife --"

"Sara." She gave Harald a quick glance.

"I am honoured with your names," the man said. "You may call me Rodrigo. It isn't my name, but I answer to it."

He led the way to the east, so Harald took their bag from Sarandia and followed, his left hand holding Sarandia. His right hand rested on the club.

By the time the sky lightened he had his arm around Sarandia, half carrying her.

"This will be far enough," Rodrigo said, "We can let your good wife rest. If you light a fire, I will see what I can find to eat."

Harald used threads pulled from his shirt and lit the fire. Rodrigo returned with a rabbit already skinned and cleaned and some tubers with dirt still clinging to them.

"You lit the fire without the tinder-root? You must be a magician." He pulled up a plant and twisted the root sharply. It puffed into a mass begging for a spark. Harald fingered another plant, but left it in the ground. Rodrigo put his root in a pouch. "Not as good as fresh, but still useful." He put the rabbit on a stick and set it to roast over the flames. The tubers he tossed into the fire.

"Now, tell me, Harald," Rodrigo raised his eyebrow. "What is the King of Belandria doing wandering the back end of nowhere dressed like a pilgrim?"

CHAPTER 4

“**W**hat makes you think I'm the King of anything?” Harald asked. *Bless all those years of keeping a straight face in Council.*

“The stick you're carrying,” Rodrigo said, “is covered with runes of power only a king's ransom could pay for. Nobody leaves things holding them lying around. Either you're the King, or the one bound to the King.”

“What is it to you who I am?” He poked at the fire. Sarandia slept under his cloak. He remembered the first time he'd seen her, coming into the grand ball room on her father's arm the day of their betrothal. A slip of a girl then, but she looked him in the eye and smiled. He fell in love and dreamed of her every night until they were married three years later. That was the second time he saw her. Harald's lips curved up at the memory. Sarandia looked dark and exotic next to his boring blond and fair skin.

"Memories are pleasant, are they not?" Rodrigo sighed and sat back. "My pledged walks with my mother on foreign shores. We speak in dreams now and again. If either of us plans to see pleasant dreams again we will need to work together."

"Trust is built," Harald turned the rabbit so it would cook evenly.

"True." Rodrigo made a face as if he swallowed something bitter. "I don't know if I have the time for trust." He reached over the fire and drew a sign in the air.

Pain exploded Harald's head. He fell back with an inarticulate cry.

"Goddess Mother, what have I done?" Rodrigro leaped over the flames to kneel at Harald's side.

"Fool," Sarandia knelt beside Rodrigo. She spat other words at him which made him go pale, but Harald didn't understand them. The pain closed down his world. If he was going to die, he'd die with Sarandia's face as the last thing he saw.

"Sorry," he said to her, "love you forever. My heart is ever yours." He found strength to lift his hand to her face and touch the tears wetting her cheeks. "Salt of my salt, joy of my joy, light of my..."

He thought the pain bad when he fell, now it wrapped around him like a great serpent and crushed him. Breathing hurt, and his heart beat agony. Harald fought back. He inhaled fire and exhaled ice. His pulse became a lash on his soul, but he refused to let go.

The light touched him and soothed the serpent.

"Oh my son, what have you wrought?" An old woman's face formed in the light. Anger flashed in those dark eyes, but not for him. "No one can carry two great bindings. My son tried a lesser rune, but the great runes will have their way. I can put the binding in abeyance for a time. Break or burn the runes and your bond with the Marshal will be restored. Don't dally, this is only for a time. I cannot say if you have more than six moons. Tell my son when all is done he must take up what he refuses." She put her finger on Harald's forehead and pushed him.

He woke with Sarandia's lips on the place where the old woman had touched him. He wrapped his arms around her and held her until he didn't have to think about breathing or listen for his heart's next beat.

Rodrigo sat slumped by the side of the fire. It was barely coals now, their rabbit charcoal. Harald sat up expecting to be weak, but moved like nothing had happened to him. He went to Rodrigo and slapped his face. The pain of the slap burned on his cheek.

"We are Bound," Harald said and stood up. He reached into the fire and picked up a coal. Rodrigo screamed and held his hand as if it were burning. Harald dropped the coal and looked into the other man's eyes. They were still wild with pain. Lines of exhaustion ran under grey skin.

"He prayed over you and called on powers I've not been taught." Sarandia came and looked at Harald's hand. The coal burned him and raised a blister. She put her hand over it and sung briefly. The blister shrank and the redness faded to his normal pale skin.

Rodrigo knelt before them.

"I am a fool and more," he said. "I acted in my own need and broke our laws. I must serve you until I make recompense for my wrongdoing."

"Whatever pain I feel, you will feel, and the reverse. If one of us dies, the other will perish within the hour. That is the Bond you have laid on us." He gripped Rodrigo's shirt and hauled him to his feet. He looked at the other man. The tightness of his grip pulled at his throat. "I am well acquainted with pain as my war masters intended. You do not seem as well trained."

"No," Rodrigo said, "pain is never something I sought."

"Your mother sends you a message," Harald spoke as clearly as he could. "When this is done you must take up what you refuse."

If Rodrigo was pale, now he looked like a ghost. He sat down abruptly and put his head in his hands.

"I should have left well enough alone, but I was going to be so clever. Now look at me."

Sarandia handed Harald a blackened tuber. He cut it open and dug the steaming center out with his fingers. Rodrigo moaned and held his hands. Harald looked at the man and started laughing. Tears ran down his face and he had to drop to his knees beside Rodrigo. Sarandia looked at him and raised her eyebrow which led to more paroxysms. Harald lay on his back and looked up at the blue sky above. Warmth from the sun caressed his face.

"Life is good," he said. "I've been through this before. When they bound Marshal to my service I had a week in which I knew every twinge and ache in the old man's body. They faded in time, but I knew in my heart the Marshal experienced whatever pain I came across, though it is limited after a time to dangerous things. There are some other aspects of the Binding I don't completely understand."

He rolled to his feet and pulled Rodrigo to his feet.

"So, what is the reason you tried to bind me?"

"I am one of two heirs to the throne of the Rehego, those you probably call waggoners as we are forbidden to own a permanent home."

"Since you were banished from your homeland for your arrogance and greed and doomed to wander ten thousand moons."

"Great," Rodrigo said, "an educated King. You don't have the whole picture though. It gets better. The White Heir has found in her search of forbidden books that if we retake the land and sacrifice the ruler on the sacred stone the doom will end."

"I wasn't aware anyone knew where the Rehego homeland is."

"A few of us know. The Grandmother and the heirs of Black and White."

"Right, so if the White Heir wants to invade and retake the homeland, I'm guessing as Black Heir you think it a very bad idea."

"Cosmically bad," Rodrigo said, "It happens to be in Lusia, capital of the Vandelusian Empire. My sister wants to go to war with the entire Empire. The scary thing is if she gets what she wants, she could win."

"Against the entire Empire?"

"She doesn't need the whole thing, just the bit of it forming our homeland. The tiny bit the Emperor calls home. The White Heir is adept at magic. As you saw, the Black Heir is not. I do have other skills."

"Thieving, spying, and poetry," Sarandia spoke from where she stood by the fire.

"Poetry?" Harald widened his eyes.

"Don't ask." Rodrigo rolled his.

"Poetry is the power of song and history." Sarandia walked over to take Harald's arm. "Did you not recognize your kin?" She lifted her face to stare Rodrigo in the eye. "Your grandmother and mine were sisters."

"Princess," Rodrigo bowed low, and would have fallen if Harald hadn't caught him.

The sound of hooves alerted Harald.

"Sarandia, take Rodrigo into the trees and hide. There are too many to fight." Harald picked another tuber out of the fire and cushioning his hands with grass, he blew on it to cool.

"Hey, you," a woman on a horse rode up so close to Harald the horse snuffled at the root he held. Five men on horseback followed her and surrounded him.

"Sorry," He patted the horse's nose, "not good for horses."

The woman nudged him with her foot and the horse danced, almost dropping her to the dirt.

"Yeah, that's him." A man rode up to Harald, the pained look on his face probably caused from the way he sat like a sack of potatoes on the beast. His horse looked at Harald and blew its air out in a heavy sigh, and Harald laughed. He sidestepped the blow the mounted man aimed at him, then caught the horse's reins as the man overbalanced and fell from the horse. He bounced to his feet with a knife in his hand.

"Asper." The woman pointed at the man. "It isn't his fault you can't ride, and it isn't the horse's fault either. Walk it off."

"You attacked my men last night." The woman turned her gaze on Harald. He wouldn't want those eyes angry at him.

"They disturbed my sleep." Harald checked the temperature of his tuber.

"What of the other one, that you aided?"

"I didn't so much aid him, as not help the others. He was quiet. I must admit I hoped to gain a copper or two for my help."

"You didn't think my men would pay you?"

"Three against one need no help, but one against three deserves something."

"So what did he give you?"

"Not a mite, but he did steal my flint. You can imagine the trouble I had starting a fire without it."

"I am sorry to hear that, though not surprised." She pulled a pouch from her side and tossed it to him. "My own flint and steel in recompense." She launched her horse down the road. The others laughed at Asper as he clambered on to the horse Harald still held for him and rode, leaning to one side, away after their leader.

Harald tossed the bag he held a few times. A sharp pain pricked his hand, so he stuffed it in his pouch. The tuber was cool enough to eat, so he ate it and kicked the fire apart. The cloak he rolled up and put over a shoulder, the day warm enough he didn't need it. The club lay on the grass where it had been covered with the cloak. He left it there after pinching the back of his hand, and walked away down the road after the horses.

He hadn't gone far when he came on the woman and her companions staring at Asper who stood on the ground looking rebellious.

"I'll not climb on that demon beast again," he said to the woman.

His horse nickered and trotted over to Harald who patted its head and commiserated on how hard it must be to have such an inept rider. He led the horse back to Asper.

"Riding isn't difficult," he said. "You must ask the horse to keep you on."

"What does a peasant know about riding?" Asper turned on Harald with his hand on his knife. "If you love the horse so much, you keep it."

"Alas, the conditions of my penance mean I must walk on my own two feet. You will need to make peace with your fear."

The knife came out so quick Harald didn't see Asper's hand move. It didn't matter, he expected the attack and was careful to not be where the knife moved. He could have taken Asper down in any number of ways Marshal had taught him. Instead he swung a haymaker, connecting with the side of the man's head and dropped him to the ground.

"You'll carry this guy, won't you?" He asked the horse which huffed and tossed its head. Harald picked the man up and slung him over the horse's back. He picked up the knife and handed it to the woman.

"Keep the knife," she said.

"I won't keep the knife of a violent man," Harald put it into her hand. Two of the other men tied Asper to the horse.

"Next time he sees you," one man said, "he's going to kill you."

"You're wrong," Harald replied. The man looked at him and opened his mouth. "He's going to try." Harald slapped the horse and it went trotting along the road. The men rode after it while the woman stared at Harald.

"You are no simple pilgrim."

"Few of us are." Harald looked back at her. She turned and rode away. This time they didn't stop.

Harald stood still on the road for a long time until the creaking of gravel announced that Rodrigo and Sarandia had caught up to him.

"I don't know anyone who could look Aisa in the eye and lie the way you did." Rodrigo said. "You must be an excellent King."

"How much information can she gain from the bag she tossed me?"

"If you had opened it and touched it," Sarandia said, "It would have enthralled you. You would never let it go. Eventually it would lead you back to her. If you weren't very strong you would be her slave."

"I won't ask how you know that," Rodrigo said, "but you are correct. Aisa is not a nice woman."

"I guessed as much when she set up Asper to be a fool to test me. She knows enough to be intrigued, but she trusts her magic like Asper trusts his knife."

"And how is that?" Rodrigo asked, but Harald just grinned. He took Sarandia's arm and set off down the road.

CHAPTER 5

The Vandelusian ambassador strolled into the Great Hall flanked by two men walking stiffly on either side of him. Most people took a second to look around the Hall when they entered for the first time. Though the tallest room in the palace, the Hall had no balconies other than tiny platforms on which archers perched. Coloured glass turned the grey floor into a riot of shades and hues which often clashed with the courtiers who invariably showed up whenever Marriette received someone in the Hall.

The ambassador may have smiled slightly, much like a parent admiring their child's work. Marshal stood behind her. The slightest rustle of fabric suggested he made some adjustment to his stance in response to the ambassador's sword. The man held his hands carefully well away from the hilt, and the escorts had conspicuously empty sheaths. Though he didn't hurry, and even chatted briefly with seGraine, it took very little time for the representative of the Empire to arrive at the foot of the dais on which Marriette sat.

"Regent," the ambassador said, and bowed deeply. "Allow me to introduce myself. I am Sier Clasighi, humble servant to the Emperor Maliantgore in Lusia. I bring his greetings and his concern for his sister's health. He was much distressed to hear of the cowardly attack upon your person."

"You are too kind." Marriette inclined her head. "God's will was to preserve my life. Please carry my greetings to my brother." The ambassador froze for a split second. *So, I can be sister, but the Emperor must remain Emperor.* "May I ask what business you had with seGraine that took precedence over your greetings to Belandria's Regent?"

Sier Clasighi coloured slightly, though whether from embarrassment or anger she couldn't tell.

"My apologies," Sier Clasighi bowed again, "I let my love of fine wine rule over propriety. I'd heard the vineyards were damaged over the summer and I wished to ensure my Emperor could purchase seGraine vintage for his cellar."

Marriette kept her expression still, but a fist settled in her stomach. A man like Sier Clasighi did nothing unintentionally. He'd deliberately insulted her to test the Regent.

"I have a cask in my cellar from two years ago," Marriette flipped her fan open to cool her face. "I have been told it is an especially fine vintage. It will be delivered to your embassy as a gift to my brother." A page slipped out of the hall. The cask would get to the embassy before the ambassador.

"You are most generous." Sier Clasighi nodded, his eyes sizing up Marriette. "My Emperor asks if you have any word of King Harald. Pilgrimages are such dangerous enterprises, even for royalty."

"I trust he is well," Marriette replied, "and knows he carries the prayers of his people with him."

"Ah." The ambassador lowered his eyes and took a humble stance. "And how may we help you during this trying time of your ruler's absence?"

"Be assured," Marriette removed every shade of emotion from her voice, "if the time comes when we require your aid, we will ask."

Marshal gasped behind her, then a thud told her he'd fallen. Boots clattered on wood and stone as guards rushed to his aid. Sier Clasighi observed with gleaming eyes and the slightest quirk to his lips.

"It appears your Marshal has been overcome. I have never heard of such unless the King is in dire straits. I do hope the prayers of your people are not in vain." His gaze on Marriette became briefly predatory before he hooded his eyes. "I will leave you to see to your subject." He bowed and sauntered away out of the hall. Marriette didn't move until the doors closed behind the man. Then she stood and followed the guards carrying Marshal out of the Great Hall.

They laid him on a table in a small room used by pages and scribes. His face was grey and he gasped for breath. The Doctor ran in and peered at the Marshal.

"His bond is causing this," the Doctor said. "The King is dead or dying."

"Not dead." Marshal's colour flooded back and he sat up. "But it is odd, the Bond has been changed somehow. My awareness of him is gone."

"You've been aware of him all this time and didn't tell me?" Marriette clenched her hands to keep from shaking him.

"My apologies, Your Majesty," Marshal hung his head. "but I only know of my awareness now it is gone."

"You will tell me immediately if anything changes, Marshal." She looked around the room. The guards stood against the wall and a couple of wide-eyed pages huddled in the corner. "The news is our King is alive. If you say anything about what you have seen, that is what you will speak. No words of changed bonds. Am I clear?" Heads nodded and the pages bowed almost to the floor.

"What happened?" SeGraine came into the room. "Only something terrible could cause the Marshal to collapse." He saw the Marshal sitting up and heaved a huge sigh.

"My apologies for my unseemly entry, Your Majesty." SeGraine went to one knee in front of her, "and my deepest apology for being the tool for that snake to insult you."

"Oh, get up." Marriette motioned to the guards who helped the older man to his feet. "He was going to insult me one way or another, and at least he complimented your wine. Now when you sell to the Empire you can state truthfully the Emperor drinks your vintages."

SeGraine's face lit up and Marriette feared he would break into a dance.

"You are a wise Queen," seGraine bowed to her.

"Regent, until King Harald gets home."

"Until he sits on the throne, you will be my Queen." He bowed over her hand and brushed the ring she wore as King's heir with his lips. "If you will excuse me?"

"Of course," Marriette said. The man ran out of the room before she finished speaking. One of the pages giggled, then covered his mouth with his hand. Marriette smiled at him, then left the room. Marshal's familiar footsteps followed her into the hall.

"You are completely recovered?" she asked.

"The pain left as quickly as it came, Your Majesty."

"I am glad to hear that," Marriette said, "I suggest you find someone and begin their training. I do not wish to be without a Marshal if something else befalls you."

"As you wish." Marshal spun around and walked away. Guards from nearby doorways stepped forward and surrounded her. It said a great deal about the man that it took eight guards to watch over her in his absence.

On an impulse, she headed toward the offices of the countless bureaucrats who, she suspected, truly ran the Kingdom. The people who worked in the offices weren't noisy, but as she entered the silence became absolute. A man walked quickly over and bowed deeply, his right eye slightly discoloured. Marriette glanced down to see the same slippers on his feet.

"My brave secretary," she said. "I have been remiss. I haven't thanked you properly for your help."

"Hardly help, Your Majesty." He turned a deep red.

"You stood between me and a man with a knife," Marriette said, "I would call that help. Now, you may be able to aid me again. Walk with me." She left the room. Murmurs followed her out into the hall. The secretary scurried along beside her. He carried his paper on a board, a quill in his hand and another behind his ear.

"I have discovered a need to know what we trade with the Emperor. What does his empire buy from us, and what do we purchase from them?"

The scratching of the pen told her he'd listened.

"I would also like to know who sells what, and who buys what," she said when the scratching stopped.

"That will take some time, Your Majesty," the secretary said, "perhaps as long as a month."

"Bring me the broad strokes as soon as you are able," she said. "If I am to call for you, what name should I use?"

"I am Jeremiah Pen." The secretary bowed briefly flourishing his pen like a sword.

34

"What reward shall I give you for your bravery, Jeremiah?"

"This," Jeremiah smiled at her, "to find information for you."

"Very well." Marriette nodded at him. "You will work for me, but you had better make sure you have a good replacement for your previous work. I don't want the government to grind to a halt for the lack of a secretary."

Jeremiah snorted, then turned red with mortification. Marriette grinned at him and waved a dismissal.

"I believe I will pay my cousin a visit," Marriette said. "Have my carriage brought around. I will change into something more suitable for his company." One guard detached from the group and jogged away toward the stables, while another ran toward her rooms. Two guards attached themselves to her squad.

Her maids had a dress laid out when she arrived in her rooms, so it didn't take long to change. The maid who had been with her on the street during the attack insisted on accompanying her outside the palace.

"Certainly," Marriette said, "though I hope we will not require your fighting skills today." The girl looked down. "I'm sorry, but I don't recall what your name is."

"There is little call for you to know it."

"I wish to know the name of my bravest maid," Marriette held the woman's gaze.

"I am called Illandria," the maid said and curtseyed.

"You are from the Queen's homeland, are you not?"

"True," Illandria said. "Some longtime servants travelled here with her."

"Do you miss your home?"

"The Queen is my home."

"Yet she is far away." Marriette sighed then chastised herself for her weakness.

"Until she returns, you are my Queen." The maid curtseyed again.

"You are the second person to tell me that today," Marriette said.

They walked surrounded by guard to the carriage. Four guards rode on the carriage, and four rode horses around it. The maid sat across from Marriette.

Something about Illandria bothered Marriette. One second she was holding up a dress or fussing over Marriette's hair, then the next she was as still and quiet as Marshal.

"How many of you travelled here with your Queen?"

"Twelve, Your Majesty."

"Enough so one of you is always at hand day or night?"

Illandria nodded her head.

"Are you bound like the Marshal?"

"By oath," Illandria said. "Magic leaves traces which can betray." She set aside being a maid, like putting off a cloak. Now, she looked every bit as lethal as Marshal.

"Our Queen asked us to guard you as we guarded her. She thought it the best way to increase the likelihood of your survival."

"I see," Marriette said, "and what are the oddsmakers saying?"

"You handled the ambassador better than you might have, but Marshal collapsing will set dangerous rumours flying."

"The odds?"

Illandria shook her head.

"Perhaps one in two."

"From your tone, you are being generous." The sounds of people going about their business intruded into the carriage. People called cheerful greetings to the guards. She imagined people doffing hats and waving, and men in upper rooms, bows stretched taut ready for the hunt.

"I think we should discuss ways of increasing those odds." Marriette said. The Carriage turned and pulled up in front of what used to be her father's home, now officially hers. Every time she visited she had to fight off the shakes.

"Courage," Illandria whispered as the carriage door swung open.

A guard helped her out. The door of her home opened. Raspin came out and bowed deeply.

"To what do I owe the pleasure of this visit?" He straightened and glared at Marriette.

"I wish to speak about our House's relationship with the Empire," Marriette said.

"Very well, Duchess, if you will follow me." He turned and led her into a house she barely recognized. Art hung on the walls and greenery occupied the windows. Carpets covered the stone floors and dampened the echo. They stopped in a room with afternoon sun glowing through the windows. A tray with a steaming tea pot and cups sat waiting for them.

Raspin waved away his staff and Marriette nodded to Illandria.

"Perhaps you may go to the kitchen and see if they will serve you tea there."

"Of course." Raspin rang a bell. "My staff will take you there."

"So you suspect me of colluding with the Empire?" Raspin asked as soon as they were alone.

"Are you?"

He snorted and poured the tea. He let her pick a cup, then sipped from his.

"What goods do we sell to the Empire?" Marriette asked after tasting the tea.

"Grain, lumber, wine, some hand crafts that catch the fancy of the wealthy. Salted fish from our coastal holdings."

"And what do we purchase from them?"

"Weapons, tools, knowledge, toys for people who must show their wealth."

"Great fuss is made about our wealth, but Torrance has suggested the Houses are not as rich as we used to be."

"Mismanagement has gutted our holdings." Raspin drank again. "I've heard rumours of landowners selling peasants as slaves. None of our people—I won't allow my people to waste resources."

"Peasants are nothing but resources?" Marriette set her tea cup down carefully.

"They are resources as well as people," Raspin waved his hand irritably. "Your Torrance is right. Trained people have more value, just as lumber or ore is more valuable when it is processed. I have been trying to build on some of what I see him doing."

"I approve," Marriette said.

"You asked me to manage the estate while you played at being Queen. I didn't ask for your approval."

"You don't like that a deLanguiers is Regent?"

"I don't like that a woman rules the country. We are a laughing stock. The ambassador would never have insulted the King."

"Yet, here we are," Marriette picked up her cup and turned it in her fingers.

"The King gave us little choice." Raspin stared into her eyes. "I will celebrate the day when I am free of my oath to serve you."

"I will too, cousin. But in the meantime, I sit on the throne."

"He might have put a dog on the throne, and I would be bound by my oath to serve it."

"Very good." Marriette laughed and stood up. "Keep in mind Raspin, I too have teeth." She left the room and a girl in deLanguiers colours guided her to the door where Illandria met her.

They walked out to where the guards joined them and climbed back onto the carriage.

"So," Marriette asked after she recounted the conversation, "did we improve the odds or not?"

"It depends on the balance between your cousin's desire to keep his oath and his loathing of a woman who took the position he thinks should be his. People do strange thing when they are that finely balanced."

CHAPTER 6

Marriette walked into the Council, and seGraine stood before any of the others. ReTaggin's sour look hadn't changed.

"In my day we didn't let any ragtag ambassador waltz in and insult the throne," he said once he'd sat down again.

"I don't recall any recent wars with the Empire." Torrance sounded amused. "If we'd hung ambassadors on the city walls, I'm sure I would have heard about it from my father."

"The Empire didn't much care about us then," duSarche said. He'd returned from his estates on the coast. Marriette didn't know anything about him other than he was a loner and preferred to live on his estate as much as his wife and his duties allowed. "They were skirmishing on their eastern border. Now they've settled the border for a time, and we're getting richer. We'd give

40

the Empire a foothold on this side of the sea. They may not invade, but they'll try something to at least gain control. Don't sign anything a Lusian ambassador puts in front of you."

"We have to have some trade treaties, agreements," seGraine tapped on the table with his finger. "The Empire is our biggest customer."

"We've done fine until now," duSarche leaned back and crossed his arms. "I've seen the ships they come trading in. Wouldn't be hard to turn them into warships and blockade us. We've got nothing to match them. A few old traders and a lot of fishing boats."

"We will talk trade," Marriette said, "and we will continue to talk trade until everyone is heartily sick of it. Talk doesn't mean we will sign anything."

"What are you going to do about that Lady Joan the King sent up North?" ReTaggin spoke into the brief silence.

"Why do I need to do anything about Lady Joan?" Marriette raised her eyebrows.

"She's kicked out anyone of noble blood from her holding, and she's letting the peasants run everything. Place is going to be a den of thieves if you don't take it in hand."

"I will send a letter to her and find out what is happening."

"You need to put her back in her place!" ReTaggin thumped the table.

"So you want me to go against the direct word of your King?" Marriette let her hands open on the table. *Don't let this old fool get you angry.* She held his eyes with hers until he dropped his gaze to the table.

"The King isn't coming home." Raspin sounded bored. "Marshal's little fainting spell was the King dying. It is time to secure the throne, and which means appointing a proper heir."

"The King—" Torrance raised his hand.

"The King appointed the heir without consulting us, then coerced our oaths to her." Raspin half stood and leaned over the table.

"I'm not aware of any law requiring the King to consult us." Torrance ignored Raspin. "He is King because his great-grandfather coerced oaths from our grandfathers. His rule is absolute and he met with the Council out of courtesy. Would you allow your councils do tell you who your heir should be?"

"My people want me to be the heir!"

"You would love to steal the deLanguiers estate from Marriette."

Raspin reached across to Torrance. Marriette tapped the table with her fan. The boom of Marshal's staff striking the floor froze the men.

"Gentlemen, sit." Marriette put as much bite in her words as she dared.

"I demand satisfaction," Raspin said, still standing and pointing at Torrance.

"No." Marriette sat back in her chair and tapped the arm of her chair with her fan. "We believe any insult to be directed to us as Regent and Heir to the throne of Belandria. If you wish, you may meet our champion in battle. We will not be pleased with anything but you personally putting your life on the line. There are many eager candidates for those seats you occupy."

"But--"

"Do not test us on this, cousin," Marriette said with as much control as she could muster. "We do not wish to appoint another heir, as your management of my estate has been adequate." She stood. "We are adjourned, gentlemen, unless there are any other concerns you wish to bring to my attention?" She held the gaze of each one, then walked out of the room.

"If your Majesty permits," Marshal said, "there is a room the King retreated to when his duties caused him distress."

"A torture chamber?" Marriette asked.

"In a manner of speaking," Marshall led her to a door and dismissed the guard standing there. A bar slid across the door to lock them in.

"Be sure," Marshal held her eyes, "you trust completely anyone you allow in this room. There is only one door, and no secret passages. Royalty needs a safe place to express their rage where it won't cost anyone their head." He handed her a wooden sword. "Attack me."

"I know nothing of sword play," Marriette turned the sword in her hands.

"This isn't about learning the sword, though I can teach you. It is about releasing the anger which will otherwise poison you."

Marriette screamed inarticulately and swung at Marshal. He parried her blow and she swung again. After a surprisingly short interval her arms ached, and her stomach no longer boiled.

"I would like to know better what I am doing," Marriette handed the sword back to Marshal.

"I will arrange it." Marshal ran his fingers along the sword, then replaced it in the rack. "You will need armour and padding. I will talk to the armourer and have him come and measure you."

***

Lady Joan leaned her staff against the corner of the barn. "Thanks for the workout, Suse."

"It is a wonderful way to relieve tension," Suse stood barely to Joan's shoulders. Her blond hair hung raggedly to her shoulders while blue eyes twinkled at Joan. Joan placed her a decade or more older than her, but Suse ruled her farm with more authority than the King in his palace, or more correctly Marriette as the King's Regent.

"It put that reTaggin punk on his ear," Joan rolled her head to relax the muscles in her shoulders. "It is bad enough having those young hangers on, without them deciding to wed me with neither the ceremony nor the consent."

"Round here we don't call that wedding." Suse spun her staff until it hummed in the air.

"Well, I've sent him home along with the rest of the lazy bunch. If they don't work, they can't stay."

"Sounds fair enough to me." Suse leaned her staff in the corner, not at all out of breath from the workout. She led the way out of the barn and barred the door behind them. "Barn will be useful for storing the crop come the harvest. You might even think about putting in some animals for the summer."

"I don't know anything about farming or animals." Joan turned to look at the barn.

"Plenty of people to help you out," Suse said. They walked along a dirt path to a stone wall. Joan stepped over the wall.

"It's nice not needing to go all the way around to the gate to get to the barn now."

"Widow Frank's house is almost done, my man said. You'll need to decide what to do next. "

"You might as well get a holder's meeting put together," Joan said. "Is tomorrow too soon?"

"Should be good. Smells like rain, so the day'll be good for nothing but talk." Suse left Joan at the door of the gardener's cottage she'd claimed for her residence. The bulk of the main house loomed dark against the sunset. It could take years to get rid of the monstrosity.

"Hello, my lady," Catrin met her at the door. She was a maid Marriette had sent with Joan to this estate. There were other staff at first, but all the men left when Joan didn't immediately take their advice.

"Hi Catrin," Joan rolled her shoulders a little. "How was your day?"

"Marie showed me how to make bread, and she sent us a loaf to eat. Agnes sent some dried fruit and promised to teach me when the season is right. Her man sent a ham to us. We could eat nothing but ham for a month." She lifted Joan's coat off her as if it were a fine cloak and hung it in the cupboard by the door. "Widow Frank's house is done."

"Suse mentioned that."

"One young man actually got a blister he worked so hard."

"Really?"

"He's a new one, my lady, arrived today."

"What did the other's think of Jame's abrupt departure?"

"One less to worry about." Catrin made a face. "Can't we run them all off?"

"I'd like to, but we need their families to buy the extra food we grow."

"What extra food?"

"We're planting the whole grounds," Joan said, "and the fruit trees and vines have been pruned for harvest not for looks. We'll be in good shape come the winter, but that is assuming we can find a market for our goods."

"The next town down will buy them."

"They already grow everything we grow. We'll need to sell to the city. My father's business was split up and sold, but I'm still friends with the drivers. We'll get our goods South, but if the Houses decide they won't buy what we are selling..." Joan shrugged and sat at the table. She cut a slice of bread and slathered it with the butter Catrin put beside her.

"Maybe we can cook the ham in slices," Joan said between bites. "I'll ask tomorrow at the holder's meeting."

"I'm still not sure about you getting all this advice from the holders. I don't remember Lord leBraun ever doing that."

"Lord leBraun wasn't given a falling down, mismanaged pile of rock to make profitable." Joan cut another slice. "Good bread." Catrin bobbed her head. "If the only way I can manage the place is through the holders, then that's what I'm going to do."

"I love it when you talk like that." Catrin came and rubbed Joan's shoulders. "It makes me believe we have a future here."

"We have a future," Joan said, "but the hard part has hardly begun. The Houses aren't going to be happy I'm not choosing one of their excess sons as a husband, so my land can be ruled by a proper male hand. They will not go away."

"You want a husband?" Catrin let her hands rove away from Joan's shoulders.

"I don't want a husband." Joan rubbed her face. "But I may not have much choice in it at the end." She caught Catrin's hand and kissed it. "Let's not worry until we must. I'm tired and tomorrow looks to be a long day." She got up and led Catrin to the one bedroom in the house.

***

Catrin slept curled up against her. Joan moved into the little cottage when she saw how impossible the big house would be even with the staff she brought with her. The men slept in the servant's quarters at the house, but Joan wouldn't let Catrin sleep there fearing the men would mistreat her. So Catrin slept with her. At first to warm the bed as stone walls pulled all the heat from the cottage, but gradually it became something very much more precious they shared. Joan didn't want to lose it, but she wasn't optimistic about being left alone to live her life as she wanted.

She got up and tucked the blanket around Catrin, then went to the main room to put away the bread and butter. After washing the plate and knife she pulled the frame with its bright fabric stretched on it, and took up quilting where she'd left off. By the next winter she planned to have several quilts to line the stone walls and keep her and Catrin warm.

The noble punk threatened her in a way none of the drovers had ever hinted at. She expected his version of events would be wildly different, though she wondered how he'd try to justify rape as a tool for courting his bride. Though maybe that was normal for the nobility. She never wanted this, but the King gave it to her, and now she wasn't giving it up without a fight.

She finished her line, then crawled back to bed. Catrin cuddled around her until Joan was warm again.

***

If the sun pouring in through the cracks in the shutters didn't wake them, the birds singing outside would have. Catrin rolled out of bed and stretched. She winked at Joan before putting on her dress for the day. Joan climbed out and got dressed quickly. The fall progressed slowly, but mornings still held a chill. A closet full of fine gowns waited at the big house, but Joan wore a working dress she didn't need help putting on. She wasn't having Catrin play the servant any more.

The other girl put bread and butter on the table along with some dried fruit, but she sat down to eat.

"We're going to enjoy every day we get," Joan said. "There's time before we need worry about anybody from the south."

Catrin went back to her friends for the day while Joan walked to the tiny town to meet the holders.

The path led her through green woods, flowers pushed their way up through last year's litter. After living amongst the stone and dead wood of the city, Joan forced down nerves every time she walked alone in the woods. The polished staff she carried helped, as did the number of times she'd walked this path through the summer and into the fall.

The first cottage was Widow Frank's. Joan took some time to watch the village men and some of the holder's sons lay stone. The widow's house had fallen under weight of time. Joan suggested they rebuild it with stone from the manor wall. There were a few indolent young men sitting in the shade. Joan frowned;

she didn't trust one of them. The man she'd sent home with his servant and a goose egg on his head didn't help matters. A new person carried a stone and discussed with an older villager where it should be placed. He looked up and finished placing the stone and testing its seat before he came over to speak to Joan.

"You would be the Lady of the estate." He bowed. "I'm Sam. I heard you welcomed hard workers."

"Perhaps you heard I didn't welcome the lazy." Joan spoke loudly enough for her words to reach the shade.

"Is that not the same thing?"

"Not quite." Joan shook off her irritation. "Every extra person is one more to feed and the harvest is months away, but now you are here, I won't send you away." She looked at the young men lazing about.

"No one without blisters will be fed." she said, again loud enough for everyone in the clearing to hear her.

"You wound me." One man in a ridiculous red outfit pouted and put his hand over his heart. "I know what work you could have me do and there would be no blisters, at least not on my hand."

"Do you wish me to teach him a lesson?" Sam asked.

"No." Joan ground her teeth. "It would cement in his tiny head that women are weak and to be used." She walked over to the lounging fool. "You have outstayed your welcome."

"My dear," he took her hand, "I haven't begun to show you --"

Joan swept her staff behind his leg and knocked him to the ground. It buzzed through the air to stop at hair's breadth from the man's eye.

"I didn't give you leave to touch me." She put the ice in her gut into her voice. "What would be the punishment for handling your Lord without their permission?" The man blanched and tried to scramble away. She tapped him on the head with her staff. "I asked you a question."

"A peasant brushed against Lord reTaggin's sleeve and the Lord had him flogged."

"Shall I have you flogged?"

"I'm no peasant."

"No, you're a fool who thinks he can get an easy bit of land by sweeping a delicate girl off her feet. I want you off my land by noon." She lifted her head to glare at the others. "And the rest of you may follow, if you will not work. I have no place for the indolent."

The men stood with mouths open staring at her.

"Sam," she asked without turning around, "did or did not the King personally deed me this land?"

"He did," Sam said. "I heard him with my own ears." The other men looked at him sharply. *He must be older than he looks to have been in court that day.*

They picked up their things. Joan allowed the buffoon in red to stand up and lead them away.

CHAPTER 7

"**Y**ou are welcome to store harvest in the barn at the manor, even use the ball room in the manor. The place isn't going to fall down anytime soon."

"We are used to storing our harvest in our own barns," Seth said. "What is to keep you from claiming any harvest we put in you barn or your house?"

Joan rubbed her eyes.

"I am not ordering you to store anything anywhere. I am making an offer. Just as I offered to let you use cut stone from the wall to repair homes in the village. Just as I am offering to broker the sale of your excess harvest in the city so you can get a better price for your crop. If you don't want to get a better price—if you want to spend the money building new barns instead of using buildings which already exist, you are welcome to do so."

She lifted her head from where she'd carefully been staring at a spot on the table so the holders didn't see the frustration Joan held back.

"I am not going to steal your land, your children, or your crop. I'm not even taking the levy I'm due as your Lady. It is time for you to decide if you want my support or not. If you want in, you will share the risk and you will share the reward."

She stood up and wobbled on her feet. Suze stepped up and steadied her.

"I'll walk you home, lass."

The night air caressed Joan's face and stole the heat of her anger away.

"They don't know what to do with you, Joan." Suze walked surefooted along the pitch-black path to the cottage. "They are so accustomed to mistrust they have a difficult time trusting their reflection in the mirror. You won't change them overnight. You've intrigued them by not giving orders. Likely you'll get the surplus from our fields to carry down to the city to sell. When you bring back the extra profit it will convince them to put more in your hands. Some of their families have lived on this land longer than the King's family's been on that throne of his."

They turned the last corner to where Joan expected to see the welcoming light of her cottage. The windows were dark, and Joan's heart pounded. She imagined scenes of destruction like at her father's business. Suze's hand on her shoulder kept her from running. When they reached the door, somehow the older woman entered the cottage first and lit the candle.

Catrin slept with her head on her hands, a candle burned out beside her. Joan ran to her.

"Catrin," she said, "Catrin, wake up!"

The girl groaned and lifted her head up.

"I was going to wait up for you, but I'm so tired."

"It's OK." Joan got an arm around Catrin and helped her off to bed.

"A word of advice from an old woman," Suze said. "When you go to the city, don't wear your heart on your sleeve. I love that you're a kind and loving girl, but they'll eat you alive."

"I'll keep it in mind," Joan said from the bedroom.

"Goodnight, lass." Suze blew out the candle and left the cottage in darkness.

***

Joan watched the last of the crop placed in the barn and made a note on her clipboard. Catrin tallied the grain stored in the ballroom. The wagons were loaded with grain and vegetables that would travel well. The rest would wait for the more traditional trade up and down the road.

"My Lady," Catrin walked up beside Joan. "The ballroom is full, and a couple of other rooms besides. Seth and I compared our tallies and they match."

"Thank you, Catrin," Joan said.

"Did you know there is a fish pond in the garden?" Catrin asked. "It is so surrounded by hedges you wouldn't know it was there."

"Must be pretty cold," Joan looked at the dust in her friend's hair.

"Cold is better than itching all night," Catrin said, "I just washed the sheets."

"Let me finish the tally, maybe get some blankets to wrap up in."

She checked her tally against Suze's list, then followed Catrin into the garden.

After the first shock of cold, the water in the fish pond was pleasant. Joan scrubbed at every part of her body and got the fine dust off her skin and out of her hair. Even after they were clean, they laughed and splashed each other.

"Well, well," the young man Joan had driven off stood by the hedge. He wore a blue dark enough to be black. Behind him stood one of his cronies.

"I told you to get off my land." Joan stood, too angry to care she was naked.

"I don't take orders from women," the man sneered.

"Run, Catrin." Joan jumped between the men and her friend.

Catrin ran into the garden. The crony ran after her, but Joan got a kick into his ribs sending him against a tree. He fell to the ground bleeding from the side of his head. Strong arms seized Joan and pushed her to the ground. She reached for the knife at the man's side, but he laughed and tossed it out of reach. Then he covered her mouth with his hand.

"You're not the nicest looking," he whispered in her ear, "but I'll manage. Once I'm done, I'll come back and hang the man who raped you." He reached down to fiddle with his pants. Joan struggled, but he was too much bigger and heavier. Then he coughed and blood dripped from his lips. He fell to the side and Joan looked up to see Catrin holding the knife.

"You murdered him!" The other man scrambled away.

"Let him go," Joan went back into the water and cleaned the blood off. They wrapped up in blankets and went back to the cottage.

"They are going to try you for murder," Joan said when they were dressed. "I am not going to let them punish you for protecting me."

The door crashed open and the crony stood there with Sam.

"There she is," he yelled at Sam. "Arrest her!"

"Catrin will remain in my custody until trial in the Regent's court." Joan dared the man to disagree.

Sam opened his mouth to argue, then shut it again. He nodded at Joan.

"Let's go." He dragged the crony out the door.

"You aren't going to do anything?" Sounds of a scuffle sounded outside the door.

"You disobeyed the Lady of this estate by staying here." Sam looked down at the man lying huddled on the ground. Joan closed the door on them as Sam yanked the man to his feet. "I'm holding you in custody until we get to trial. I'll have no attempts to circumvent the Queen's justice."

Catrin sat shaking, tears running down her face.

"What did I do?"

"You did what you had to," Joan said. "You saved my life. Now, I'm going to save yours."

***

"Heard there was trouble," Suze said to Joan as they walked into town. "The kind of trouble that means digging graves."

"No graves here. I'm returning him to his family. Sam is taking him. The idiot is a reTaggin brat, so they won't be taking it lightly."

Suze spit to the side.

"The holders want someone to go with you to the city."

"Fair enough," Joan said, "as long as they can leave without holding up the wagons."

"My gear's already loaded." Suze put her hand on Joan's shoulder. "I'm thinking you're going to need someone watching your back with all the grieving relatives out there."

"Thanks Suze." Joan fought away the lump in her throat. "But I can't ask you to be part of this mess."

Suze laughed.

"My Lady, I'm the only chance you have of surviving." She spun her staff and planted it between her feet. "Before I came here to the farm, I had command of King Hastirix's body guard. Then he sent me away and murdered the rest of my girls so he could join the Empire without the trouble of a fight." She went to one knee and offered Joan her staff. "This is going to get ugly fast. You are my Lady and I ask leave to protect you."

"You have my leave." Joan put her hand on the staff. "But you have to keep training me, and Catrin too, 'cause you'll need us to watch your back." She picked up the staff and hefted it. It was much heavier than hers. "Let's get on our way." Joan handed the staff back.

***

The wagons rolled into Bellopolis without any fanfare. The guards at the gate barely glanced at the waybills. It helped that hundreds of other wagons were also bringing food into the city.

"How are you going to sell anything with all these other people bringing in food too?" Catrin looked at them with a frown.

"All the food on all those wagons might feed the city for a day or two. They need a lot of food." Joan directed the wagons toward the market for higher quality goods. "We'll do well, you'll see."

They reached the market and parked. The drovers unhitched their horses and led them away.

"Where from?" A man in royal colours walked around the wagons.

"The north—the highest quality grain and roots and squash." She handed the man a turnip. He peered at it closely and cut away a piece with his knife.

"How much do you want for the entire load?" the man asked.

A short time later, the man held the waybills for the wagons they'd brought to the city, and Joan had an order drawn on the royal bank for her payment for the shipment.

"I'm impressed." Suze looked at the payment amount. "That's more than I make on my entire harvest."

"Let's put this on deposit," Joan said, "then find a place to make ourselves look respectable." She led Suze and Catrin into the city.

The hotel wasn't the priciest in Bellopolis, but Joan knew the proprietor from the days when she worked for her father. She took a room for a week, then paid for a meal to be sent up.

"Here," she handed Suze a paper. "If I don't make it back north, you can cash this in or take it home for security. I have a duplicate copy." Suze rolled the paper up and put it in her pouch.

A knock at the door announced the arrival of their supper— stew with actual meat in it and biscuits on the side.

Joan gave the bowl one last polish and ate the tiny bit of biscuit. Licking the bowl would be pushing things too far, so she regretfully set it aside.

"I hadn't realized how used I'd gotten to being hungry."

"You should never be hungry." Suze set her bowl on top of Joan's. "We always have enough."

"I didn't want to impose."

"I can understand not wanting to be someone who only takes." Suze leaned back in her chair. "But you are giving plenty. It should shame us that you are going without." Catrin nodded in agreement. She opened the chest and started hanging dresses to let the wrinkles loosen.

"I'll not want anything fancy for tomorrow," Joan said. "I want them thinking Lady of the estate, not belle of the ball."

"Speaking of tomorrow, what is your plan?"

"I'm sure reTaggin has been already shouting for my head. It would explain why there was an investigator there."

"I think Sam likes you." Catrin shook out another dress, then started on the rest of the clothes.

"He may, but it doesn't matter much. He took home a body with a knife wound in his back. His family will be crying murder and wanting blood. It's the only way they don't have to accept his cowardice.'"

"...And you're going to go in and shove his cowardice in their faces."

"A full trial, we lose even if we win. They'll say whatever they need to say and we have no witness to say otherwise."

"Good grief." Suze stared at Joan. "you're setting up for trial by combat."

"It's simple," Joan said, "I let them accuse me, then I challenge them."

"Not so simple," Suze said. "They will have a champion who will take you apart. You have to set them up to expect you will fight your own combat, then you send in your champion when they send in theirs."

"I have a champion?" Joan asked.

"Pray I'm still half as good as I used to be." Suze gave a twisted smile.

CHAPTER 8

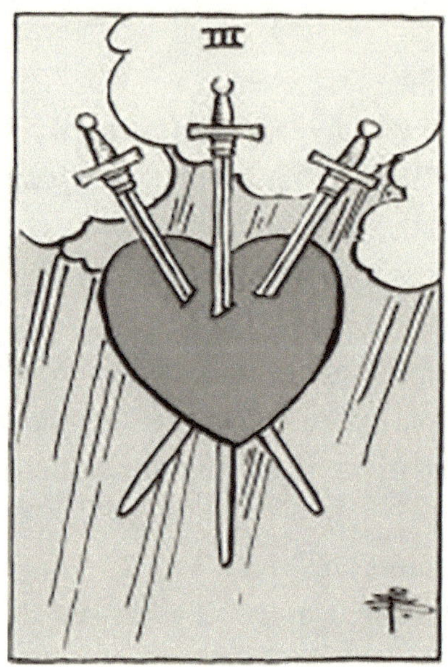

"You must send out to them and bring them back for punishment," reTaggin stood on the first step of the dais to harangue Marriette. If he wasn't careful, he would trip and slice himself open on the sword standing in the stone a step or two away from the throne.

"Don't you mean, *Please Regent, ask Lady Joan to present herself so she may give her account of events.*"

"My nephew was stabbed in the back," the old man said. "It doesn't matter what he was doing."

Marriette bit her tongue. Illandria had turned out to be a wealth of information about the state of the other Houses. The young man had a reputation.

"Your Majesty," the major domo broke in to announce. "The Lady Joan wishes to present herself at court."

58

"Finally," reTaggin said.

"Marshal," Marriette spoke casually. "If reTaggin opens his mouth before we give him leave, you have my permission to muzzle him." The old man opened his mouth to argue, but a growl from Marshal changed his mind.

Marriette almost groaned out loud when Joan walked in, her maid bound with a token thread in front of her. Behind walked a large woman in a cloak, leaning on a staff. She had blonde hair, and wore no makeup to hide the wrinkles. Her hands on the staff were rough and strong. *She no more needs the staff than I do.* Marriette lifted her fan slightly. Marshal shifted position slightly.

"Your Majesty," Joan bowed deeply to Marriette. "I regret I bring you a need for justice. My maid here," she lifted the hand holding the thread, "killed a man while acting in my defense. It is unfortunate she had to stab him in the back, but given he was occupied with his attempt to rape me, she didn't have time to act otherwise."

"You lie!" A young man shouted and ran toward Joan. "You seduced Robert so your maid could kill him."

Marriette lifted her fan to order Marshal to restrain the young man, but the grey-haired woman tossed her staff to Lady Joan who spun in a vicious arc stopping a hair's breadth from the young man's face.

"You recognize this, don't you?" Joan said. "Remind me where you saw it last." Marriette looked at the young man's white face.

"We are all ears." Marriette leaned forward. Her fan spread and in front of her brought Marshal to stand one step down from the throne.

"You used it to knock Robert down," the young man said. "A coward's attack as he wasn't armed."

"Is rape more or less cowardly than striking an unarmed fool?" Joan didn't shift the staff, but her posture screamed attack.

"But I must apologize." The staff spun away from his face. "You can't testify about your friend's cowardice because you ran into a tree while chasing my maid."

The assembled people laughed a little more loudly than the comment called for.

"Why were you still on my land, when you'd been told to leave?" Joan leaned on the staff and raised an eyebrow.

"Robert said we weren't going to do what some stupid..." he trailed off.

"I beg your indulgence, Your Majesty," Joan turned and bowed again. "Was I not given my estate by the King's very word? Not as a dalliance, but to exercise a firm hand?"

"That is true."

"How many of you Lords would tolerate an unwanted person on your land simply because they didn't feel like leaving?"

"You could have sent him off instead of murdering him," reTaggin almost screamed the words at her.

"If he hadn't been busy attempting to rape me," Joan said, "I might have tried. This one knows I tried, though he lies to protect his friend."

"So you say." ReTaggin's face turned an unhealthy shade of red. "I'm expected to take the word of a woman over my flesh and blood?"

"Yes." Joan smiled sweetly at him. "When you know your flesh and blood is a worthless pile of dross you don't allow into your own home because he won't leave your servants alone."

"I demand satisfaction for these insults!'" ReTaggin screamed. "You can't expect me to stand here and not respond!"

"So, draw your sword, Sir, and we will have this decided."

"I'm a Duke," reTaggin waved his hand. "I will let my champion fight in my stead."

"Oh, so that's how you do it," Joan said. "I admit to some curiosity at how to get someone else to fight for you without admitting you're a coward." She looked at the man who shouldered his way out of the crowd and stared at Joan. "Suze?"

"Ready, my Lady." The grey-haired woman dropped her cloak. Marriette heard Marshal swear under his breath. reTaggin went from red to white.

"I will allow my champion to fight, because she is stronger and more capable than I, but hear this, Duke reTaggin. If you choose to take up the sword in your own honour, I will meet you."

The Duke didn't look like he'd heard her.

"Marshal, have a square formed and let us have this nonsense done with. We will have no death blood in our hall. Combat is to first blood, permanent injury done will displease us greatly."

"Understood, your Majesty." The combatants bowed to her.

"Bring the reTaggin champion his sword," Marshal drew his sword to stand between Marriette and the soon to be armed champion.

A young man walked in carrying a sword in a scabbard. The reTaggin champion drew it and held it with one hand to salute his opponent. The woman—Suze, Joan called her—saluted with her staff.

"You are the one to prove the truth," Suze said. "Strike first and we'll see the strength of your conviction."

The champion swung his sword so it whistled as it cut the air. Suze tapped the sword with the staff and stepped slightly to the side. The man brought the sword back in a reverse cut and Suze again stepped out of the way.

"Not bad, you've practiced against the staff before. Allow me to test your skill." The staff blurred in her hands. He moved his sword to block the first blow and managed to dodge the second. The third blow caught his arm midway between wrist and elbow. The fourth knocked the sword from his hand then the staff stopped, touching the man's forehead.

"It is difficult to draw blood with a staff without doing a lot of damage. Do I need to continue?" Suze didn't even breathe deeply. The man bowed and went to one knee.

"Very well," Marriette had to fight back a grin. "Since we are sure, Duke reTaggin, you would have claimed Lady Joan's estate in the event your champion won, it seems fair you pay an equivalent fine to her as damages for allowing one of your kin to trespass on her land and lay violent hands on her. You will also withdraw all complaint against Lady Joan or those who serve her. We will hold you personally responsible if some excitable member of your very extended family were to try to gain vengeance on your behalf."

Marriette stood.

"Lady Joan, if you will accompany me. I'm afraid I must ask your champion to remain here."

"Your Majesty." Joan bowed, then stripped the thread from the maid's hands and followed Marriette.

Marriette led her to the same room they'd laid Marshal in not long before.

"Quite a show you put on." Marriette shooed out the pages and closed the door.

"It was his word against mine," Joan said, "and nobility is not known for paying attention to women."

"If you had let me know…"

"You mean told you I couldn't manage my own estate. Then they would have pushed even harder. If I'm going to manage this thing, I need to do it my way so there is no question about whose estate it is."

"There will be others." Marriette frowned. She didn't remember Joan being so prickly. "Maybe not from reTaggin's bunch, but someone will decide to put you in your place."

"I'm sure you will know who has tried by the bruises on their faces." Joan said. "Suze took it easy on the guy. She used to be a bodyguard for some King."

"That would explain Marshal's reaction. I've never heard him swear before. Speaking of which, I will have to warn you against smacking the head of anyone who talks to you cross eyed."

"I don't want to alienate the major houses." Joan let her shoulders slump. "But it will hard to ignore those who are determined to prove me false or incompetent."

"Don't seek out trouble." Marriette wrapped her arms around Joan and hugged her. "Now you must tell me what you've been doing all this time." She let Joan go and opened the door.

"Tea for Lady Joan and me." She sent a page running, then closed the door again.

***

"You said you would muzzle that Duke, then you let him talk." Illandria brushed out Marriette's hair. The bath was the only room she'd talk to Marriette like an advisor rather than a maid.

"As I recall, I told Marshal he had permission to muzzle the old crank. I wanted him to be angry and not thinking clearly."

"Very good, your Majesty," Illandria picked up another lock of hair and started brushing it. "Though reTaggin will tell himself he was manipulated."

"I want him knowing he was manipulated. I want him complaining about it to the other Lords, so they start wondering how I am manipulating them. It is time they stopped treating me like a well-trained puppy and started acting like I am their Queen."

"You are playing a dangerous game." Illandria braided Marriette's hair.

"It's a little late to worry about that now."

***

"You must tell that wife of yours," General Kouza said to Torrance, "the Empire is up to something. Sailors are getting off Empire ships and wandering away. The Empire doesn't allow deserters, so they are acting on orders."

"How many?" Torrance asked.

"Five here, ten there." The General shrugged and took a drink from his tankard. "Perhaps a hundred, perhaps five hundred."

"What are that few soldiers going to do in this city?"

"Think rather what half a legion is doing in our city." The General pointed at Torrance. "The Empire plays a deep game. You'd better be ready for it."

"How many do you have in your stronghold on the coast?"

"We have half a legion, but if we move them inland, we could lose the port. Need I remind you the port is but half a day's march from the capital?"

"Thank you for the information." Torrance played with his own drink. "I will bring it to the Regent's attention."

The General bowed and left. Torrance paid the bill and headed back to the palace. His boots echoed in the streets. There were few people out and most of them gave Torrance and his sword a wide berth. Someone followed him. They wore soft boots, but he could make out their footsteps. A man, shorter than him, but not by much. He would turn at the next corner and try to capture and question the man.

He concentrated so hard on the person behind, he walked right into the group waiting for him. The flash of moonlight on a blade sent him ducking and rolling to the side. He drew his sword and put his back to a wall and faced them. Four of them, wearing masks too. Without a word, they attacked from both sides.

Torrance blocked the first stroke and almost blocked the second. Fire burned on his ribs, but the leather deflected the worst of it. His sword slashed an attacker's throat. Another sword scraped across his ribs. Torrance tried for another throat, but had to settle for marking an arm. A sword skewered his leg and twisted. Torrance went down hard on the cobbles. He tried to roll to bring his sword into play. Steel touched his throat and he threw himself desperately away, but too slow.

He fell on his back and dropped his sword to clasp his hand to his neck. Moonlight gleamed on the edge of the blade as it descended toward his throat.

A dart came out of the darkness and struck the mask where the eye would have been. The sword fell and missed him. Two more darts hissed through the air and the other two attackers fell.

Soft boots stepped out of the shadow and cursed at the blood pouring from Torrance's throat. He whistled a complicated tune, then tore a sleeve from a dead man to hold against Torrance's wound. Torrance couldn't see the figure properly, but he wanted to thank him for his aid, late as it came.

"Hush," soft boots spoke in a soprano voice, "don't speak. We have one more cast of the die before the night is done."

Running steps approached. A whistle echoed briefly before a young man led an old woman into the moonlight. With the help of the young man she knelt beside Torrance and put her hand on his throat. Humming made his teeth ache, but Torrance drank it in. The agony in his throat receded and he knew he could speak if he needed. He stayed silent while the old woman touched each of his wounds in turn. When she'd finished, Torrance reached out to her.

"My Lady," he said as quiet as he could, "my thanks for this healing and for the healing of my wife. Whatever I can do for you that will not hurt this land or my lady wife is yours."

"Do not go out so foolishly alone," the old woman said, "There are more enemies than you know in the night."

"Empire soldiers." Torrance sighed. "I'm guessing they want a widow on the throne, though they don't know Marriette if they expect her to wed anyone else."

The old woman nodded.

"Your lady Queen and I must talk, but the day is not right. Your Marshal searches for me, believing me a greater danger than this." She waved her hand at the corpses. "He may be right. If you need to send a message to me, Halonde here may carry it." Soft boots nodded at the name.

Hands helped him up and gave him a shirt to put on. It fit loosely over his leather, then a rough towel scrubbed the blood off his face. Men came and carried away the four attackers. He bet they'd be back to rinse down the cobbles. Halonde shadowed him home and vanished as he walked through the gate. The last he saw of her was her finger on her lips.

Torrance bathed properly and threw the shirt away. He dressed in his own clothes then went to find Marriette. She had come out of the bath, her hair still damp. Illandria, Marriette's favourite maid, adjusted the robe Marriette wore and placed a pillow beneath her feet.

"You spoil me," Marriette said.

"It is our duty to remind you of your station and duties." Torrance tried not to start at the soprano voice behind him.

The maid put a tray with tea on the table near Marriette. She crossed behind Marriette and put her finger to her lips and made a sign that someone listened. Torrance poured tea and made small talk until the maids finally pushed them off to bed and carried away the tray.

"Halonde warned that someone listens," Torrance whispered into Marriette's ear.

"Illandria says Master Tiron doesn't spy solely on our enemies."

"We have trouble on the streets," Torrance murmured. "Empire soldiers have left their ships and live here."

"I can't do anything official," Marriette said, "or the Council would have us declaring war on our own people."

"We can't leave them free run of Bellopolis."

"You will have to come up with a plan, Torrance." Marriette nibbled on Torrance's ear and the discussion got put off until later.

CHAPTER 9

The leather armour laced into the approximate shape of her belly. It obstructed her movements more than a corset.

"I've fit men with bigger bellies than this," the armourer said. "Keep the shape as close as you can to your real stomach. It will be more comfortable."

"I'm having a hard time imagining it less comfortable," Marriette tried adjusting the leather to sit better.

"You will get stronger with time," the man said, "and you only need wear it when you are in public."

"Very well," Marriette waved to Illandria who helped her put a dress over the armour."

"This will turn a knife blow." The man pointed to her stomach. "But it won't stop an arrow or a sword."

"It's a start," Marriette said. "Thank you."

The man bobbed his head and left.

"Now I suppose you want to go find Marshal and try it out?" Illandria put out her arm.

"I'm barely five months," Marriette headed out the door. "I am not helpless." They walked out into the hall and toward the practice room. Marshal met them there. He handed Marriette a wooden sword after closing and barring the door.

"What about a staff like Joan's champion wielded?"

"Suze," Marshal took a defensive stance. "once known as Suchianrze, the Right Arm of King Hastirix. A few years ago, the price on her head was a thousand gold coins. The emperor apparently decided she must be dead. There is no price on her head now. She may be the only person in the country who might challenge me successfully."

"Is the staff harder than the sword to learn?"

"Different," Marshal said. "She used the staff because King Hastirix didn't trust women with edged weapons. I've seen her hold off five men with swords. I don't know many swordsmen who could manage one person with a staff never mind five."

Marriette held up the wooden sword.

"This will do for now." *Wrist straight, swing from the shoulder, use my legs.* The sword cracked against Marshal's sword, again and again. He swung his sword and she beat it away with hers—annoyed he obviously moved in slow motion, yet pleased that slow motion or not, for these few minutes of the day, she need only worry about this one length of wood.

***

"This piece," Master Tiron held up a black disc. "is unique in the game." He showed her two black sides. "It is the only piece which will not turn. Every other piece on the board will turn under the right set of circumstances. The pawn will turn if a piece on either side of it turns. The spy will turn if it is surrounded, the mole waits until the time is ripe, then turns. Even your ruling disc can be turned if all the other pieces on the board turn against it. This one stubborn piece refuses." He tossed it in his hand and put it back into the bag. "It is best if your opponent doesn't know which it is. You must play it far enough into the game it doesn't immediately come into play, but close enough to the center to have an effect."

They played every night after Master Tiron gave his report. He put the number of legionnaires at a century, possibly two.

"It isn't unusual for a foreign power to want soldiers at hand, if not obvious, especially if there is likely to be turmoil in the country. If you continue to hold the throne confidently in expectation of Harald's return, you have little with which to concern yourself."

"The General, on the other hand," Master Tiron put the game away after destroying Marriette's careful defense, "is old school and a friend of reTaggin's. He won't be happy with a woman on the throne. He won't deliberately go against you, but he will go to people he is comfortable dealing with, and let them talk to you."

"So what Houses have the closest ties with the Empire?"

"All the Houses depend on the Empire for their profit. There isn't enough wealth in Belandria to make them as rich as they want to be. What works in your favour is they are richer now than they would be under the Empire. SeGraine sells his wine to the Empire and claims the emperor drinks it. LeBraun sells timber, and cheese of all things." Master Tiron shrugged, "ReTaggin sells ore, timber and, according to rumour, slaves. DuSarche has his fish. VonFrome doesn't do much beyond a few books. They never had the stomach for rule." He hefted the bag and dropped it on the board. "Even you have a connection with the Empire. You collect a tax from every ship to drop anchor in the port. Without the tax, your treasury would be very much poorer."

He nodded at her and let himself out through the secret door.

Torrance came in a minute later and saw the game.

"So what did the spymaster have to say tonight?"

"We talked about how the Houses are connected to the Empire."

"Connected," Torrance sat down across from her, "not ruled by."

"So he said." Marriette picked up the bag and weighed it in her hand. "Though he made it sound much more portentous. He makes my head spin."

"If information is your trade, you are going to make it sound as important as possible."

When they lay in bed, Marriette whispered in Torrance's ear. He kissed her briefly, then they slept.

***

"My Lady Regent," Marshal said the next morning, "my apprentice." He indicated a man who didn't quite have Marshal's height, but whose shoulders were every bit as broad.

Marriette examined him carefully.

"Are you from one of the Houses?" she asked.

"My mother is a cousin of seGraine. My father a man at arms with duSarche."

"He will follow me for the next several months." Marshal glowered at her. "If he passes the tests, I will take him to the next level of training."

"Very well, Marshal," Marriette nodded at the pair. "I will leave him in your hands."

The apprentice didn't say a word the entire day. Marriette put him out of her mind. She had seGraine convinced to her cause and reTaggin still stung from the public rebuke. He could hardly blame Marriette for his humiliation. He'd brought Marriette a bank letter for the amount of his fine. She'd passed it on to Joan.

Raspin still made himself a pain at council meetings, but without support from seGraine or reTaggin, he remained a nuisance. DuSarche returned to his coast muttering about the number of ships the Empire had in their waters. Even he admitted they didn't have the time or money to build a navy.

Torrance missed more meetings than he made. He helped Lady Joan make a tour of the schools in the city and try to make sure the education they offered would be sufficient to improve the lot of the students. There were schools charging fees for people to learn at them. Marriette didn't want to shut them down, but she needed to know they weren't stealing from their students.

"I fail to see why it matters who teaches what."

"Would you allow a baker to teach your son swordplay?" the archbishop asked. It was worth sitting through Council to see the archbishop poke gently fun at the other men.

"Of course not," seGraine looked shocked at the idea. "swordplay is noble art."

"If you've ever eaten bread made by a swordsman instead of a baker," the archbishop smiled ruefully, "you'd agree the making of bread is also a noble art."

"Exactly," Marriette took control of the conversation, "we don't need to control what the schools teach, but simply be assured they are qualified to teach."

"Bookwork," reTaggin sneered. "Leave it to the clerks."

"Very well," Marriette dismissed the Council. She headed down to the office where she'd set Jeremiah to do his research for her.

"Wait out in the hall," she ordered Marshal. "You make him nervous and it takes him twice as long to report. With the two of you, it would be four times as long."

She entered the office and sat at the desk. Between her stomach and the armour she wore, every chance to get off her feet was welcome. Jeremiah handed her a report to read while he talked.

"The Houses' relationship with the Empire is complex." Jeremiah's words took on the cadence of teachers at the schools.

"Most of the trade happens through markets or ship captains. A small amount of trade goes through the ambassador but is especially valuable as the ambassador can be said to be buying for the emperor himself. As you know, such a claim can make much higher prices obtainable for the same product."

While he rattled on, Marritte read his report on the work Torrance and Joan were doing which had little to do with accreditation of the schools.

The initial training of the century is under way. Suze identified ten people who already had some skill with the staff. She is working with them. Those people have chosen their decade to train. The emphasis is on an oath to serve the Regent personally until the return of King Harald. It is short, but specific that they will drop everything to answer the Regent's call to defense. Suze is pleased with the progress her ten are making. Joan describes her as calling them 'surprisingly adequate.'

"Thanks," Marriette handed the paper back. "I have some more work for you. I think you'll have to recruit some help. I'd like to have a list of what the schools in the city are teaching and how the teachers are qualified to teach their subject."

"Lovely," Jeremiah almost rubbed his hands in glee. "I have a couple of boys I can send around with forms. I'll have a report for you within the week.

Marriette returned to her rooms to rest. Halonde drew her a warm bath and washed and brushed Marriette's hair.

"Illandria is working," Halonde whispered behind Marriette. "Your husband is too confident the people around him mean no harm. She watches over him."

"You think there are people who would try to get to me through him?"

"Illandria watches." Halonde tugged a little harder at the brush. "All is safe."

The baby kicked inside Marriette. Too bad Torrance isn't here. He'd love to feel his heir's vitality

CHAPTER 10

"Harald." Sarandia grinned broadly. "The baby is kicking."

He put his hand on his love's belly and felt the kicks.

"A good strong son," he said.

"Or a good strong daughter." She covered his hand with hers.

"I don't know what is more annoying." Rodrigo rolled his eyes. "Wandering the back roads with a couple so deeply in love they barely know I exist, or wandering with the couple while they gush about a baby who is causing us nothing but grief."

"It isn't the babe's fault," Sarandia frowned at Rodrigo, "if people are so unused to the idea of an expectant mother on the pilgrimage."

"Perhaps because the pilgrimage is known to be hard on healthy adults."

"I am a healthy adult." Sarandia put her hand out; Harald jumped up and pulled her to her feet.

Rodrigo took a long shuddering breath.

"Allow me to try again. Would you rather have your child in the Holy City with the best of care about you, or in the back end of nowhere in a stable with a goat for a midwife?"

"Well, if it was good enough for our Saviour..." She grinned mischievously at Rodrigo. "But it would be nicest to have my child at my father's home."

"Yes, we should cross into one of the few remaining enemies of the Empire!"

"I'm sure you could manage it if needed," Harald slapped the other man on the shoulder.

Rodrigo made a show of fixing the fall of his shirt.

"We need to pick up the pace, or the kid will be eating steak by the time we get there."

"Very well," Harald said, "walking is slower than I counted on. I am enjoying the time spent with Sarandia, but I agree it is time we got a move on. I keep expecting Aisa to show up again."

"She will when she realizes you haven't been enthralled by the flint and steel you are carrying around."

"I can hardly leave it out for someone to find and lose their soul."

"They may not--

"May not is not sure enough." Harald crossed his arms and glared at Rodrigo.

"Boys, we have company." Sarandia tugged on Harald's sleeve and pointed to where a large bear snuffled through the underbrush looking for berries. It wouldn't take long for it to realize they had the berries in a bag at Harald's waist.

"I have an idea." Rodrigo's eyes lit up. "Give me the heel of bread and the flint and steel."

Harald handed him the stale bread and the tiny bag. Rodrigo hollowed out the loaf and pushed the bag inside the bread. He put some bread into the opening to hold it.

"May I suggest we walk slowly away?" Rodrigo dropped the bread on the ground and pulled Harald and Sarandia with him. Harald kept his hand on the club at his waist, but the bear watched them with curiousity rather than malice. They were at the path when the bear reached where they'd been standing. It sniffed at something before it swallowed it down.

"Let Aisa deal with that." Rodrigo crowed in delight. "Now we need a wagon or something to speed up our pace. Even with a wagon we have a solid month on the road before we can take the ferry to the Holy City."

"I have to admit I had no idea of the size of the Empire," Sarandia said. "It makes it even stranger they are so determined to take my father's country from him. It is such a tiny place in comparison. No border is more than a day's ride."

"Your home is the one place I might consider settling in if I were allowed," Rodrigo looked at her, his face serious for a change. "The learning and love of arts there goes back centuries, maybe longer. I know the royal line is related to us and my people have married into yours. There must be some lifting of our curse within your borders." He picked up the pace a little. "Its very pleasantness is a trap."

"That still doesn't explain --"

"There are some who will not be happy until they own the world," Harald said. "The Emperor is one such."

"So is the White Heir," Rodrigo clenched his fists. "Mother expects me to challenge her openly, as no Black Heir has ruled our people in generations."

"I don't understand," Harald relaxed his hands to counteract the tension in Rodrigo's. "How did you become the Black Heir if you didn't want the job? Why not let someone who wants it become the King of your people?"

"It would be too easy," Rodrigo shook himself. "I think it goes back to the doom, and leaders who were willing to destroy the world to get what they wanted. The Heirs are chosen by lot once every five years. We have five years to convince the people to support us. If we don't get at least two-thirds of adults supporting an Heir, new lots are drawn and we start all over again. Most of the history of the Rehego is about the heirs; I don't know if we've had more than a handful of rulers. It is considered bad form to murder the other heir, but there are many ways to inconvenience them without killing them. I fear I have stretched my sister's patience too far. She expects to be Ruler of our people in a year's time and I am in the way. It is not healthy to be in Lasheimre's way."

"Can't you quit and let her do what she wants?"

"What she wants is to plunge the Empire into civil war. Our homeland is under the Emperor's city. If she takes the City and kills the Emperor, it would be horrific. I'm not a big fan of the Empire, but it is better than what would replace it."

"It sounds like you need to get serious about being the Black Heir," Sarandia sped up to walk beside Rodrigo.

"My mother says the same, but how do I go about convincing my people to vote for me when I'm a banished criminal?"

"A criminal!" Sarandia put her hand to her mouth.

"Sadly, yes," Rodrigo looked down. "With the reputation we Rehego have of being somewhat ... light-fingered ... You'd think we'd have more tolerance toward thieves. The truth is though we don't own property as you do, we are still strongly attached to our things. I got caught stealing from another's wagon. Given the choice of returning what I'd taken or exile, I chose exile. I hardly made it out of camp when I discovered I'd been chosen the Black Heir. Fate does have her sense of humour."

"How did you know you were Black Heir?" Harald asked.

"The clothes," Rodrigo sighed deeply. "You can't imagine I dress this way from choice, do you? Whatever clothes I obtain, they turn black as soon as I put them on. This is fascinating and all, but it isn't getting us closer to a wagon to ride to the Holy City."

"Perhaps the backroads are the problem." Harald rubbed his chin. "Most of the people we meet don't have a wagon, much less a wagon they could sell. It may be time to head to the main road."

"You have some secret stash of money on the main road?" Rodrigo waved his hands.

"There are caravans," Harald said. "Caravans need guards."

"You want me to be a caravan guard?"

"You are good with the blade you carry." Harald looked Rodrigo up and down thoughtfully. "We just need to convince them you are trustworthy."

"You are the Heir of thieves, spies and liars. It should be easy enough." Sarandia laughed and nudged Rodrigo's shoulder.

"Joy," Rodrigo sounded like he was headed for the gallows. "The highway is this way, maybe a day or two's walk."

***

"He looks like a waggoner," Dedrick shook his head and peered suspiciously at Rodrigo—the third caravaner to turn them down because of Rodrigo's looks.

"When was the last time you saw a waggoner wearing black?" Harald raised his eyebrows.

"I don't know..."

"How do you plan to get through Hella's Gap?" Rodrigo leaned against a wall. "I'd heard there's a new lot of bandits holed up in the caves there."

"The Legions will take care of them." Dedrick said.

"The Legions are designed to fight on an open field, not in caves. Besides, the Seventh is up North keeping Hastirix honest, the Sixth is on the coast chasing pirates, and the Fourth and Fifth are in the south waiting for an excuse to invade Uphramede. The Third is broken up after their disgrace in Nola, and you know the Emperor will never let the First or Second out of the capital."

"You know a lot for someone who looks like a thieving waggoner."

"It's the talk of your fellows over beer," Rodrigo pulled his knife and cleaned his nails. "Since no one will talk to me, I might as well listen."

"What is Hansdolf carrying in those wagons of his?"

"I could go and look." Rodrigo put the knife away and held his hand out to check his work. "But I heard him asking after a guide through Gronton. I'd guess leathers, probably tanned from the lack of people vomiting as they walk past his wagons."

"And Grendel?"

"I can hardly be expected to work for free," Rodrigo pushed himself away from the wall. "My friend and his wife are on pilgrimage. I thought I'd tag along for the amusement of the thing. Hire us and I will tell you whatever I hear."

"You won't steal my horses?"

"What would I want with your horses?" Rodrigo looked offended. "I'm sure they are fine horses to pull wagons, but no waggoner would give them a second look. Spotted horses are unlucky."

"Okay, then," Dedrick said. "The girl can ride on the second wagon. Rodrigo and Harald, one of you stays on the front wagon and the other on the last one. No sleeping while we're on the road."

"Thank you," Harald went to the inn to fetch Sarandia. She waved goodbye to the girl she sat beside.

"Poor kid wants out of town," Sarandia whispered. "She knows nothing about what life is like out there."

"Sounds like her father needs to send her with a safe person to learn the ropes."

"I suggested it, but her father's never left the village and sees no need for the girl to."

"I hope when she sneaks away she chooses a safe caravan to do it." Harald hoisted Sarandia up on the wagon and passed up the tiny sack holding everything they owned.

He let Rodrigo take the lead wagon and headed to the third. The innkeeper sidled up to him.

"My daughter is planning to hide in Dedrick's caravan. Let her get cold and hungry, then send her back to me."

"Send her back with who?" Harald asked, "Any caravan which happens by may decide they need a girl to keep the men happy. Perhaps some legionnaires will be happy to take care of her for you."

"She's going to run away, the fool girl. Dedrick's the only one I trust."

"Then trust him," Harald met the man's eyes. "Let him hire her on right and proper and have her for the whole trip. She will get what she wants and you know she will be as safe as she can be."

"I can't let her know or she'll take some other caravan to spite me."

"I will take care of it," Harald said, "Sarandia will keep an eye on her, but I don't want to come back to tales of abduction and woe. Once she's safe and gone, you be sure to tell the truth. It will be a good story."

The innkeeper pushed a small bag of coin at Harald.

"Keep it for when she needs it." He wiped a tear from his eye.

"Let's go," Dedrick shouted to his drivers. "Keep your mind on driving, I've guards to watch for the pretty girls and thieves."

The wagons rolled out the gates of the town. Harald saw the tarp on the second wagon move a little as their stowaway peeked out at the world.

Harald saw few pretty girls and no thieves as the rolled through fields that were at the end of harvest. By afternoon the fields gave way to open forest. Now they needed to stop frequently to rest the horses.

"Dedrick," Harald came over to meet him at one of the stops. "If I may have a word?"

"What, you bored already?" Dedrick pushed himself to his feet. "I hired you to do a job."

"You did," Harald said. "I've had worse jobs. But what I wanted to talk to you about is the innkeeper's daughter who's been hiding out in the second wagon all day."

Dedrick turned red and turned to go to the wagon, then he stopped and glared at Harald.

"Why are you telling me now, rather when we could have sent her home with no loss of time? I can't send her with the first group to pass by."

"So I said to her father."

"Oh, you did?" Dedrick dropped his voice. "And how much did the father pay you to take on his daughter? Next I know there will be cries of abduction and worse."

"No." Harald put his hand out to stop Dedrick. "There will not be. He told me she was planning to hide away on a caravan anyway. He trusts you more than any other caravaner to do right by his daughter."

"So I have another mouth to feed and nothing to show for it."

"She's the daughter of an innkeeper," Harald didn't drop his arm. "I expect she knows horses, cooking and a few other useful skills. She can keep Sara company on the wagon. You can feed her out of my wages. I don't need the money, just a way to get to the Holy City."

"I will decide how to feed her. Never let it be said I tried to cheat an employee." Dedrick pushed Harald's hand aside and walked over to the second wagon to bang on the side.

"Ok, girl, you can come out now."

The girl who clambered out of the wagon stood perhaps Sarandia's height, but she was built more solidly. Her hair tangled around her face and she kept her eyes down.

"What's your name?" Dedrick asked.

"Siana," the girl spoke in the lightest of whispers.

"So, Siana, what do you expect me to do with you?"

"I want to come along. I can cook and carry water. I can..." Her face turned bright red beneath her hair.

"We aren't that kind of people." Dedrick frowned at her. "You will cook and clean, help out with whatever else you can do. Anyone bothers you, speak to me. Understand?"

"You mean I can stay?" Siana looked up at Dedrick. A birthmark covered one cheek with purple skin, but there was no mistaking the spark in her eyes, one blue and the other brown.

"Go sit with Sara." Dedrick pointed to the third wagon. "Let's go people, horses are rested. Unless there are any more surprises for me?" He jumped up on the lead wagon and they were off again.

Sun glinted through the trees. Occasional gaps hinted at how high they had come. Dedrick pulled into an open space beside the road. Siana grabbed the bucket and began watering the horses as they were unhitched and hobbled for the night. Harald got a fire going as Rodrigo walked around the campsite. Siana peeled roots for the soup pot. Dedrick watched her for a while then nodded his head.

Harald and Rodrigo split the night. The drivers slept under the wagons they drove. Dedrick followed their example. Harald made a tiny lean-to for Sarandia and Siana to share. He had first shift, so Rodrigo curled up in a blanket under the last wagon.

The chill in the aid kept Harald moving. He'd never had to fight a battle, but his father had sent him out into the mountains of Belandria to get trained. Harald missed those trips once he started ruling. The moon rose to turn everything stark black and white.

The world used to look like that to Harald. As King he'd thought whatever looked to be best for him could be assumed to be best for the Kingdom. Marriette upset his assumptions, and he saw how he used his position to serve himself before his people. As he walked around the sleeping people, Harald tried to decide what he needed to do differently. None of this mattered if he didn't become a better King. Nothing happened to interrupt his reflections, but he wasn't any closer to an answer when he woke Rodrigo, then curled up in the warm blankets to sleep.

CHAPTER 11

The Gap didn't look dangerous. A broad valley meandered through mountain peaks on either side. Flowers filled the fields lining the road with dying colour.

"Lots of people have tried to settle here." Dedrick waved at the fields. "It would be a profitable place for an inn, but there are too many bandits robbing caravans who go through the Gap." He walked out ahead of the caravan with Harald and Rodrigo. "I didn't have any women with me last time; I paid the toll they demanded and got on my way. I've heard of caravans who argued, or tried to sneak through and were slaughtered to the last man."

"They can't interfere with shipping too much," Harald shaded his eyes to look along the valley, "or the Emperor, or whoever he's put in charge here, would come in and clean it out.

They haven't because it would cost more than they would save. I wonder how many rumours they started themselves."

"It's how I would do it." Rodrigo nodded. "And send a little something to the governor to keep his eyes elsewhere."

"What do you recommend?" Dedrick asked. "I have the usual toll set aside in the third wagon, but I don't want to risk the women."

"I'll go ahead and scout the situation," Harald walked a little aside with Rodrigo. "Do you feel that?" He poked his hand with a sharp rock.

"I have no idea how you can stand poking and prodding yourself," Rodrigo winced. "My hands ache from you chopping wood."

"Good." Harald slapped Rodrigo on the back. "One means move the caravan through the gap, two means wait, three means all hell is breaking loose and you're on your own."

"Thrilling," Rodrigo peered at his hands. "Messages through pain."

"Our scouts have an entire language of taps and hand signals. It might be useful to develop a system."

"Useful indeed," Rodrigo said, "I twinge in anticipation."

Harald headed along the road looking up to the peaks. There was more than enough cover to hide an army, never mind a band of brigands. He suspected they operated more by threat than force of numbers. He wouldn't want to try to feed more than a few men up this far away from civilization. He should have asked how much of the 'toll' was food.

A flicker of movement caught his eye, but Harald pretended to not see it. At the end of the valley the road took a sharp turn between high rocks—the usual place to pay the toll. Dedrick told him it took twenty minutes to maneuver each wagon through the turn. Plenty of time for even a small band to wreak havoc.

The sharp turn afforded a view of the winding trail down to where patches of fields showed farmers had claimed land to grow on. *Where do all the extra people go? In Belandria, clearing new land gives them five years of freedom from taxes. The new holders are wealthy, while the older farms grow good crops but lose money to the nobles. For all that the nobility holds and works more land than anyone else, they lose money at it.* Something about it bothered Harald. The nobles were losing money, when a generation ago they had made plenty of money even with lower tithes from their landholders.

"Hey, you," a man stepped out from the rocks, "you must be with the caravan holed up at the bottom of the valley."

"Yes," Harald held his hands out to show he carried no weapons. This bandit looked clean and well fed. His clothes were newer than Harald's. They were getting regular supply from somewhere, probably the south side of the Gap. The governor on the north side lived a week away by wagon. Of course, the governor didn't need to be personally involved, but it would be hard to manage this without at least his knowledge.

"So, you do have the toll for us?"

"Never!" Siana rushed out of the rocks swinging a stick. The bandit dodged her easily and tripped her to the ground. The stick went flying and Siana scrambled after it.

"Stupid cow." The bandit stalked over to where she finally grabbed her stick. He twisted it out of her hands and drew a knife. "I should keep you for the men, but you're too ugly."

"That is no way to talk to a fine lady." Harald wrenched the knife from the bandit and tossed it to Siana.

"Come over here, Siana." He dragged the bandit kicking and screaming to where he'd enjoyed the view earlier. Since the man was beating and scratching at Harald's hands he bit once hard on the inside of his cheek.

Other men came out of the rocks. A couple held bows, the rest had swords or clubs. They looked more like what Harald expected bandits to look like.

"This is how it is going to work," Harald held his man at the edge of the cliff. "You will stay there and watch our wagons go through the gap. If you behave, I don't drop your friend with the political connections down the cliff. If you try to shoot me, he drops. You try to attack the caravan, he drops. You slow them down so my arm gets tired, he drops."

"What if we don't like him anyway?" one of the men with bows asked.

"You could shoot me, and we both go over the cliff. Then you try to figure out how to sell the stuff you steal, how to stay away from this guy's friends while you do it, and how you are going to survive the winter without his help."

"I'll kill you all," the man shouted. "You're dead! I know important people." He squirmed and managed to pull a second knife from his boot. He stabbed at Harald's hand. When Harald let go, the man tried to sidle sideways, but a rock turned under his foot. He screamed briefly as he fell.

Harald shrugged and looked at the men who were clustered together.

"I don't want a fight," Harold sucked at the back of his hand, "but if you're determined." He reached for the club at his waist.

"Can we still get our toll if we don't bother you?" One of the men asked.

"Deal's still on." Harald said.

The men sat down and waited. The first wagon made the corner.

"Now I have to move it back and forth to get it on the road down," Dedrick unhitched the horses and had Siana walk a little down the road. "I hate this part." He climbed up on the wagon.

"Push until I yell, then we need to push it back a little to get it lined up to go down the road. Horses make it too long and they get skittish near the edge."

They worked the first wagon through with the help of the would-be bandits. Once they knew what they were doing they had an easier time with the next two.

The wagons started down the trail, but Harald hung back to talk to the men who were pouring over the boxes Dedrick had left them.

"You like it up here?" he asked.

"Never much good at doing what I was told." One of the men said as he tried to pry a lid off the box. Harald used his knife to pry up one slat, then wrenched it off. The crate held clothes. The next had boots, the last had a mix of root vegetables and squash.

"It may be safer to find a different occupation," Harald pulled a splinter from his hand. "My friend was saying as how he thought having a shelter or even an inn up here would do well. Helping wagons through the gap will earn you some favours."

"What do I know about running an inn?"

"Don't need to know much," Harald said. "Have a place where folks feel safe. You don't need to feed them, but they will be happier knowing they won't be robbed, and you can charge as much for the use of the inn and your help as you get in your toll."

"We'll think on it," the man looked uncertain. "Likely some smooth-talking fellow will show up to take that guy's place."

"Cliff isn't going anywhere," Harald headed down the road toward the wagons. They were going slower downhill than they had going up.

"So, did you convince them to give up their evil ways and leave the Gap?" Dedrick looked over as Harald climbed up on the wagon.

"Suggested they open an inn," Harald made himself comfortable. "Probably more profitable than robbery and they don't have to try to figure out what to do with a crate full of boots that don't fit them."

"I always give them stuff I can't sell, my little revenge for the inconvenience. Their help in the turn was nice, don't think I've ever gone through so fast."

"Keep that in mind when you go back and there's an inn. Don't get cheap—it will only work if people pay."

"Hmmph," Dedrick said. "It will still be robbery."

Harald sat beside Siana at lunch.

"How you doing?"

"Did you have to drop him off the cliff?"

"He stabbed me in the hand." Harald stopped himself. "No, I didn't need to drop him off the cliff, I didn't even want to. If he'd stayed quiet, he'd be up there plotting to rob the next caravan. He didn't think far enough ahead about what he wanted, and definitely not about the cost of getting it."

"I ran away from my father's inn." Siana looked down at her feet. "I wanted to see the world, not people falling off cliffs."

"Why did you follow me?"

"In all the stories, the bandits are sitting around a campfire making plans. I was going to listen in on their plans."

"Life is more complicated than stories. Bandits don't sit around campfires making plans. The only thing they want is to survive another day. Campfires don't help. Kings don't sit on their thrones plotting how to make their people miserable or less miserable. They sign papers and get bored as old men rant about how everything is worse now."

"Sounds dull." Siana looked up at him through her hair.

"It is dull if you let it be, but it doesn't have to be." Harald stretched until his back popped. "I dug out a stable with a guy who told me all about how he built his stable different than other people. He thought he could make the horses more comfortable."

"Were they?"

"I don't know. They didn't say anything. But the guy's life wasn't boring. He was on an adventure to learn how to care for his horses better. I've met farmers who were the same way about growing food. I even met someone who felt that way about teaching people."

"So what are you saying?" Siana asked. "I should be a stablehand or a farmer?"

"You should be something which makes you happy to get up in the morning."

"I don't know what that is," she said. "This is stupid." She got up and went to the other side of the fire.

"See you haven't lost your touch," Sarandia snuggled against him and he put his arm around her.

"Reminding myself life is not about entertaining myself. I have to think about how I am going to do things differently when I get home."

"It will come to you." She nudged him gently. "Don't try to force it. Part of pilgrimage is humility. Live for the day."

"Okay. I hope tomorrow doesn't involve any cliffs."

"How is your hand?" Sarandia picked it up and poked at it. Rodrigo sucked his breath.

"Not as bruised as my conscience," Harald said. "I didn't intend to drop him."

"He was an idiot begging to get dropped." Rodrigo said from the other side of the fire. "Wherever you go, there will be people who don't believe you're serious until you drop them off a cliff."

"How do you convince them you're serious before that?"

"Drop someone else?" Rodrigo shrugged. "I try not to get into those kinds of discussions."

"What would you have done?"

"Probably run him through, then kicked him over the cliff," Rodrigo said. "I wouldn't have been trying to convince a ragtag lot of bandits to take up innkeeping."

"What's wrong with innkeeping?" Siana asked.

"Absolutely nothing, if you're an innkeeper." Rodrigo poked at the fire.

She stuck her tongue out at him. Rodrigo rolled his eyes then helped himself to more soup.

***

Rodrigo woke Harald for his shift. Clouds covered the stars. A breeze played in the trees beside them. The horses whuffed and shifted.

"All clear. Maybe now would be a good time to learn your code. I had no idea what you were trying to say. My hands were burning. My cheek hurt and then my shoulders ached. I had to pretend to get a splinter when the idiot stabbed your hand."

"I guess the first thing is to find out what you can feel and what you can't."

"I only feel pain," Rodrigo said, "A relief as much as a nuisance. I can't imagine how embarrassing it would be to have to feel other things."

"A relief to both of us. Yet there are levels of pain. I shouldn't need to stab myself to get your attention." Harald tapped his fingers on the back of his arm. He kept striking harder until Rodrigo stiffened.

"I felt that!" Rodrigo looked over at Harald.

"Good, now you try."

"I had forgotten this worked both ways." Rodrigo took his turn tapping until Harald felt it.

"So we need to tap hard," Harald said, "or devise a way to hold a pin on our fingers that won't interfere with whatever else we are doing."

"It depends on the situation," Rodrigo waved his fingers. "Sometimes we won't be carrying weapons and could use a pin. Maybe I'll have to start wearing a pin."

"I'm a pilgrim," Harald looked up at the night sky. "I don't know if I'm supposed to wear jewelry."

"Never mind, now you need to teach me the code."

"When the scouts use it, they tap on their neighbour's arm, thus." Harald tapped a quick message on Rodrigo's forearm.

"What did that say?"

"We are being observed, on my right hand."

Rodrigo peered into the darkness and grunted.

"I wouldn't have noticed her at all."

"Her sleep has been restless this night," Harald said. "Her stories didn't prepare her for how easy it is to die out here."

"Now, the code starts simple with 'yes' and 'no'," Harald demonstrated and quickly got more complex. Rodrigo was an apt student.

"I can't believe we don't have something like this. We have a rough finger talk to communicate while others are standing around us, but nothing like this."

"You wouldn't need it."

"There were a few nights this would have saved me a lot of grief."

"Would it have stopped you being banished?"

"Nothing would have prevented that." Rodrigo rubbed his hands across his eyes. "I'm going to hit the sack. We can practice tomorrow."

CHAPTER 12

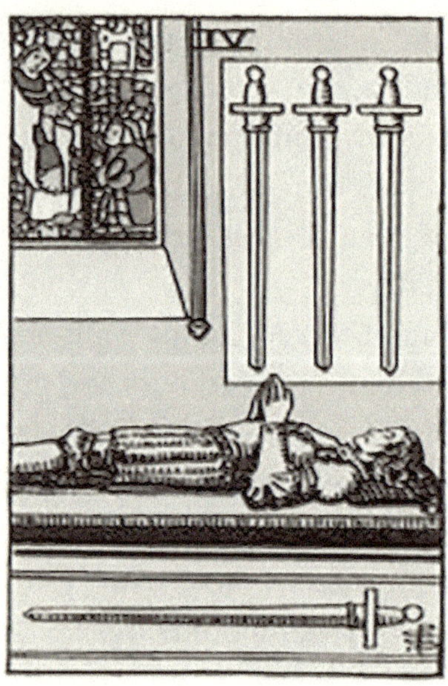

Lady Joan walked into the cathedral with Catrin beside her.

"Should we be here?" Catrin whispered. "You know the priests don't like people like us."

"I refuse to apologize for whom I love." Joan smiled at Catrin. "Priests or no priests."

Lady Joan was welcome to visit the cathedral in a way Joan Carter was not. She planned to take every advantage of her new status. Suze kept busy training people day and night. Joan worried she was overdoing it, but Suze grinned and declared she'd never had so much fun.

The light from the windows painted abstract patterns on the floor. An acolyte appeared at their side as they looked up at the stained glass.

"Welcome." He bowed, his hands hidden in long sleeves. "Perhaps I could tell you a little about the cathedral?"

Joan smiled brightly at him.

"That would be lovely. I am Lady Joan, and this is my friend Catrin."

"Lady Joan." The acolyte's eye went wide. "Are you the one who's brother became an angel?"

"It was a little more complicated." Joan apologized to her brother for using his memory in such a way. "But yes."

"What was it like being held by the angel?"

Joan closed her eyes and opened the door to memory. Light flooded into her and tears squeezed out of her eyes. A hand brushed against her cheek and Joan felt cleaner than any bath could make her. She opened her eyes and dabbed at them with a kerchief Catrin handed her.

"Imagine being filled with light." She pointed to the pattern on the floor. "But it speaking to you, saying you are loved. Not in some general *we are all loved* way, but you, Andrew, are adored beyond measure."

"How did you know my name?" Andrew took a step back.

"Sometimes, when I let the light into my soul, I hear things."

"If I had such light in me," Andrew stared at the dappled floor in awe. "I would dwell in it all the time."

"I would never get anything done." Joan smiled and handed the kerchief back to Catrin. "It is always there when I need to be reminded, but I'm sure the reason I have it is to pass it to others."

Andrew sighed deeply and took them around the building. He showed them odd nooks and crannies. Things most people would never see. To Joan's delight he didn't introduce her to the other people of the cathedral. Monastics and priests bid her welcome with a smile and went on with what they were doing.

"Quick." Andrew pulled them through a door. "Let's take a short cut down this hallway, the Archbishop often comes this way to get a snack from the kitchen."

This hallway stretched grey and utilitarian. Not a picture or a crucifix broke the expanse of stone. It came to a T-junction. Joan guessed one way led to the kitchen and the other up toward the Archbishop's office. Meeting the Archbishop might be a bit too much. She remembered how much Marriette glowed when she spoke of the old man, but he led the church which officially condemned her without knowing her.

They'd almost reached the junction when a cry came from around the corner ahead, then the sound of someone falling. Joan ran around the corner with Andrew and Catrin close behind. The Archbishop lay crumpled at the foot of the stairs. Their footsteps echoed oddly in the hall, then Joan realized she'd heard another person running away from the scene as they ran toward it.

"Don't try to move." Joan let Joan Carter take control. Wagons were sometimes dangerous. She'd learned how to respond. "Andrew, go get help. We'll stay here with him."

Andrew ran down the hall, while Joan knelt on one side and Catrin the other.

"Warn Marriette," the words bubbled out through blood on his lips, "treachery in the church and maybe elsewhere." He shuddered. "May I make my last confession to the light I see shining in you?"

Joan let the light into her. She didn't hear the old man's words; the light swelled and took them, then fell like rain on him. When she opened her eyes, the Archbishop had died and Catrin looked at her with wide eyes, breathing fast.

"Please, my love." Joan caressed Catrin's cheek. And Catrin's breathing slowed. "Never fear me." Catrin covered Joan's hand with her own. The approach of running feet made them sit back.

"I'm sorry," Joan said. "He's gone."

The priests told Andrew to see the women out, then surrounded the Archbishop. The quavering voice of a priest leading in prayer followed them out into the sanctuary.

"Please don't tell anyone." Andrew bowed deeply to them. "The cathedral must make its own announcement in its own time."

Joan put her hand on Andrew's shoulder.

"Let light be always present in your life," she said. They left him there with tears streaming down his cheeks.

"We must go to see Marriette." Joan looked around for the carriage they'd hired.

"Andrew asked us not to tell anyone."

"Marriette is the Regent." Joan climbed into the carriage she'd hired for the day. "Take us to the Palace, please." When Catrin was in and the door closed, she leaned close to her friend. "I need to tell her the old man may have been pushed."

"Are you sure?" Catrin asked.

"No." Joan stared out the window, not seeing the passing city. "But I heard footsteps running away from the scene. Why would someone run away if they hadn't pushed him?"

"Maybe he was going for help?"

"Maybe, but we ran toward him first." Joan sat back in the carriage. She wanted to ask the Light, but she never got that kind of answer. Catrin reached out and took Joan's hand. The warm strength of her hand steadied Joan, so when the carriage pulled up in front of the palace, she knew what she needed to do.

"Please beg the Regent's indulgence," Joan held herself straight and spoke like she knew already her request would be granted. "Ask if she has a moment for her friend, Lady Joan, Arthur's sister."

The servant at the door nodded and let them into a hall filled with paintings and sculpture.

"Wait here, my Lady."

They'd made half a circuit of the room when the servant returned.

"If you will follow me." He led them through halls filled with people walking purposefully from one place to another. Joan never considered how many people worked behind the scenes, running the country. He knocked on a plain looking door. A maid opened it and waved Joan and Catrin in.

The room formed a stone cube with wooden and steel weapons hung on the walls. Marriette sat in a chair against one wall. The maid barred the door and put her back to it.

"We have a few minutes," Marriette's eyes held steel Joan hadn't seen in them before. "I'm told this is the only room with no passages or listening holes. What do you need to tell me?"

Joan curtseyed, and Catrin dropped to the floor.

"It's OK, we're all friends here." Marriette waved at Catrin to rise. "But mention of your brother suggested matters of urgent and private nature."

"We came from the cathedral. I bring grievous news." Joan flung herself at Marriette's knees. "The Archbishop fell down a flight of stairs," her voice broke and she could barely force the words out. "He is dead, Marriette, and a great light of faith died with him."

"Yet, as grievous as this news may be," Marriette spoke evenly in spite of the shaking of her body, "it does not demand privacy such as this."

"I fear someone pushed him," Joan said into Marriette's skirts. She lifted her eyes to look at her friend. "Footsteps ran away from him as we ran toward him. In his last breath, he asked me to warn you of treachery in the church and elsewhere."

"Thank you." Marriette put her hand on Joan's head. "You have put yourself at risk, coming to me like this. Untrusting souls will see conspiracy everywhere. You must be doubly careful. They will try to destroy you by destroying what you love."

"I understand." Joan stood and curtsied again with Catrin by her side. "We will be watchful."

"You may go," Marriette nodded at them.

***

"What do you think?" Marriette said after the door closed behind Joan and Catrin.

"They are sheep for the slaughter." Illandria shook her head.

"Can you watch them?"

"I will do what I can." Illandria rubbed her forehead. "We are busy guarding Torrance from another attempt to make you a widow."

"What!" Marriette half stood. "He said nothing of this to me."

"He was asked not to by the woman who healed you and him."

"Who is she to command my husband?"

"Her mother and the Queen's grandmother were sisters. The closest word we would have for her title would be Grandmother, but she is Queen and high priestess and Grandmother all in one. She wishes to speak with you."

"Then let us speak." Marriette leaned back on her chair.

"If it were that easy," Illandria said. "She is Rehego, what you call waggoners, and since last year they have been forbidden entrance to the Kingdom."

"I will repeal that at once," Marriette said. "It is foolishness."

"Say malice rather." Illandria held her hand up as if to hold Marriette in the chair. "Some had been waiting such an opportunity for many years. It will not be easy to overturn on a whim."

"So how do we meet, she and I?"

"She is ready to reveal herself. We will be watching to learn who is most adamant about her imprisonment. Once she is in prison, you will be able to visit her to question her. There will be witnesses, so you will need to be circumspect.

"Keep me posted, Illandria." Marriette looked down, suddenly tired of the labyrinth of politics.

"You haven't asked about the Archbishop," Illandria came to help Marriette to her feet.

"He told me he was poisoned." Marriette let Illandria settle her gown. "He tried to warn me this was coming. Learn what you can, but be careful."

"Always, your Majesty."

Illandria opened the door and Marshal and his apprentice stood in the hall with identical frowns. Marriette had a vision of the apprentice practicing before a mirror.

"I needed a quiet moment, Marshal."

"Would the quiet moment have anything to do with Lady Joan's visit and the rumours the Archbishop is dead?"

"This binding you carry," Marriette asked as she took Marshal's arm. "Does it allow you to feel your sovereign's grief and heart pain?"

"Just pain of the body," Marshal said.

"Count yourself blessed. We will go to my rooms and find suitable dress to mourn an Archbishop."

At her rooms, Marriette sat on her chair while Marshal stood guard outside.

"It wouldn't be right to wear mourning before the official announcement from the cathedral, but this dress is close enough." Illandria held it up. Marriette nodded her head. She struggled to her feet so Illandria and another maid could strip the dress she wore and replace it with the dull purple fabric. Deft hands straightened creases and checked that it fell properly. They politely ignored the sobs wracking her body. When they were done, they left her alone with her grief.

CHAPTER 13

The bells tolled in grief for the Archbishop. They'd rung all day and night since the cathedral announced his passing. Torrance almost stopped hearing them, then a word would get overlaid by the ringing of a bell and he would remember again.

He went from one part of the city to another checking on schools, watching secretaries look over papers or interview instructors. While he watched, they would serve him tea and biscuits. Often on the napkin lay a sign. Nothing obvious, often a toothpick, but it told him Suze's training had reached another part of the city.

Nobles and citizens had always moved in different circles, but in the last few years, they barely acknowledged each other at all. He was a rarity; he knew no other noble well outside of his own holdings.

"We're done for the day," Torrance told his helpers. "I know it's early, but my wife needs me. She may be Regent, but her grief for her friend is no less painful." They nodded and put their books away. The carriage ride to the palace gave him a chance to listen again to the endless bells.

As he climbed out of the carriage, the bells stopped; their absence echoed within him. The new archbishop would lay the old one to rest and life would go on—except life was ever more dangerous and complex. Marriette whispered to him the Archbishop had been murdered. The young acolyte who had run for help had gone missing. Torrance grieved him as well. His disappearance didn't bode well for Joan and her maid, though a landed Lady would be harder to remove than an unknown young acolyte.

The halls of the palace were subdued as he walked to the rooms he shared with Marriette. The room held the particular silence signalling Master Tiron had just left. Marriette played with a piece from the game, flipping it from white to black and back again.

"What did the rumour monger have for you today?" Torrance took the piece and put it away.

"His sources suggest strongly the Archbishop's death is too convenient to be coincidence. The poor boy being gone cements things. Nothing is official, nobody is even investigating. The next piece to fall in place will be the interim Archbishop. The bishops are supposed to meet and pick one of their number to hold the office until the Holy Father appoints a replacement. It's winter and the sea is rough. It could be months before the word even goes out. A few new bishops have come in from the Emperor's City over the past year, and are trying to push our cathedral to match their model in the Empire. The Emperor is not above playing politics with the Church. It is rumoured he and the Holy Father are not on speaking terms."

"On a different subject," Marriette picked up a book and pulled some papers from its center, "look at this and let me know what you think. While you read, I'm going to take a bath." One of her maids came to help her up and out of the room.

Torrance looked at the papers in his hand. He saw a statement of his House's finances on top. They were specifically about his financial relationship with the Empire. As he would have expected they showed he didn't buy much from the Empire. He sold some, but mostly through intermediaries. *Where did she get this much detail?*

His stomach clenched when he looked at the records for the other Houses. VonFrome bought more than they sold from the Empire, but they weren't bad next to reTaggin who owed most of his estate to the Empire. He had purchased so much it was surprising he had any money left at all. SeGraine's sale of his wines improved his balance. SuDarche, like Torrance, didn't buy much. What he bought were ships. Four ships in the last two years, costing almost as much as Torrance's city house. He would have expected Raspin to have some interaction with the Empire, but he did less business with them than Torrance did, preferring to do all his trading through brokers and middle men.

Did the people the Empire owned plan treachery, or did the careful distance between House and Empire show a deceitful face? Torrance didn't like sending his money away in Empire ships. He made do with local artisans, and paid people who would in turn buy his goods.

Torrance got himself ready for bed and crawled in. Marriette joined him shortly after.

"We are sending too much money to the Empire," he said softly. "It weakens us and leaves less wealth to build up our land."

"So I thought," Marriette whispered back, "yet I can hardly ban trade with the Empire."

"You might forbid debt to the Empire. Debts can be called in more than one way."

"You don't think any of our nobles would turn traitor?"

"It is hard to imagine." Torrance's gut grew cold. "But the Empire has a gift for finding people to prepare the way for their invasion."

"So you think invasion too?"

"It may be harder here," Torrance said. "There may be five centuries or more of Empire soldiers out there in the city. They have to be holed up somewhere because there is little talk on the street about them."

"I heard you met a few of them yourself."

"True." Torrance's throat twinged slightly. "The woman who healed me asked me to wait before I told you."

"So some woman asks and you agree to hide things from your wife and Regent?"

"She healed you and then me." Torrance rolled to his back. "I owed her a debt."

"Those are dangerous debts," Marriette said.

"What happened to my wife who wanted to change the world and be damned to anyone trying to stop her?"

"A knife in the street happened. Master Tiron with his talk of sacrificing pawns happened. The Archbishop being murdered happened."

"There is always a cost to what we do," Torrance said, his heart heavy.

"But others are paying the cost!' Marriette spoke into the pillow to muffle the rising wail.

"That's the way it is. We can't pay the whole price any more than we can do everything needed. We do what we must, and pray it is enough." Torrance held her tight and rubbed her back, wishing they were back at his home so she didn't need to fear being overheard. "Hold on until Harald returns."

***

The acting Archbishop presented himself to Marriette at Council. He didn't look at all familiar.

"Bishop Velagoa," he introduced himself. "As often the temporary replacement is not retained as Archbishop, my election was seen as expedient." He sat back in his chair and listened to the ebb and flow of conversation. SeGraine had moved from wanting protection from the Empire's goods to pushing for more open trade. He had dressed in clothes clearly intended to show the latest fashion in the Empire's Capital, though how he knew what that might be was a mystery to Marriette. She'd already seen courtiers of the seGraine House, but also reTaggin and suDarche taking up the style.

As she usually did, Marriette noted the conversation, though lately she hardly spoke at all. The Council knew she would make no major changes as Regent. They were testing each other's strength, positioning themselves for when Harald returned.

"One thing." Bishop Velagoa held up his hand as Marriette was about to dismiss them. "The church is concerned there is no properly consecrated ruler on the throne of Belandria. We admire the courage and conviction you've brought to your months of Regency." *He looks more like the cat that ate the canary.* "But it is time the Kingdom has a proper Monarch. We have received no word from the Holy Father if the King has made it there. It has been six months; he should have been there and back by now. While there are undoubtedly significant discussions to have, I want to state the church has no objection to Her Majesty Regent becoming Her Majesty."

"Nonsense," reTaggin banged the table. "No woman can sit on the throne, they don't have the constitution for it."

"If she is to become Queen in actuality, rather than in form," Raspin spoke very slowly as if he were inventing each word as he said it. "Then according to law, she must give up ownership of any estate she holds under a family name."

Marriette almost laughed at the thought of Raspin supporting her as Queen to gain control of her father's estates.

"We will give this suggestion due consideration," Marriette said into the brief silence following Raspin's statement. "Thank you, gentlemen." She rose to her feet ending the meeting. Bishop's Velagoa's mouth opened, but he wisely closed it without making any sound.

***

"What can you tell me about this Bishop Velagoa?" she asked Master Tiron over their evening game.

"He was the Holy Father's ambassador to the Emperor. The two aren't on speaking terms so Velagoa became go between. A few months back he was suddenly attached to Sier Clasighi as a spiritual advisor. Church people suggest it is a penance for something and he will never advance past bishop."

"Unless he can get himself appointed as Archbishop in Belandria," Marriette placed a piece and flipped over several from black to white. "I have heard much of the animosity between the Holy Father and the Emperor is over the appointment of Bishops and Archbishops in the Empire. Perhaps he is hoping supporting me as Queen would translate into me supporting him as Archbishop."

"A reasonable supposition," Master Tiron made his play and took control of a large section of the board. "My sources suggest he has become a creature of the Empire. His pressure for you to take the throne comes from someone behind him. The Empire would delight in having someone weak on the throne. Sier Clasighi wines and dines your noble Houses and listens avidly to their complaints. It may very well be the Emperor wants you on the throne and will manipulate events to make it happen."

"Manipulate, as in murdering an Archbishop to put his mouthpiece in place."

"It wouldn't be the first time clerics have died for politics." Master Tiron held up a piece from the board. There is a reason why in this game priests are not to be counted on. They turn too easily, or they are playing their own game. No one in the church above the rank of priest is unaware of politics." He put the piece back down on the board with a slap.

Marriette looked at the game. She'd found it difficult enough when they play with pawns who were simple black or white. Trying to keep straight the special pieces and under what circumstance they would turn made her head hurt. The baby kicked as if it wanted out now, though she had two months before the due date. She wanted a warm bath to take the ache of winter out of her bones.

Master Tiron left, as ever, a minute or two before Torrance came in. Marriette had set herself to figure out how he knew Torrance approached. The timing was too tight for it to be guess work. She listened for boots in the hallway. Tiron had vanished by the time Torrance greeted the guards. Perhaps the man had extraordinary hearing.

"Come rub my back in the bath," Marriette said when Torrance came in.

"It will scandalize the servants," Torrance tossed his coat over a chair.

"We haven't done anything to scandalize them for a while." Marriette tried to smile.

"Then it is my duty to serve my Queen," Torrance wiggled his brows suggestively. Marriette sighed and allowed him to pull her to her feet. The bath steamed as Marriette allowed her maid to strip the dress from her. The girl rolled her eyes when Marriette informed her Torrance would stay. She laid out the towels, soaps and the implements of Marriette's bath then left.

Torrance ignored them all. He helped her lift her bulk into the tub and poured water over her. He rubbed her back and shoulders and whispered ridiculous things in her ears to made her giggle most unlike a Regent.

"Tell me what you've heard out there in the streets," Marriette said as he finally picked up the soap and lathered her back and hair.

"People are uncertain," Torrance poured water over her head. "The King has been gone six months and some now. There are rumours he's dead, or he's abdicated and become a shepherd outside the Holy City. Even rumours he returned and is locked up in the dungeons below the palace."

"We have dungeons below the palace?" Marriette tried to turn to look at him.

"I believe there are a few cells down there. Most prisoners are held at the City Armoury where there are plenty of guards and kitchens and the rest to feed people in the cells. The only people who are kept here are prisoners of political importance."

"I suppose the King would be a prisoner of political importance." Marriette pushed some soap away from her eyes.

"You thinking of checking out the cells?" Torrance ladled more water over her until she was rinsed clean.

"If I knew where they were, I could order people locked away if they displeased me."

"I'd better make sure I do a good job of drying you off then," Torrance picked up a towel and wrapped it around her as she stood. He lifted her out of the water, then gently dried her off.

"What do you do when you come to the palace?" Marriette asked. "Master Tiron always leaves not a minute before you arrive. I don't know how he knows you are here."

"I come in the west door, because it is closest to your rooms, check with whoever on duty if there is something I need to know and if you are in your rooms. Then I come to your room. I wave at Jeremiah as I walk by if he's in his office, which he invariably is."

"No one runs ahead to warn him," Marriette said. "He up and leaves, and a minute later you walk in."

"Does he always sit in the same place?"

"Yes, but then I do as well."

"Try sitting in a different seat tomorrow and see what he does."

CHAPTER 14

"Do we have anyone in the palace cells?" Marriette asked Marshal.

He looked at her and shook his head.

"Your sources are improving," he said. "Do you wish to see her?"

"Of course." Marriette bit her cheek to keep from asking *Who?*

"Where is your apprentice today?" she asked as they walked down the hall past the room where she still escaped to even if she didn't beat at Marshal with a wooden sword any more.

"Family issues," Marshal said. "He may as well deal with them now. Once he's Marshal there is no time to worry about that."

"Come now." Marriette looked up at him. "You must have family somewhere?"

Marshal opened a door and ushered her through. This door had guards on both sides of the door.

"My father still lives in a village to the north, not far from where you spent the winter last year." Marshal said. "My brother runs the farm and complains about the cost of the brood he's raising. Six sons and a daughter, all like to be taller than him. None of them have the slightest interest in anything but farming, thank God. My sister married a fellow down the road from him, but her husband died so she and her daughter live with my brother. My younger brother has an inn in the nearby village. He comes once a year to bring me the news."

"If you retire will you return home?"

"I hated the farm. I'd go crazy after the first day. So, I send them money as I can and for the rest, they're on their own. Marshal before me told me to grieve them as if they were dead, because I'd have no time to grieve them later."

"That seems harsh." Marriette kept her hand on the outside wall as they started down a circular stair case.

"Being Marshal is a harsh job, your Majesty."

Marriette saved her breath for the stairs. If she got this puffed going down, what would it be like going up again?

At the bottom of the stairs were two more guards standing in the light of lamps hung high on the walls. One of them nodded at her before opening the door.

The cells were dry and slightly chilly.

"King Harald's grandfather was terribly disappointed the rock down here didn't weep moisture. He complained no proper dungeon should be dry and comfortable." Marshal walked her along the hall to the single closed door. He knocked. "She's here as you said she'd be," Marshal called through the door.

"Bring her in," an old woman's voice said from the other side of the door. Marshal opened the door and waved Marriette into the cell.

A pallet lay on a raised platform of rock. A bucket with a lid sat in the corner.

The old woman sat on the bed as if waiting for Marriette to arrive; from what Marshal said, she had been.

"My apologies, your Majesty, my legs aren't what they used to be." She made a bow from the waist, but remained sitting.

"Stay," Marriette held out her hand, "we have no need of formality here and now." Marshal left the cell door open and leaned on the wall across the way.

"Do you still have your cards?" Marriette asked.

"Not with me," The old woman shrugged. "I'm surprised you remember."

"They started me on the path to here," Marriette said. "I still dream about that reading."

"If you are dreaming about it, then you haven't done with it, but then there are always new devils and new decisions." The woman patted the bed beside her. "Sit down, I remember how much my feet hurt when I had my boy."

Marriette sat and sighed as she stretched out her legs.

"You are in grave danger." The old woman's voice carried the cadence from when she'd read the cards. "You were safer when your enemies wanted you dead. It is harder when they want your soul. Know who you trust and trust them with your life, but don't trust them to make your decisions. When all your hopes are shattered, you will know what you need to do."

"Cheerful." Marriette rolled her shoulders.

"You want cheerful," the old woman said, "you should have lived a different life. But you were shaped for this time." She patted Marriette on the leg. Marshal stiffened, but Marriette waved him off. "You'll do fine." A smile changed all the lines on the old woman's face into joy.

"What do I call you?"

"I am Grandmother," the old woman sounded wistful. "though my son has yet to make me a grandmother in truth. It is a title."

"You're waggoner," Marriette said. "Are you their ruler?"

"We prefer Rehego, and not so much their ruler as their Grandmother. I give them advice which they mostly ignore."

"Why did you heal me? Why heal Torrance?"

"Do you not think you are worth healing?"

"Everybody around here has at least three reasons for doing anything." Marriette heard bitterness creep into her voice. "It wasn't just charity that put you on the side of the road."

"And that is why your Marshal has me locked so comfortably in this cell," Grandmother waved at him. Marshal frowned back. "He doesn't believe I saw you dying on the street in a dream before I healed you."

"That doesn't explain why."

"No, it doesn't." Grandmother didn't say anything else. Marriette waited until her feet stopped aching enough to consider standing up. She put her hand out and Marshal helped her up. He closed the door and offered her his arm.

The stairs up were much worse than coming down.

"Did they make these stairs deliberately awkward?" Marriette asked as they reached the top.

"Yes, the lower gate to the cells is well guarded, but if it falls, then anyone coming up these stairs is at a disadvantage." He waited until her breathing slowed before guiding her back out the door. "The Council has asked to meet with you at your convenience," Marshal said as they walked out into the hallway.

"You tell me now?" Marriette glared up at him. "Shouldn't you have told me before you took me down to the dungeon?"

"You are Regent," Marshal's face might have been carved from stone. "They must know you aren't to be bullied."

"I suppose then putting on a proper dress to meet with the Council would be a wise course."

"Indeed," Marshal said. "All rulers must arm themselves before going into battle."

Marshal waited in the hall as Illandria dressed Marriette for battle.

"If you were King, you'd carry a sword and wear armour. But as Regent and Queen, you must be more subtle." Illandria pulled out a black dress that looked deceptively simple. When Marriette examined it, she saw stitching running through the entire dress. "Those are patterns of power. We wear them to show we are fearless, but they are subtle so only those who know to look will see them."

"The Council is not subtle," Marriette ran her fingers across the dress.

"Their purpose may not be, but the men at the table have played the game of power for years. Don't think you know them by what you see on their faces. They show you what they wish you to see, and for their own design. They each have a use for you that doesn't account for your wellbeing."

Marriette swept out into the hall in the dress. It filled the hall and hid the belly carrying her child. Marshal nodded once and led her to the Council chamber.

VonFromme and the old men were there, but none of their aides and courtiers. Even duSarche had travelled up to attend the meeting. Torrance's seat was empty.

"He is off with Lady Joan," reTaggin said as soon as Marriette had seated herself. "She is dashing about the city asking the most ridiculous questions. No one wants to talk about next year's harvest. The young men will go where they will. If she doesn't want them, she should marry and let her husband keep her safe."

"You called me here to complain about Lady Joan?" Marriette asked. "Perhaps a better discussion would be how you could learn from her."

"Learn?" reTaggin turned red. "Don't be absurd."

"She made her estate turn a profit in her first year." Marriette held up a finger. "She brought a group of recalcitrant holders into line." Another finger. "And she is making it clear she won't allow interference from young men looking to marry into land."

"She will never be more than the Lady of a parcel of hill and rock."

"She is our friend," Marriette said.

"She is running around with your husband making a fool out of you," seGraine almost shouted.

"Ah," Marriette sat back and contemplated her Council. "You think you are telling me my husband is committing adultery. Perhaps goading me into a rage to make me set him aside. If a Queen is desirable on the throne, an eligible Queen would be more so." She leaned forward and slapped her fan on the table. "I trust Torrance with my life. Whatever he does, he does with my knowledge and approval." She leaned back and tapped her fingers with the fan. "I would be interested in knowing what promises are being made to you by Sier Calighi."

"Sier Calighi is the ambassador of the Empire." Acting Archbishop Velogoa leaned forward, his mouth turned down. "He doesn't involve himself in local politics."

"He is the servant of the Empire." Marriette sent her words at him like darts. "He would dance naked in the streets if the Emperor instructed him to do so. It is his place to meddle in politics. I wish to know the extent of his meddling. Surely my Council is not afraid to share with their Regent the wealth of advice the ambassador has for them?"

"It is unseemly to intrude on private conversations," the Bishop said.

"So now the ambassador is a priest giving confession?" Marriette pointed the fan at the Bishop. "You are here without our leave and your voice is irritating us. Be silent or we will have Marshal remove you. Shall we ask the Bishops to reconsider their choice?" She held his gaze until he ground his teeth and dropped his eyes. She looked around the table.

"What has the Empire been promising the nobles of our realm?" Marriette threw out the challenge. The men looked down at the table. "Let me tell you what he is promising then." Marriette pointed her fan at seGraine. "Increased access to trade your wine in the Empire, permission to use the Emperor's name, perhaps even a seal?" SeGraine coloured slightly and his lips thinned. She thrust at reTaggin like the fan was a sword. "You get better terms on your debt. It can't be fun discovering you sold your soul to the devil and didn't get near what you thought it was worth." She looked at suDarche. "How many ships? What will it take to turn your Duchy from being a fishing village to a center of trade? You will bring trade agreements to us before you sign them. If you sign something which puts our land at a disadvantage we may decide to see it as treason. The Empire has bought as many kingdoms as it has conquered. Belandria will not be one such land."

She stood and swept out of the room before the men could push themselves to their feet.

"Dangerous game you are playing," Marshal muttered at her.

"The Empire wants a weak Queen on the throne. Maybe I can slow down their plots by refusing to be weak."

"Can you slow the rain by being strong?" Marshal asked.

CHAPTER 15

The rain pounded down on Harald's head like fingers drumming on his skull. Siana and Sarandia huddled under their tarp on the wagon. The drivers and Dedrick wore wide brim hats to protect their heads.

Harald couldn't see very far into the downpour, but he didn't think any bandits would be out in this weather. Bows would be impossible, so it would be hand to hand fighting to take the caravan. Most bandits weren't interested in putting their lives on the line. From the glimpses he got, they were riding past plowed fields.

They'd been moving through the rain for three days. As soon as they came out of the mountains it had started and poured without let up day or night. Harald tried to hunch a different way to relax muscles that cramped in the damp.

village ahead

Rodrigo signaled from the lead wagon. He'd taken to the scout code eagerly and spent a lot of time trying to refine it.

The village turned out to be eight houses around a central square. One house had a shingle hung out so Harald sat with the wagons while the others went in to eat and get warm. The innkeeper brought Harald an oiled cloth to sit under and a bowl of fragrant stew. He used the bread accompanying the stew as a spoon. With a full belly and shelter from the incessant pounding Harald kept an eye on the caravan while he let his thoughts wander.

He'd planned to be gone for four months, six at the most. Their plans hadn't lasted past the ship which foundered on shoals trying to avoid the black sails of pirates. The sole things Harald rescued were the signet ring in his pouch and Sarandia. He hadn't paid much attention to passing time as they meandered through the backroads of the Empire. Now Dedrick obsessed about every passing day on the road and Harald wondered how long they'd been gone. Five months? Six? Sarandia hadn't known she was expecting when they began, now she needed to be lifted up and down from the wagon and had to waddle everywhere.

Dedrick came out the inn.

"Hoy," he said, "the innkeeper's son will watch the wagons for the night. I thought you might like a chance to cuddle up with your pretty wife. Siana is in with the innkeeper's daughter for the night."

Harald's grin made his face ache in the damp.

"You can't imagine."

"When I'm on the last leg home after a trip, I have no trouble imagining." Dedrick slapped Harald on the shoulder and leaned against the wagon. "I'll wait for the kid to come out so I can show him what to do."

The innkeeper pointed up the stairs and grinned at Harald. Sarandia waited for him in a room holding a bed with a little space to sidle around the edges. Harald closed the door and stripped off his wet clothes. He toweled himself dry with a cloth his wife handed him then sank down on the bed with a deep sigh. Sarandia lowered herself down beside him.

"So, husband of mine." She trailed her fingers across his chest. "How does the work of a caravan guard suit you?"

"I could enjoy any occupation if I have you to come home to." Harald enjoyed the weight and warmth of her head on his arm. "I have to admit I enjoy not needing to worry about what new problem the council wants me to solve, or think how I can politely refuse the advances of the Empire without offending them."

"It seems so much like a dream," Sarandia said. "I can't imagine worrying about what gown to wear to a ball, or who I should notice or invite for tea. What will happen when we go back?"

"I've been thinking the same thing; for all that I'm King, I didn't know what I was doing half the time. That's how Tamas got his hooks into me. I'm not sure I know any better now."

"God sent us on this journey." Sarandia squirmed up against him. "We will be guided when we need."

Harald pulled the thin blanket over them. She wore a thin shift and all his clothes were hung about the room. He tried to find a position which didn't push his need at her. She trailed her fingers from his cheek down his side until he gasped.

"I am your wife," she whispered, "I'm your lover. I've been yours since the first time I saw you and you treated me with kindness and respect."

***

Harald put his clothes back on and grinned at Sarandia. When he had dressed he helped her with her clothes, then they went downstairs hand in hand.

Dedrick waved at them from the side of the common room.

"I'm glad to see the night was good for you. Sit and eat. I'm told the rain is supposed to let up in midmorning so I'm not in much of a rush to go out and get wet again."

"Is it always like this?" Harald asked.

"There are usually heavy rains this time of year," Dedrick drank from a mug of tea. "Sometimes they are heavier and sometimes lighter. We need be careful over the next stretch. There are mudslides off the hills which can block the road."

By midmorning the rain had slowed enough Dedrick decided to start on his way. Rodrigo handed Harald a hat.

"Won it last night in a game of bones." He laughed as Harald put it on. "But then again maybe he lost on purpose." He unrolled his hat and arranged it carefully. Harald shrugged and went out to help get the caravan rolling.

The road wound between hills covered with trees. There were a couple of spots where he saw fresh dirt spread at the bottom of the hill, but nothing to threaten the road. The rain stopped and a heavy mist came off the hills to shroud them in grey.

The fog magnified sounds. The creaks and groans of the wagons echoed off unseen hills and he listened to the chatter of Sarandia and Siana in the wagon ahead. They talked about Sarandia's baby and joked about names.

Harald heard a roar from the right along with the cracking of trees. His first thought was some kind of huge beast, then Siana screamed.

"Sarandia!" the girl cried, then a crash told him the wagon had tipped over. Harald jumped to the ground and ran forward as the wagon halted. He sank up to his knees, then fought through mud up to his waist. The noise stopped and the ground tried to solidify around him. Siana still screamed so he pushed on toward her voice.

He came out of the fog to see the girl holding Sarandia's arm. The earth covered the rest of his beloved. He threw mud aside as he tried to free her, but the earth fell back in to cover her. Then Rodrigo helped at one side, and Dedrick on the other, two drivers flanking them. They uncovered Sarandia, but she lay grey and unmoving on the ground. Harald picked her up and held her, but he couldn't tell if there was any breath or warmth in her.

"Let me," Siana pulled her away and forced Sarandia's mouth open. She used the sleeve of her blouse to wipe out Sarandia's mouth, then covered her mouth with her own and breathed air into Sarandia.

Harald watched and held his own breath. If that was what was needed to make her live, he'd gladly never breathe again.

Sarandia choked and vomited while Siana held her head. Carefully Siana cleaned Sarandia's mouth again when Dedrick handed her a clean cloth. Harald knelt beside his wife, hardly believing he had her back.

"Whatever is in my power to give," he said to Siana, "anything at all, ask and I will make it happen." He held Sarandia in his arms celebrating each breath she took.

"It is something I learned from the shepherds." She turned deep red and looked down. "Sometimes lambs are born with something in their throats. If you clear it out, you can breathe into them."

"You learned it from the shepherds," Harald didn't want to let go of Sarandia to wipe his tears, so Siana's face looked blurred. "You have used the knowledge to save my wife. That is no small thing."

"I saved her because she's my friend, not because I want a reward."

"Understood," Harald said, "but you saved her and I have given you my word."

Siana nodded and sat holding Sarandia. Rodrigo tapped Harald on the shoulder.

"A minute, friend?" He took Harald aside. "A mighty promise to give to a young girl."

"I meant it." Harald glanced back to where Siana sat with Sarandia.

"Of course you did," Rodrigo said, "but be careful of the day she learns who you are and what kind of power your promise has."

Harald nodded and went back to Sarandia. Dedrick had sent the driver of the last wagon back to get help from the village. They'd found the second driver up against a tree with his leg snapped like a twig. He rode in the wagon and would be left at the inn.

People arrived with shovels and wheelbarrows and started digging out the wagon. It had blocked the flow and protected the women. Miraculously, nothing on the wagon broke so they righted it and loaded it up again. The horses weren't caught in the mudslide so once their harnesses were untangled, they were ready to start off again. Dedrick took over driving the first wagon to make up for the missing man. Harald sat with Sarandia in the third wagon.

Two days they drove through fog, then light mist and finally sunshine. The villages got closer together and the people spoke with an accent Harald had to work to understand.

On the third day, Sarandia woke with cramps.

"The baby," she said, "but it is too early."

Harald signaled Rodrigo who ran back to tell them to find a village close by. He ran ahead but didn't stop at the first wagon. He sped around the corner and vanished up the road.

Harald held Sarandia and prayed as she screamed. Rodrigo appeared in a donkey cart with an old woman beside her. She wore the riotous colours of a Rehego woman, but Harald gladly set up the lean to for the woman to work. She whispered encouragement to Sarandia and had her breathing hard. Siana fetched water and Harald was vaguely aware people were doing things like lighting fires and warming blankets. Sarandia stopped screaming and he heard her weeping.

"Poor wee one," the old woman said, "sometimes they are too early." Harald walked around the tarp and took his child from the old woman. She was perfect, but she lay inert in Harald's hands. Without thinking he opened the little one's mouth and swiped his finger through it then breathed gently into the infant.

"I tried," the old woman said. "I tried everything I knew."

Harald's knees shook and he let himself collapse, still holding the motionless body.

Arthur, he flung his prayer into the sky, *I beg you, I plead with you, I will give my life in place of my child's.*

Light surrounded him

My son, the light spoke in his mind, *I am who created the one you name.*

Please.

Live, love, be filled with joy.

Harald wanted to object until he realized the light was speaking to the baby he held. She moved and squirmed in his arms, then wailed.

The light chuckled.

I offered the girl who saved my wife whatever I had in my power to give. Can I offer God any less? I know I am not worthy, but my life is yours.

It already was, my son, the light laid a hand on his head, *but now you know it too. Rule wisely and kindly in my name.*

Harald opened his eyes as the old woman took the baby from his arm and put it on Sarandia. The babe cuddled up and she put her to her breast and she fed.

"If God healed my child," Sarandia looked at her daughter and the air almost glowed with her love. "I was sure He'd make sure there was milk for her."

"I am blessed beyond measure." The old woman bowed down. Harald thought he caught a glimpse of tears.

"Will you join us for a meal? We need to give Sara and the girl some time to rest." Dedrick arranged a blanket on the ground for her. Harald left them to talk and went to sit with Sarandia.

"What happened?" Sarandia caressed his face with her free hand. "You were holding our baby and weeping, then light surrounded you and she moved and cried.

"I called out to Arthur." Harald whispered, "The only name I knew the angel by."

"And he came?"

Harald shook his head and tried to find words.

"God came," he said, "and spoke to our daughter. I tried to give my life in exchange, but God told me it was already his."

Sarandia nodded and rested her head on his chest.

"What shall we call her?"

"I'm thinking Arthuria Siana. We can add more later if we want."

"What," Rodrigo put a hand on his chest. "She doesn't get called after me? Probably just as well."

He handed Harald a bowl of stew.

"Thank you, my friend." Harald clasped Rodrigo's arm. "I know how much I owe you."

After the meal, the old woman declared Sarandia could ride with the infant. She refused to take any payment for her part.

"I need nothing beyond what I've seen." She nodded and rode off in her donkey cart.

They reached the village a short time later and the priest came out to meet them.

"I've been praying since your friend showed up and asked for the local midwife. I know she's not what most people expect, but she is very good."

"She is indeed," Harald said, "Would you care to bless our daughter?"

They trooped into the church where the priest blessed and baptized Arthuria Siana. Siana turned red when she heard her name, but then grinned from ear to ear. She stood as godmother for Arthuria, and Dedrick as his godfather. Rodrigo laughed when they asked him and told Harald the kid didn't need that kind of trouble.

As they left the church, Harald dug out what coins he had and gave them to the priest.

"I'm sure you can find people to help," Harald said.

"Bless you." The priest laid his hand briefly on Harald's shoulder.

As they left the village, Dedrick pointed ahead.

"You see there? You can see the waters of the sea and the glitter of Lusia, the gem of the Empire."

Home, came the signal from Rodrigo, *trouble.*

CHAPTER 16

For all they'd seen the city from the hill, it took another week for the caravan to arrive. Sarandia carried Thuria in a sling on her breast. Harald watched her check a hundred times a day that she breathed and thrived. She chuckled and laughed through the days and had an incredible appetite. Siana found some cloths to swaddle her.

They rolled up to the city and Harald had to force himself not to gawk. Bellopolis had no true wall. No need, for it had been built after his great-grandfather made peace among the Houses. Walls and defenses stood only at the port where pirates had been known to make lightning raids.

Lusia was walled with stone, white and blinding in the afternoon light. The walls stretched away in either direction at least forty feet tall. The road cut through a broad swath of green.

126

"Killing zone," the driver said back to Harald. "I'm always a bit nervous until we get to the gate. Not that there isn't a hundred ways to get killed inside the city too."

The guards barely glanced at the wagons or Dedrick's papers. The drove through the gates, then the stench of the city hit them. Lusia had more poor than his own city. Harald hadn't thought much of the poor beyond what the church demanded of him. Not until Marriette challenged him. He vowed he would pay more attention when he got home.

Beggars ran up to the wagons, but Dedrick drove on without slowing. They turned off the main road and followed a narrower way for a while before he turned through an open gate in a high wall. Boys ran and shut the gate behind them, then started to unhitch the horses.

A woman came out of the building who looked very much like Dedrick.

"So you finally made it?" she said. "I had made up my mind to start worrying tomorrow."

"We are here and whole," Dedrick hugged the woman. "My sister Margarite," he introduced her to Harald and the others.

"Harald is a guard I hired along with Rodrigo here. Sarandia is Harald's wife and the babe is new born. Siana is the daughter of an old friend who has hired on for the trip."

"Welcome all." Margarite smiled broadly at them. "Come in and get cleaned up while I get supper started.

Harald washed in the water set out in a bowl in the room they'd been given. Then he held Thuria while Sarandia washed. He still struggled to believe this perfect babe was his. Thuria gurgled at him and Harald's heart overflowed. She then gladly returned to her mother.

"All she does is eat." Sarandia put the infant to her breast.

"She does something besides eat." Harald grinned. "We'll need more cloths."

They went out into the main house where Rodrigo already sat with his hosts. The table held fruit and bread. A woman in a plain dress carried in a plate of steaming fish then vanished.

If he hadn't known he was in a house behind a wall within a city surrounded by a wall, Harald would have thought they were on a spacious estate. Light poured in through open windows and greenery hung inside and outside the openings. The air wasn't as thick as when they entered Lusia, or maybe he'd adjusted to it already. They sat at a low table and ate quietly.

When they were done and the dishes cleared Dedrick broke the silence.

"What are you up to next?" he asked. "I can still use you as guards."

"Didn't have much to do." Harald sat back pleasantly full.

"Enough," Dedrick said, "this was an easy trip."

"I still have a pilgrimage to complete." Harald sat back. "I need a ferry across to the Holy City."

"Sadly that is easier to say than to accomplish." Margarite frowned and shook her head. With the Emperor on the outs with the Holy Father, the traffic between the cities has slowed."

"The Empire is interfering with pilgrims?" Harald shook his head.

"Not directly," Dedrick said, "but where they once had free hostels and a free ferry to the Holy City, the hostels are now expensive hotels and the ferry costs a month's wages and there is a line up to get a ticket."

"Are there other boats we can take?" Harald asked.

"The Holy City is very particular about who lands on their docks. You must have a license from the Holy City to land." Dedrick shrugged his shoulders.

"And a license to land here, now." Margarite looked up at the ceiling.

"So, how do we get tickets?" Sarandia asked.

"I've heard you can go to the Cathedral of the Ascension of John, which is the Emperor's cathedral." Margarite said.

"How do we get there?" Harald asked.

"I'll walk you there," Dedrick said.

"I'm going to stay here with Thuria." Sarandia looked down at her babe. "The noise and heat won't be good for her."

"I will stay and rest as well," Rodrigo said. "You will do better without my presence. May I suggest you leave your club here? You wouldn't want to try to explain bringing those runes into a church. You may carry my sword if you wish."

"I don't want to carry a sword either, it doesn't fit with being a pilgrim." Harald put the club on the table. "We should be safe enough in a church."

While they walked in the shade of the walls and houses lining the streets making the day cool enough, even if the shouts of children and vendors echoed painfully off the stone and brick. When they entered a market, heat and the stench of the city were like a club. Harald's eyes watered and his shirt clung to his skin. The echo vanished, but the number of people vying for his attention increased. Dedrick forged through the crowd ignoring fish and vegetables vendors shoved in his face. Harald stayed close. They entered another shadowy avenue, but the stench stayed with them—though it changed as they walked.

"People say they love the smell of the sea," Dedrick said, "but I don't understand how."

"Maybe they mean the smell when they've got away from the docks." Harald breathed through his mouth until his nose adjusted. They reached another broad expanse of pavement, empty of vendors. Clumps of people scurried across it, but the birds claimed most of it. On the other side loomed a building which made the cathedral in Bellopolis look like a country parish.

"Why did you say it is the Emperor's Church?" Harald asked massaging out the stiffness from staring up at the towers.

"His father started it and the Emperor finished it. They paid with their own money, and so claim the right to choose who stands in the pulpit. Technically it is not the Cathedral of Lusia, but for all practical purposes, nothing happens in the church not first approved in there."

"I hope the Emperor isn't there," Harald muttered.

"You think he knows you?" Dedrick started to laugh, then looked at Harald. "You're serious, aren't you? The Emperor might recognize you. I'm going to pretend I don't know who you must be."

"It is better if I stay Harald, the caravan guard." Harald started out across the square with Dedrick beside him. They meandered past the flocks of birds creating their own cacophony of coos and thumping wings. His shirt stuck to him again and Harald sighed; no one would want to be anywhere near him.

They barely crossed into the cool shade of the building when an acolyte appeared at Harald's shoulder.

"Welcome pilgrim," the young man said. "Congratulations on reaching the pinnacle of your journey."

"I must travel to the Holy City." Harald looked around briefly.

"Crowded and dirty," the acolyte said. "There is illness there, so we had to restrict travel. You can finish your pilgrimage here and not risk taking sickness home with you." He walked quickly as they talked, not stopping to show windows or crosses to them. At home, a visitor would be lucky to look at everything just once. The stained glass sent light glowing across the huge space, but as Harald examined them he saw they were all similar. The faces had the same look of peaceful disdain, pushing Harald's gaze in search of a more welcoming figure. The statues also stood apart from the people who wandered through the church.

Harald fought his impatience down. He needed to travel quickly to the Holy City. He had to jump through whatever hoops were needed to make that happen.

"Here." His guide bowed slightly. "You may light candles for whomever you wish. I must leave you to give your prayers of thanksgiving for safe travel." He tapped a box on his way past the candles.

"I'm a caravaner, not a pilgrim." Dedrick scowled at where the acolyte vanished into the crowd. "But I know when I'm being sold a bill of goods."

"True, but we must stay and light a few candles and make our offering. I don't want the priests marking a too quick departure." Harald lit a candle and offered up a prayer for Marriette. Another candle and another prayer. Each one added to the stillness in his center. The church might be false, but his prayers were real.

When enough time had passed, he led Dedrick out the door not far from the bank of candles into the street. It wasn't so much a street as a narrow alley. Harald could have reached out and touched both walls.

The silhouettes of three men with swords blocked them in front. A scrape of a foot on the cobbles betrayed the men behind them. The alley was bare of anything he could use as a weapon.

"We just need the big blond," one man said, "kill the other."

Harald spun to go back into the church, but the door had closed after them. The men behind him carried clubs instead of swords. Harald charged them and bowled them over. Dedrick stayed right behind him and picked up a club.

"No, go." He took the club from Dedrick and pushed him down the alley. A couple of taps on the head convinced the two men he'd knocked down to stay down.

One of the men with swords hung back.

"You must be the officer," Harald lifted his club. "Sending the others to do your dirty work." A hand tried to grab his foot and he stomped on it. He hadn't hit that one hard enough. The scream filled the alley, so Harald jumped forward to attack. He beat one sword aside and brought the club down hard on the sword hand of the other attacker. The man swore and dropped the sword. Harald jumped back and parried the lunge from the other with the club. He stepped inside the man's reach and tossed the club to his left hand. He pulled the man into him with his right hand on the man's sword arm. The club made a satisfying hollow sound as Harald hit the attacker's head. He snatched at the sword but a length of steel pierced his right arm, then seconds later his left. The blade hovered at his throat for a second before a club hit him from behind and Harald fell to the pavement. His cheek burned as the tip of the sword followed him all the way down. Blood dripped from his face as he tried to push himself up. A foot shoved him down and rough hands bound his arms

Harald tapped his fingers in what he hoped looked like an attempt to untie his hands. A bag covered his head and they picked him up and dropped him on a cart that creaked as it moved through the alley.

"Sorry, your Majesty, but we can't have you awake on a cart meant for corpses." The blow on his temple was measured and firm. Lights burst into being in Harald's eyes, then they vanished and carried his consciousness with them.

***

Rodrigo played with the club. The runes fascinated him. They were so close to the runes of binding, but not quite. He'd heard of the binding of Marshals to the Belandria royalty and knew it to be Rehego work, but he'd never expected the complexity of the runes. As if using them to bind two people together was too small a task for them.

The pain ran through his right arm and he dropped the club, then it hit his left arm.

"Trouble," Rodrigo groaned, "behind the cathedral, Dedrick is free, Harald..." The pain drove him to his knees. *Not mine, not mine.* He pushed himself to his feet. "They've taken Harald. He's unconscious but alive. I'm going to go and look for him."

"How are you going to find him in this city?" Sarandia stood wide eyed as she nursed Thuria. "And if you find him what can you do about it?"

"First," Rodrigo put the club on his belt. "I will find him, then we will decide how to rescue him from the Emperor."

"How will you find him?"

"I'll follow the pain." Rodrigo ran out before she could ask any more questions. He'd made it sound simple, but it was anything but. Rodrigo gripped the club in his hand and tried to get a bearing on the agony flooding through him. It surrounded and mocked him. Maybe if he started closer to the scene. He loped through the streets heading for the cathedral. People ducked out of his way with curses, but Rodrigo didn't care. He needed to find Harald. Easy to tell himself he wanted to save his friend from almost certain torture and death; but a tiny voice in his head shrilly insisted he feared the pain he knew was coming.

At first he thought the dart was Harald's pain so he was slow to remove it. Then it was too late. The street blurred and distorted. His steady lope became a stagger sent him into a wall. Strong hands gripped his arms and dragged him away. Voices said he was sick and they were taking him to the doctors. Rodrigo knew he couldn't get sick; as the Black Heir no illness would be allowed to get in the way of his duty.

He could, however, be drugged.

The distorted world didn't fade away. He saw people with faces like clowns or wild animals. They peered in close at him, then left him. Rodrigo's head slowly stopped spinning and the faces in front of him looked like real people not carnival masks.

"I would have thought the famous Black Heir would be harder to catch." Aisa nudged him with her toe. She shifted her weight and Rodrigo tensed waiting for the kick to land. A soft cough turned the shift into a step back.

"Brother." Another woman's voice caressed his ears, eased his pain. He'd travelled across the Empire to hear this voice.

"Enough, sister," Rodrigo said. "I am immune to your wiles."

The kick landed in his gut and he curled around the foot. He made sure some of the vomit landed on Aisa's boot. She jumped back cursing. Rodrigo pushed himself up. He peered through the last of the drug's effects at the White Heir. His sister had always pushed him around. The many beatings he'd taken cured him of the need to answer the magic in her voice with obedience.

"Foolish," she said. "You always liked that role."

Pain struck him like his face had been slapped. Blood should leak out of the wound on his cheek.

"You're bound," his sister laughed. She lifted his face with her finger and considered his eyes. "Who could bind the Black Heir without negating the vote?" She turned his face back and forth. "Not a Rehego, but who else would..." She dropped his face then took a step back. Her hum buzzed faintly in his ears, then she laughed. If he didn't know her better he'd have called it a girlish laugh of delight. "You actually messed with the royal binding of Belandria!" She shook her head. "You should really leave magic to those who know what they are doing. Did you kill him or turn him into a vegetable?"

"Neither, sweet sister." Rodrigo gritted his teeth. "Grandmother took a hand and sent him back." He arched his back as someone on the other side of the city applied a hot iron to his back. He laughed through the pain. "When the Emperor's men kill

King Harald, I will die in the Marshal's place." He sat up against the wall and gasped for air. "When I die, the lot will choose again. Tell me, in all our millennia of history, has a person ever been drawn twice as Heir?" He tried to laugh more, but it came out as a wheezing cough. Pain lanced through his arms and he barely snatched the scream back.

But his sister saw it. She frowned and took hold of the club.

"Concentrate on the other end of the link."

"No. It will be worth my death and his to defeat you. If I'd known it was this easy, I would have done it ages ago."

"Brother!" She stomped her foot, "I do not desire your death."

"Swear you will let me and those with me go free without any of your tricks. Swear, or the lot chooses again."

"Fine!" She drove her fist into her leg, then held it over her heart. "I swear I will not interfere with you, or the King or those he chooses to travel with him. There will be no retribution this day. That is as far as I go, brother. I will not endanger the cause for you."

"Oath accepted." Rodrigo thought of Harald and the pain as hair-like roots joining them. His sister's humming ached in his head, but he held the vision.

She walked to the other side of the room to instruct Aisa, then crouched down by Rodrigo.

"Why won't you believe I have your welfare in mind?" she asked.

"I do," Rodrigo whispered, "that is why you terrify me so."

"Come, you fool." She put out her hand for him to take, "We have work to do."

She dragged him to his feet and her grip siphoned away the pain. A faint vertical line appeared on her forehead as she led him to the street.

"Take me to these others. I've given my oath; they are safe enough, but the Emperor has given no oath and will not hesitate from sentimentality." Rodrigo forced himself to focus on the streets. "Quickly, we won't have much time once he is free."

"You are assuming Harald will be freed so quickly."

"If I put Aisa up against a Legion, who would you bet on?"

"Right, of course." Rodrigo led his sister through the streets. More than one person stopped and pointed at them. They had to be a striking couple—him in Black and her in White. She held the club and tapped her fingers on it nervously. She'd never been nervous before. He picked up his pace as the drug wore off and his surroundings grew more familiar.

He pushed open the door of Margarite's home and dragged his sister in.

"Hello," he said to Margarite, "my sister, the Rehego White Heir. White Heir, my host Margarite."

"Sarandia is in her room with the babe." Margarite spoke as if mad people in black and white burst through her door every day. "I got a runner saying Dedrick has followed the men who have your friend. He is being held in a barracks by the docks."

"Convenient." Rodrigo rubbed his arm. "It so happens we will need to take a boat a very short time after my friend is rescued."

Sarandia came out.

"Have you heard anything?" she asked. Rodrigo watched as the colour of his sister's clothing sunk in.

"I thought you didn't like her," she said. "Why is she here?"

"I don't like what she is doing." Rodrigo's head ached. It usually did around his sister. "It has nothing to do with whether I like her or not."

"What a darling baby!" The White Heir smiled at Thuria. Thuria smiled back and a truce was formed.

"We need to get to the docks." Rodrigo looked over at his host. "Soon would be best."

"The wagon is hitched." Margarite nodded. "I'll take you there. We have some goods to pick up anyway."

They climbed onto the wagon. His sister never let go of him or the club with the runes on it. Margarite drove down to the dock region, then along the wharfs until Rodrigo's sister told her to stop.

"Now what?" Sarandia asked.

"We wait," the White Heir said.

***

Harald came to, mostly naked and strapped on a table. Wheels held the table at either end. Hot iron cloyed the air.

"Not often we have a King to play with." A man in a plain smock waved Harald's signet ring at him, then passed it to a guard. "Take this to the Emperor." He stepped up closer to Harald. "We are able to wound." Ice ran along Harald's back. "Or heal." He poured from a cup he held onto the wounds in Harald's arms. The ache in them vanished in a spike of pain. "I can keep you alive a very long time. It may even drive your redoubtable Marshal insane." He shrugged. "One can hope. He is in the way. Let's start with something easy. There is a secret way into your palace only you as King would know. Describe for me that passage."

"There is no passage," Harald said. "Master Tiron might know, but I know nothing of such a thing."

The edge ran across his back. Did it go high enough to damage his sword arm?

"Really." Harald kept his voice conversational. "This is most inefficient. I'm sure you already know everything there is to know about my palace. It isn't the most secure building. Did you know we designed it that way intentionally? It placated the Houses."

"Nowhere royalty lives is completely insecure." The man pulled an iron out of the brazier. "I want to know all the weaknesses and strengths. If your Kingdom was invaded, where would you defend yourself?"

"I'd abandon the palace and take over one of the Houses. Those places are built to last." The red-hot iron ran down his left arm. His mind wandered away while Harald's arm spasmed with pain. Something tore in his elbow. Harald's ragged breathing dried his throat and made him cough.

"No one is coming to rescue you." The torturer gave Harald a sip of water. "Your people think you dead or in exile. There is you, me, and the pain."

"Give me another shot of that iron," Harald said. "You're wearing thin on me."

What is Rodrigo trying to say? He's talking like he's drunk. Who would rescue me from the Emperor?

"Brave words, but we can make this so much worse. Some things no man wants to lose, especially if he has no heir." The torturer cut Harald's pants off and picked another iron from the fire. "Let's find out how brave you truly are."

Harald screamed when the iron came to rest on his thigh. The straps were so tight he couldn't move without tearing himself apart.

"I own you." The man in the smock whispered in Harald's ear. "When you know this to be true in the depths of your soul, we will get along splendidly."

"I gave myself to God," Harald said. "Take it up with him."

"I work for God." The man grabbed skin and twisted. "I am his arm. I punish those who get in the way of God's anointed."

"You mean you do the nasty work for the Emperor on people who are bound so tight that spitting on you is impossible." Harald breathed deeply as he'd been taught. "You are a coward and a fool."

The man snatched a red-hot rod and beat Harald with it. He shattered an elbow and knee cap, then stood panting and glaring at Harald.

"Pain has no power over me," Harald held the torturer's eyes. "I'm trained to handle the worst pain. Were you?" The man jumped as Aisa behind him pricked a knife by his ear.

"Release Harald." She growled.

"Never!"

"Fine, I don't need your help," Aisa rapped him sharply with the knife.

Asper pulled Harald from the table as the torturer fell to the floor.

"Watch him," Harald said. "He's a snake."

"Let's make him comfortable, shall we?" She pointed at the table and two men hoisted him onto the rack and strapped him in. She kicked at something on the floor and a blade ran through the table and sliced the torturer's back.

"Don't play with him." Harald picked up a red-hot rod and plunged it into the man's heart. "There is nothing we need to know so badly we must become as bad as him."

"I like you." Aisa's smile was more a wolf baring her fangs. "I don't know how you're going to walk."

"He had something in a cup." Harald searched the room to find another cup like the first. He poured a bit on the burn on his thigh. It vanished with a final blast of pain. "Cheers." Harald drank the cup in one swallow. All the pain in his body hit him at once and knocked him to the floor.

"Crazy, that might have killed you or worse."

"It didn't," Harald said, "so if one of you will loan me some pants."

"Asper," Aisa nodded. He ran off and came back with a legionnaire's tunic and leggings.

"Not pants," Asper shrugged. "but they'll do."

Harald pulled the clothes on quickly and grinned.

"What's so funny?" Aisa asked.

"Few minutes ago I faced death by torture." He laughed quietly. "Now I fear dying of embarrassment. How do these guys live in this outfit?"

"I think they wear a tougher skirt when they're fighting. Time to go." Aisa left the room at a run and Harald stayed at her shoulder. He hadn't felt this good in ages. They passed through stone halls with an occasional pair of legs sticking out a door.

"Now I see why Rodrigo has so much respect for you," Harald said when they were out in the sunlight. Aisa didn't answer, but raced through narrow streets. They were running downhill, toward the sea. Rodrigo told him he had Sarandia and the others on a wharf. He didn't sound drunk now.

Harald saw them standing by a wagon. They talked to an old man in a priest's robe. Shouts came from behind them, then a clatter of hard boots on the cobbles. He didn't bother looking, but he guessed these soldiers were wearing the tougher looking skirt.

Harald ran up to his friends and stopped. He barely panted while Aisa struggled to draw breath.

"You will come with us immediately." The lead soldier pointed his sword as they stomped up to them. Harald was happy to note Asper and his fellows had vanished.

"No," the old priest leaned on a staff. "They are on the Holy Father's dock. Will you risk his wrath to abuse his guests?"

The guard's face showed he didn't want to be having this conversation.

"Let's get on the boat, shall we?" Rodrigo pushed Harald along the dock to a rickety boat. Sarandia and Thuria were right behind him on the right; Dedrick and Margarite on the left. They climbed on board and Rodrigo slipped something beneath the seats.

"We will meet again, brother." The White Heir said as she stood over them.

"I am certain of it, sister." Rodrigo had a rare serious look on his face. "We don't need to be enemies,"

"In the end, we will not be." She walked away.

"What did you do with my flint and steel I gave you?" Aisa asked.

"Fed it to a bear," Harald said.

Aisa laughed and slapped her leg. Then she too walked away without saying anything else.

"Let's go," Rodrigo looked a bit nervous.

The old priest hopped nimbly into the boat and cast off. The White Heir screamed in fury and pointed back at them. Aisa started in a sprint down the dock, but the boat caught a current and whisked away from shore. The woman stopped on the edge. A feral grin passed so fast across her face Harald wasn't sure he'd seen it. Rodrigo shuddered.

"What was that all about?" Sarandia asked. "She just helped to set us free."

"She is missing a treasure." Rodrigo pulled the carved club from beneath the seat. "Next time I tell you to leave this behind, feel free to ignore me."

Mist came up from the water and covered them. With the mist came a silence Harald had no desire to break. He pulled Sarandia close to him and made faces at his daughter.

CHAPTER 17

“What good is it to tell me there is a traitor, if you can't tell me who?”

“Not so loud.” Illandria put her finger on Marriette's lips. “We are safe from being overheard, but only if we talk quietly.”

“So, quietly then, please explain.” Marriette sighed and leaned back. She couldn't be commanding while naked in the tub.

“There are rumours about your husband and this Lady Joan he is escorting all over the city. Tongues wag, and adultery against royalty is treason.”

“Torrance is doing what I asked of him,” Marriette said.

“You want him the subject of rumours and innuendo.” Illandria scrubbed at her hair carefully. “There is no purpose in removing a player who might be turned. He may be approached by someone offering alliance.” Her hands paused as if in question.

"No, it's too much. You two made such a show of your devotion not a year ago."

"What other treachery is happening around me?" Marriette cupped water in her hand and watched it drain out. "I can hardly be expected to rule if I don't know who is out for my blood."

"They are all out for your blood," Illandria said. "It is the nature of power. The question we must ask, is who is willing to act?"

"They've already acted. Someone killed the Archbishop."

"The person who pushed the old man is undoubtedly already dead. It is hard to determine who pulled the strings. You told me he was being poisoned, but the server who purportedly administered the poison hung himself."

"Who gains the most from a new Archbishop?" Marriette asked.

"A difficult question. What do any of the Houses gain? They have their own priests and bishops."

"The Empire gains a voice in council." Marriette laid her hand flat on the water. "A voice trying to turn the Regent away from her duty."

"The Empire is ever wary of unrest," Illandria rubbed soap into Marriette's hair. "Unless it is the Emperor's hand causing it."

"The Emperor can't really think I'm going to suddenly declare myself Queen."

"Stranger things have happened." Illandria massaged the soap into Marriette's scalp. "But he doesn't need to convince you to declare yourself, just to convince someone else you are going to."

"How lovely." Marriette shifted in the water trying to find a pocket of warm water.

"Let me rinse you off, your Majesty." Illandria helped Marriette to stand and poured warm water over her to rinse the soap away.

"So my people think I am a traitor."

"Say rather some may be convinced for expediency's sake."

"What can we do to confuse the issue?" Marriette stepped out of the tub. "I don't want to push anyone into hasty action, but we need to know more."

"Maybe it is time to pick a fight." Illandria steadied Marriette on her feet. "And see who lines up where."

"Did you speak like this with Sarandia too?"

"Frequently, your Majesty, but keep one thing in mind. We missed Tamas' treachery completely."

"Why?"

"Most people who plan treachery have people they meet and plot with. Messages needing to be sent. Those are things spies can catch wind of and follow. Tamas didn't have any conspirators we know of. He sent no messages we could detect. We didn't even detect the scent of magic on him. He positioned himself as the King's mentor and corrupted him slowly. We also didn't see you coming—you who arrived like a bolt from the blue and shook the King to his foundation. Tamas betrayed him, but you tested him. Now, he is being reforged for God's purpose."

"You believe that?"

"Why else would God have sent you and the angel?" Illandria toweled Marriette briskly. "God has a plan, but like usual God doesn't let us mortals in on it." She wrapped a robe around Marriette. "Pick a fight with Torrance, and make it most definitely not about Lady Joan so everyone will think it is. We will see who whispers what."

"I can't attack Torrance over nothing,"

"You two must come up with a believable argument. Make sure he knows his part."

"I think we can manage that." Marriette curled her lips into a smile. "It sounds like fun."

***

Torrance ran in late and bowed quickly to Marriette. She heaved a sigh.

"The discussion we have concluded might have been more productive had you been present," Marriette said, proud of the tone, not barbed, but weary. "Do you wish to speak or shall we move on?"

"Since I don't know what it is I should have been here discussing," Torrance dropped into his seat, "let's move on."

"If you had been here on time, you would know." Marriette played with her fan sending the apprentice into seizures of readiness.

"Marshal," she spoke without turning around, "we need to work on subtlety." She hated to come down on the young man, but she didn't want him attacking anyone by mistake.

"Now, as we were saying, gentlemen." She slid her fan into her sleeve, "I believe a relief on taxes for money invested in schools is fair, but only if those schools are educating future workers. We have sufficient bored thugs with swords; we hardly need to train more."

Raspin rolled his eyes at her and reTaggin harrumphed, but seGraine took the bait and ran with it.

"Any money we spend on any school is worthy; if educated peasants are valuable, how much more an educated nobility?"

"Perhaps, if you educate them to think and not move from one estate to another preying on the weak."

"Perhaps, it is education they lack." Torrance rubbed his chin thoughtfully. "If they were to learn more they might be less lazy for it."

"And pigs may fly." Marriette glared at him. "All they have shown any desire of learning is how to further shirk their duties."

"How can you demand duty without education?"

"Can you offer education without duty?" Marriette raised her voice slightly. "These young nobles are more like a pack of dogs than rational beings."

"That's what your father thought of the peasants we now train in our school." Torrance leaned forward.

"You speak to me of my father?" Marriette's hands trembled. If she could have snatched her fan she would have silenced him. Instead she pushed herself unsteadily to her feet. The men leaped up.

"We are done. There will be no tax reduction for support of schools not teaching a trade. If young nobles wish to be educated, let them become carpenters." She waddled out of the room.

Marshal closed the door behind her and took her arm.

"If I may speak," the apprentice said.

"No."

"Go," Marshal pointed down the hall. "Practice subtlety." The young man saluted and walked away.

"You were hard on him."

"And I shouldn't be?"

Marshal sighed and opened the door to the sparring room. Marriette went and sat down on the chair.

"There is who you are." Marshal stood like a statue. "And who you think you must be to rule. Do not confuse the two."

"Now my bodyguard is schooling me?"

"I have seen three people on that throne." Marshal refused to drop his gaze. "I saw what destroyed them."

"Any word of the King?" she changed the subject.

"I woke up one night in a sweat with my body aching, but by the time the morning came it had passed."

"We come to this," Marriette said, "reading omens in your dreams?"

"The bond is set aside," Marshal said. "I don't know what is happening. I don't think he's dead, because it would break the binding and mean my own death. I breathe yet. We all hang in the balance. A stonemason may drop a rock on me and strike me down."

"Perhaps, or they will drop it on the King and you will still be struck down."

"People think the binding is to convince the Marshal to work harder at keeping the King safe. What it's truly about is reminding the King that at least one person will pay deeply and inevitably for their failure. It isn't about the Marshal at all, it is about the King. Sometimes the path to humility is reminding them I am prepared to die for their mistakes."

"You won't die for me." Marriette studied the wall covered with weapons. "We have no binding between us."

"We do." Marshal's voice shook. "Your husband stood between the King and a demon when I did not."

"It was treachery of the worst kind."

"Treachery I didn't detect."

"No one did, Marshal."

"Didn't they?" Marshal's mouth quirked, "Interesting."

"Yet you will not perish, if I am killed."

"There is only one end for a Marshal who lets the King, or Queen," he nodded at her, "die. You don't escape humility that easily."

***

Joan looked down at the hulking youth who rubbed his shoulder and glowered at her.

"Do you wish another round?" she asked.

"My shoulder hurts. How'm I going to fight with a hurt shoulder?"

"You aren't. You took the oath, same as the others when you picked up that stick." She pointed at the broken staff lying beside the youth. "We aren't training you to fight. Not stupid fights like beating on the City Constables. They decide you've been learning weapons skills, you hang, and all your friends with you."

Her staff hummed in the air and stopped a hair from his face. To give him credit he didn't flinch, or maybe was too stupid to.

"I get you." He brought himself to a kneeling position. "My Da always said I's too eager for a fight. No more." He bowed to the floor. "I have put myself under your command."

"Very good, start by getting someone to work on your shoulder. Can't hold a staff with a bad shoulder." Joan grabbed his sleeve and pulled him to his feet. "Don't make me come back here."

"Nice work," Suze said as they left the yard. "The perfect mix of iron and humour."

"I don't know. I always feel silly acting like that."

"When you get used to it, we'll all be in trouble." Suze walked unerringly through the city. There were few people out at dusk and none bothered to look twice at the women.

Lamps lit the hotel, and they were welcomed by the staff. Joan had rented the top floor for the winter, so they got royal treatment. She still liked eating in the common room, but she regretted her choice when she saw Sam sitting with Catrin.

"Hello." Joan sat down. "How are you this evening?"

Sam looked at her and rubbed his face.

"What is it going to take for me to get back on your good side?"

"Why does the King's Justicer need to be on my good side?"

"I'm not the Justicer," Sam smiled at her. "You know I'm merely an investigator."

"Investigating me." Joan waved at the woman serving drinks.

"Investigating the situation at your estate." Sam took a swig of his drink before exchanging it for a new one as the server put food and drink in front of Joan. "I had already reported to the Regent my findings."

"Findings, how comforting that is when --"

"Joan." Catrin laid her hand on Joan's. "Please don't go there, you know how the nightmares keep you up at night,"

Joan glared at Sam. He didn't glare back. No matter how angry Joan got, he stayed calm and reasonable.

"Very well." She took a long drink of the bitter ale. "I suppose it might be useful to have an investigator on my good side." She turned to face Catrin. "What did you do today?"

"Pastry, we were trying to make edible pastries. We mostly succeeded." Catrin licked her lips and smiled broadly. "That's why there is nothing for you to sample." She giggled and Joan laughed.

The innkeeper brought out some cold meats and a pastry for Joan to try. It melted in her mouth. Suze showed up and took a sample. After a while she and Catrin left to go upstairs.

"A word," Sam said, "not all people will take such joy in your love as I do. Be careful, this can be a dangerous place and you have enemies who would use those your care about against you."

"Not my brave investigator?" Joan let her mouth twitch.

"Not if my life depended on it." Sam put his hand on hers. "If you would count me as one of your friends, I would be content."

"Friend, I can live with," Joan toasted him with the last of her ale. They clanked tankards, then she left him to finish his drink while she went to see if Catrin was ready for bed.

CHAPTER 18

Marriette shifted uncomfortably.

"Sorry."

"Your Majesty," the armourer said. "You are much more patient than most people I fit. They will invest great time and effort on a sword, which I admit is important, but if you don't have a well-fitting bit of armour, the sword will do you precious little good."

"You must admit this has to be the oddest piece of armour you've created."

"I haven't fitted a pregnant woman before, but to be honest, I've fit armour over larger bellies." The armourer stood up. "Move around, make sure it is comfortable."

Marriette walked around the room. Illandria whispered something to the armourer and he ran over to adjust a strap.

150

"It is much better," Marriette put. "My thanks for your time."

"It is my honour to serve," the armourer bowed. "And this is a more pleasant tale than most of what I have to tell my wife." He reddened, Marriette guessed worried about talking of her secrets.

"No worries," Marriette said, "if there is anything I do not wish you to speak of, I will inform you. Take my greetings to your good wife and let her know if the Regent were any bigger, she'd need guards to carry her belly for her."

"My Janna's the same." The armourer smiled broadly. "She always looked ready to burst a month before her time. We had five healthy children from it. The last born this year."

"Wait a minute," Marriette waddled from the room to fetch a soft toy from a pile in the corner.

"Here, for your youngest. I have so many clothes and toys for my child they fill half my room."

He turned even deeper red and bowed deep.

"We are honoured, my daughter will treasure it."

"Make sure she plays with it." Marriette pretended to scowl at him. "If you are going to put it on a shelf, I have an uglier one for you."

"As you command." The armourer left, carrying his tools and bags in one hand while cradling the toy in the other.

"Within days," Illandria shook her head, "servants will be telling you tales of their wee newborns in hopes of a royal gift."

"Perhaps you could keep an ear to the ground to make sure only people with legitimate claim on a toy is given one. Not the frog."

"I insist it is a knight."

"Either way it is far too hideous to be given to a child. Let me know who is lying the most and I will give it to them and watch them try to thank me for it."

"Your months as Regent have made you cruel." Illandria laughed.

"I would walk for a bit." Marriette patted her stomach. "Before I grow any further and require another fitting."

Illandria and another maid put an overdress on Marriette, then she walked out into the hall. Marshal fell into step behind her.

Marriette meandered through the palace, more concerned with avoiding stairs than worrying where she went. One door had steam pouring from it and she went to the top of some steps.

"Your Majesty." A servant tried to curtsey while still on the stair; a quick grab by Illandria kept her from tumbling. "What brings you to the laundry?"

"Ah," Marriette said, "this is where you do the laundry."

"Well mostly the linen." The woman kept her eyes down. "Sheets and towels and tablecloths. Your dresses and other clothes are washed somewhere else."

"So you are the people who put that wonderful scent on my sheets."

"Lavender, your Majesty." The woman blushed and curtseyed again. "If it pleases you, it's to help you sleep."

"It does please me, thank you." Marriette nodded and made her way out the door before the woman fell down the stairs.

"What other fascinating corners of the palace can I discover?" Marriette started off again. She stopped and spoke to servants whenever they bumped into them.

"I think it may be time to return to my rooms," Marriette said at last.

"This way, your Majesty," Marshal took the lead and in a couple of turns had them back outside Marriette's rooms.

Once they were in her suite, Marriette looked around. Between her pregnancy and the challenges to her rule, she spent most of her time in this room, the council chambers or the sparring room.

"Remind me that walking is good for me." Marriette settled into her chair.

"I would hate to be a bother." Illandria poured water from a jug on a sideboard.

"I need someone to bother me, and keep me feeling human. You know, I think I will sort through those toys to decide what to keep and what to give to my councilors to give them nightmares." She took the cup from Illandria and drank it down.

"They were probably the ones who gave you the ugly ones to begin with."

"Then they deserve to have them given back to them."

Illandria carried an armload of toys and clothes and put them on the chair in front of Marriette.

Master Tiron came into the room to discover all the chairs in front of Marriette piled with toys and clothes of all description. He went to move the pile from the chair he usually sat in.

"Please don't," Marriette held up her hand, "I've just got them sorted the way I want. Bring a chair from over by the wall."

He picked up the chair and carried it back to place it carefully in front of Marriette.

"I see you have the board covered with your toys," he said, "may I ask why the sudden urge to sort the largesse?"

"I am going to give some away. I don't want to look like I'm giving only the ugly ones away." She pulled out a multi-coloured thing with bulging eyes and what might have been a sword in one hand. "There are a few like this one, they will go to especially deserving people."

"It is times like this which make me glad I have neither wife nor child," Master Tiron smiled briefly. "What is the purpose of this gifting?"

"Several reasons really," Marriette said. "The first is I have far too much stuff for any one baby. I don't want to lose my child amid all this. Secondly, it will get the people talking about the Regent with stories other than my disagreement with my husband."

"Rumour is you almost set Marshal on him."

"Highly exaggerated." Marriette laughed and waved her hand. "I considered it for no more than a second. We have always had times we've disagreed. This is simply one more of those times."

"You are Regent," Master Tiron frowned, "Simple doesn't come into the equation. People will be maneuvering on whether they think he is in your favour or not."

"Let them." Marriette said, "In the meantime the common people will be thinking of me in positive terms."

"The common people don't matter. They aren't the ones plotting how to use you to increase their own power."

"So tell me about these plots." Marriette sat back and looked at him.

"These aren't conspiracies like Tamas', or those fools on the road."

"Those fools almost killed me, and Tamas came close to killing the King."

"Tamas worked alone as far as I have been able to tell." Master Tiron looked annoyed. "No one has showed up to take control of his assets. The crown has taken them over. We've watched for interest and there is none. If he had accomplices, they are dead or gone."

"And the fools on the road?"

"They didn't yell any slogans, they were trained, but not terribly well. I couldn't track them back, couldn't even find out who they were. It is likely they were a professional group hired to assassinate you."

"Why haven't they hired another group and tried again?"

"No opportunity, and perhaps whoever hired them has changed their mind. Perhaps they no longer have the significant outlay of money it would take."

"So none of the plotting you hear about involves mercenaries and knives."

"Nothing so obvious." Master Tiron steepled his fingers. "There is someone who has a person following Lady Joan, possibly two people. It is known you are friends with the Lady, they may be looking for a way to get in your favour or to distract you at an important moment. Similarly, there are several people following your husband. His guards are aware of it and keeping watch. He is another person whose value on the board is closely linked to you."

"It might be a shorter list to tell me who is *not* being followed."

"No one follows Marshal," Master Tiron said.

"That seems wise."

"The binding gives him some expanded perception making him difficult to shadow."

"The people on the road knew they had to draw him away before the real attack started. They gave him something to focus on."

"It worked in short term." Master Tiron looked up at the ceiling. "It would be much harder to fool him over a longer period."

He sat back and shook his head.

"Most of what is going on is the normal maneuvering between Houses. Some appears to be more intense because of the Regency, but as you have made it clear you aren't making huge changes while the King is away, it has moved away from you."

"What isn't normal?"

"Some of your Council have found religion, or at least religious observance has taken on new meaning for them. Raspin, seGraine and reTaggin have all entertained the new Archbishop.

SuDarche is sitting outside of the activity, though he remains in the city for some reason."

"I wonder what promises the new Archbishop is making." Marriette said.

The door to her rooms opened and Torrance walked in.

"Hello, Tiron." Torrance handed his cloak to Illandria. "What brings you here?"

"It is my work to keep the throne cognizant of what is going on in their kingdom."

"Shaping policy by giving a little weight here, a little less there." Torrance picked up the frog/knight toy and raised an eyebrow. "Tiny things to make a King suspect someone of treachery."

"I present information," Master Tiron jumped to his feet. "It is up to the throne to interpret. Good day, your Majesty." He nodded to Torrance and left through the door Torrance had come in.

"I wonder why he didn't go through the secret passages," Marriette said. "Some guard will try to arrest him as an intruder."

"If I knew where the door was." Torrance tossed the toy aside. "I'd nail it shut."

"Over here." Marriette pushed herself to her feet and showed Torrance the panel on the wall which opened. "I have no idea how it works, I've looked. It opens back into the wall, but there is no catch I could find. She pushed on the panel and it swung open.

"So this is what the secret passages look like," Torrance walked in a way and his voice got muffled. "No peep holes or slides I can see. The worm can listen to us but not see us." He came back and pointed at a lantern on a shelf. "Light for him to find his way about." Torrance peered closely at the mechanism to lock the door.

"From this side it is a lever to move, it must be more complicated on our side if he leaves the door unlocked." He pushed a knife into a slot in the frame and was rewarded by a faint click.

156

"Let's step away from the door." Torrance made them move out into the room. The door swung softly closed. He pushed the door open and again it closed. "Either I've fixed it open, or there's something missing."

"You've never explained to me what happened to make you and Tiron avoid each other."

"I don't know him well enough to dislike him." Torrance frowned slightly. "Occasionally the King would do some odd thing and hint he acted on inside information. Once he admitted Tiron's information had sent him in that direction. No one else has the unchecked ear of the King. All he'd need to do is not say something at the right time. He certainly never seems to have any insight when a major thing is happening."

"You think he should have known about the attack on the street?"

"He should have at least heard rumblings of sufficient discontent to make an attack possible. Nothing. He's a rumour monger, who uses his mystique to get the ear of the King."

"Or Regent. Forcing him to sit in a different chair meant he couldn't make his escape before you entered." She sat in the chair Master Tiron then Marriette got up and went to the wall. A tiny lever pointed to the left. There was a hole in the end of the lever as if it had once had string on it. It didn't move up, but it did move down when she pushed it. She tried a couple of times, then there was a knock at the door.

"Let him in," Marriette said.

The door opened and Jeremiah came in.

"You called me?" He bowed to her. "The bell in my office rang."

"Thank you, Jeremiah," Marriette nodded to him. "I've been considering making gifts of some of the toys I have been so generously given. I would like to make a list of servants who have had a child in the last year."

"People who serve within the palace, or the outside staff as well?"

"Inside staff for the time being." Marriette said.

"Very well, your Majesty." The secretary bowed and left.

"Interesting," Torrance peered at the lever. "It would make sense if this were a guest room for there to be a bell for servants. Since you would never be without your maids as Regent, you didn't need the bell and the servants' room became an empty room to make Jeremiah's office."

"But why all the fuss?" Marriette sat down heavily. "Does Tiron really have to play spy to the point of using my secretary to avoid my husband?"

"He knows I'll challenge his stories or push him to add to them. You've probably noticed he talks in generalities most of the time. He's probably terrified I'll catch him out in the thing that gets spy masters executed."

"What's that?" Marriette raised her eyebrow.

"Telling a lie," Illandria came in from Marriette's bedroom. "If he's lying to you, even subtly, then nothing he says is to be trusted. If you can't trust your spy master..." She shrugged and pulled her finger across her throat.

"So, figure out what he's telling me that is a lie," Marriette said.

"As you wish," Illandria curtsied and left.

"You always talk spies and politics with your maid?"

"Of course." Marriette smiled at Torrance. "Who else?"

CHAPTER 19

The bells sounded for prayer like auditory dusk falling on the Holy City. Harald focused on emptying himself of all desire but of hearing God's voice again. Sarandia bowed her head on her side of the tiny room. Even Thuria quieted for the moment.

Like other nights they finished too soon and Harald was left with a part of him in a different world and part laden down with the cares of this world.

"I'm going to go out and get supper." Harald stood up and stretched.

"Be careful." Sarandia picked up their daughter. "Remember there is sickness in the Holy City. The priest told us to stay in this quarter."

Harald kissed her and the babe.

"I won't be risking you."

The people of the Holy City did their business around him, calling out their wares and inviting pilgrims to enjoy pleasures Harald didn't believe should be part of the journey. Not his problem. He found an ever-increasing pleasure in reflecting problems which weren't his to fix. Time in the Holy City was fluid except for the bells for prayer. All business and commotion stopped at the first sound of the bell, and picked up as the last tone faded away.

Harald stopped listening for the bell. For the first days, his neck hurt as he held himself in anticipation of the sound. When he stopped waiting for it, the Holy City swept him away. He couldn't say if they'd been there a week or a month. The prayed, they talked, they made love, sometimes all three at once.

A vendor on a corner sold sticks with tiny cubes of meat on them. They were a favourite of Sarandia's so he bought a handful and meandered back through the crowd. As he walked back a disturbance in the crowds eddied toward him. He stepped to the side to avoid whatever was upsetting the rhythm of the people.

A woman burst out of the crowd. She looked around more like an animal than a human. Her clothes hung in rags off a body showing more bone than muscle. The woman looked like carved ebony with a feral beauty that left Harald stunned for a second. She jumped on the skewers and tried to eat them whole. Her saliva splashed hot and sticky on his hand. A skewer poked out the side of her neck but she didn't stop pushing them into her mouth. The people of the City walked around her, giving her space. Even the fever couldn't stop their work.

Harald backed away. He thought of Sarandia, thin and bestial, Thuria dying as her mother lost her humanity. He stopped a passerby with a wave.

"Greetings, brother. I must have the medics look at me in case the fever passed to my hand. Please take greetings to my wife and child." Harald gave the man directions, then turned to walk to the city within the city where the people with the fever lived. They lived a long time if fed properly. The woman must have escaped or been caught unawares. The sickness had been in the Holy City for centuries.

Harald presented himself at the gate and passed in after being given a tablet on a string to wear.

"You lose this," the man said, "we'll give you another one and we start again. A week, forty-nine ringing of the bells and if you don't show the disease, you'll be free."

"How do I keep track of the bells?"

"Don't," the man said, "come see anyone at the gate, and we'll tell you how long it has been. If you fret too much, you'll imagine yourself into the fever. Many people here are sure they are fevered, but have no sign of the disease."

Harald wandered into the city of the sick. The sparse crowd moved with frenetic rhythm he didn't try to match. He found himself a blank pavement where there may have been a door once. The stone warmed him as he sat. He had nothing to do so he set his mind to be ready for the next ringing of the bells.

Whining brought him back to full consciousness. Across the darkened street a child sat like a dog. She tilted her head at him.

"There's room for both of us." Harald shifted over. "If that's what you want."

She bounded over and curled up beside him on the pavement. Harald shrugged. Not like he could catch it twice. He went back to his prayers, but fell asleep sometime after the midnight prayer. His mind heard bells through the night, but he didn't make it awake before they faded into silence. Harald curled up and slept.

Morning bells woke Harald. He couldn't move as fevered people curled around him and even on top of him. Harald prayed as well as he could with the people packed around him. They woke immediately after the morning bells faded into silence. They jumped to their feet and ran along the road. Harald followed at a slower pace. The first girl to join him stayed with him, holding his hand. Callouses caught on his skin, but her grip was warm and comforting.

There were tables set up with food. The fevered rushed at them and tore at it. A lot got trampled underfoot.

"Hey," Harald said, "Take it easy." He walked to a table and started tossing bread and fruit to the fevered at the back of the crowd. A few scuffles broke out, but stopped as more bread and fruit came their way. Other fevered at the table copied Harald and in short order the whole mob munched away. People took more food or dropped what they didn't want and wandered off.

"Blessed brother," someone called from behind a grate. Harald walked over to it.

"Morning, brother." Harald said. "Thanks for the food. I woke with this crowd around me."

"If you push at them enough, they will go somewhere else."

"Why would I?" Harald asked. "This is their City. God willing, I am but a visitor."

"We will pray vigorously for your health, blessed brother."

"I don't feel blessed." Harald looked around. "But I thank you for your prayers."

"You don't understand," the man on the other side of the grate said. "Most people hide in the houses and stay away from the fevered. They come when the fevered are not present to get food."

"It is too late to worry about whether I will sicken or not," Harald shrugged.

"Most do not think so." The man looked sadly at the empty courtyard. "But every once in a while we get someone like you who does not panic or descend into rape and cruelty. Your presence reminds the fevered of what they once were. You are a blessing."

Harald bowed to him and wandered through the city. The people moved quickly and suspiciously. A man looked ready to beat another with a stick, so Harald intervened and sent them off in opposite directions. It wasn't only the fevered who forgot their humanity.

The girl found him in his exploration, so he let her take his hand and lead him where ever she wanted. He ate when the food was placed out and prayed while the bells rang. Most of the people, whether fevered or not, no longer paused for the bells. Yet around Harald at each sounding, a pool of silence formed.

They slept in a different cubby in the street and once more Harald woke surrounded by warm bodies. He lay still and prayed, then followed them to breakfast. It became his routine until he lost track of the days and existed on an ocean of prayer broken occasionally by the sound of bells.

He needed nothing, wanted nothing, feared nothing.
***

Sarandia sat in the room and tried not to clutch Thuria too hard. Harald with the sickness? The messenger hadn't entered the room, just spoke the news once as Harald had asked him then left.

She tried to breathe and calm herself, but all her grandmother's teachings failed her. Harald had been her rock since they met. She couldn't be sure of who she was without him. The pilgrimage terrified her slightly less than being without her husband.

A priest stopped in later in the evening and gave her a tablet.

"Your husband wears one with the same number. When his week is done, if he is without fever, he will be returned to you. Patience and prayer, sister."

"Thank you, Father." Sarandia nodded her head.

She tried to pray each time the bells sounded, but instead of peace the time brought her an ever more frantic worry. She and Thuria huddled in the room, barely sleeping. The morning bells woke her from a fitful rest. Bread and fruit had been left inside the door.

Sarandia ate and paced the tiny room. Thuria picked up on her nerves and became restless and weepy.

"I must be strong for you." Sarandia caressed Thuria's head. She inhaled long and deeply, then exhaled until there was no air in her. Then she repeated it. A mat on the floor reminded her of the exercises she used to do with her grandmother and mother. If ever she needed stillness, it was now.

Stillness turned out to be hard to find. Thuria breathed so much faster than her it pulled her away from the trance. She had needs, so she fed her, but her suckling kept her away from the trance.

"I can't escape this way," she said to Thuria. "You need me present." She ate some more and prayed when the bells rang. The rest of the time she played with her baby and sang to her as if Harald were going to walk back through the door at any moment.

Bread and fruit appeared each morning, so Sarandia didn't need to go out. The days repeated until the evening a new priest knocked at her door.

"Sarandia, Queen of Belandra?" the man asked. It took her a moment to remember that was her.

"Yes, Father."

"The Holy Father calls for you. I am Father Bran. Bring the child and anything else you don't wish to abandon. You will not return to this abode."

She packed up the few things they needed and snatched the club from the side of the bed where Harald had left it.

"I'm ready." She followed the priest out into the evening light. Strangers nodded at her as if they knew her, or maybe it was the priest they honoured. Sarandia clutched her bundle in one hand and steadied Thuria in her sling with the other. The club hung from Harald's belt over her shoulder.

They stopped twice for the bells, and once so Sarandia could feed Thuria.

164

"I didn't realize the Holy City was so big."

"It has grown over thousands of years as a few pilgrims each year decide to live here and dedicate their work to God, but it is also laid out as a labyrinth. At need, there are streets to carry us straight to our destination, but much of the time we are better served being reminded God's way is not our straight way, but still we arrive in the time we are meant to."

They walked through a gate and then another. The path led into a garden. Though it was black dark now except for tiny lanterns set on the path, she identified the flowers by the plethora of scent. Like the night gardens at her childhood home, the plants were chosen more for their harmonious perfumes, than colour or shape. She took a second, deep breath, but then caught up to the priest.

"Ah," he said, "you remember the gardens of your childhood?"

"I do, and would gladly linger, but I would not keep the Holy Father waiting while I indulge myself."

"He would not begrudge you a brief indulgence."

"If I needed it for healing." Sarandia waved at him to continue. "But now would be pure indulgence. God willing, there will be time for me to return."

"Very good," the priest said, "though I am curious about your talk of healing. This is a peaceful spot, but healing?"

"There are certain ailments of the body that respond well to the odors of the night gardens, I don't know much more than what my grandmother taught me."

"Yet, it is more than I know. It would be a pleasure, God willing, to learn from you the healing use of the garden."

He pushed open a pair of doors and waved her into a room that reminded her of the Archbishop's room in Belandria. Books lined the walls and scrolls filled any space left by the books. A tiny cupboard against one wall would hold a bottle of fine wine and perhaps a crust of bread.

The priest knelt on a mat and went still. Sarandia dropped her bundle and Harald's club. Thuria fussed wanting to be fed, so she was feeding her child when the Holy Father entered the room. The priest bent to the floor, but with her daughter at her breast, she could only manage a nod. The Holy Father sat in the chair and watched her with a slight smile. He didn't look much older than the priest who had stood and left the room. Wrinkles ran from his eyes, but his hair looked more black than grey. When she looked into his grey eyes she felt the burden of his position. Those eyes made her own tear up. They'd seen such grief and horror. If it had been anyone else but the Holy Father, she would have embraced him and prayed for peace for his soul.

"Thank you, daughter," the Holy Father spoke in a soft tenor. "Fear not, I am given glimpses of people's souls when they look into my eyes. Kings are routinely warned not to meet my gaze."

"How do you live with it?" Sarandia asked, tears dropping on Thuria's head. "The memory of all the pain?"

"However strong the memory of pain may be, child, the memory of joy is stronger."

She looked up at him again and met his eyes. letting the pain flow through her. Under it she heard a song, like a hint of bells, and laughed in spite of herself.

"I see I am not the only one with a dangerous gaze." The Holy Father stood. "Be welcome and your daughter as well. Your husband will join us tomorrow, God willing."

"Holy Father," Sarandia whispered. "If you find yourself wearied, sit in the night garden a while and breathe in its perfume. It will ease you."

"Thank you, child." The Holy Father nodded and left her alone in the room. The priest returned a moment later to take her to a place she could rest. Sarandia fell into a deep sleep and even the bells didn't wake her.

She woke to discover bread and fruit by her door. She ate then cleaned Thuria and fed her.

"Walk with me," the priest said to her. "Your things will be safe here." He led her out into a different garden, this one with herbs and vegetables. She wandered with him, talking about the herbs and their uses. He knew different ways of mixing the herbs than her grandmother. He made drops of the essence, while Sarandia learned to drink horrible teas to aid whenever she was sick.

They picked some ripe vegetables and left them for the kitchen. He took her through a door and into a hallway. She gasped at tiles with gold running through them. Panels on the wall were covered with gold leaf so thin she could see the grain of the wood through it. Statues and paintings lined the hallway. Windows high in the walls illuminated it. The ceiling had been painted dark blue with stars gleaming gold.

"We call this the Hall of the Kings," Father Bran said. "It is supposed to be humbling, but I don't know, not being a king."

"It is overwhelming." Sarandia looked around again. "But you have truer wealth in those gardens we walked through."

Father Bran laughed and led her through another door.

"Here is one of our libraries. Dozens of people spend their lives copying the books of this library."

He walked straight through and Sarandia stopped to watch a young woman at work. The woman smiled shyly at Sarandia, then carried her finished page over to a rack where she placed it to dry. She nodded toward the priest. Sarandia smiled at her then caught up with the priest.

They walked through another door and entered a different hallway as plain as the Hall of the Kings was ornate.

"The Holy Father told me to wait here for your husband to arrive."

"He's not going to enter through the Hall of the Kings?"

"Apparently not." Father Bran shook his head. "The Holy Father is rarely wrong about these things."

CHAPTER 20

Rodrigo hated the Holy City. The bells drove him nuts. He didn't pray when they rang, but everyone in sight glared at him if he didn't stop and look pious. What he wanted to do was rob them blind while they prayed. Rumours circulated that thieves did very poorly here, and Rodrigo saw no guards walking the streets. So, he kept his hands at his side and his eyes straight ahead.

He'd remembered his dislike on the boat as they slipped through the uncanny mist, but on the dock, the boat looked to be a better option than staying in Lusia with his sister. Her howl of anger sent shivers of fear and guilty pleasure through him. Not often did he come out ahead of her. She'd never forgive him, and never stop her attempt to return her people to their homeland.

Why couldn't they have once lived on the distant steppes and had only goats to push away from their land?

"Hey," someone stepped in front of him, which appeared to be the accepted way of getting his attention. This guy looked a little odd. Rodrigo let boredom make his choice for him.

"Yeah." He put his hands behind his back.

"Didn't you come from Lusia?"

"What does it matter?" Rodrigo clenched his hands. The fat purse hanging on the man's belt made his fingers twitch.

"Trying to be friendly," the guy said. "Only got here myself, we pilgrims need to stick together."

"I'm not a pilgrim." Rodrigo stepped away.

"Then what are you doing here?" The guy moved in front of him again. Rodrigo's fingers stopped twitching. The purse held pennies at most, probably pebbles. The man was beating the bushes for information. Information wrested from an incompetent spy was exactly the thing to take his mind off stealing.

"It seemed like a good idea at the time." Rodrigo said. "Something to do with Imperial guards and stolen items."

"So you are a different kind of pilgrim." The guy gave him a toothy smile. His hair was terrible, leftover dye colouring the skin around his ears. Maybe he was being deliberately obvious in bait.

"I have certainly traveled."

"What is your opinion of this fair city?"

"Do you really expect me to discuss it here on the street?"

The guy pointed back down the road.

"There's a bar kind of thing that way."

Either he had a gang of bullies back there, or an exceptionally bad trainer. Rodrigo had to find out. His sword lay on the bed in his room—just as well, arguments with steel always ended badly.

"Let's go investigate." Rodrigo stepped around the guy and walked, forcing the other to walk between him and the wall. If he was good, the attack would come from the right and he'd be in the way. If he was really good, they would pretend to attack him first to draw Rodrigo in. If he was brilliant, the attack would come from the left, pretend to focus on the guy and Rodrigo would be the poor slob who got caught in the middle, or...

Or they could walk into a boring looking bar and sit at a table. The guy sat with his back to the door even. Rodrigo didn't roll his eyes, barely. He caught the glance to the old looking man in a cloak nursing half a glass of red wine. The young lady with the pilgrim on the other side also had a tell. The pilgrim didn't. *Bet he's gone in five minutes, thinking it's his fault.* Much more like the quality of agents Rodrigo liked to see.

"Wine, barkeep," the guy said, "bring the bottle."

The barkeep looked to be a timid man in an apron. The hidden knives in his boots told a different story.

"This is marvelous," Rodrigo sniffed at the wine, "a seGraine vintage from four, no five years back." He took a sip. "Five years," he nodded to himself.

The guy glowered at him and slugged back a good portion of his glass.

"My name is Kosimo." Rodrigo moved his wine to his left hand to offer his right.

"Jorges." The guy shook Rodrigo's hand.

"Tell me more about your decision to take the boat to this place. I'd heard the boats are very limited."

"Yes." Rodrigo sipped at his wine. "Something about a sickness in the Holy City. I'm deathly afraid of catching the plague."

"The fever here is a strange thing, no one is quite sure how you catch it. I'd be careful though." Jorges took another slug of the wine and Rodrigo winced.

"I'm a beer drinker," Jorges said, "but I haven't found a decent beer place here. I think they're stuck on wine."

Rodrigo swirled the lovely wine in his mouth and counted the number of people and places he'd seen in the last few days selling beer or something looking a lot like it.

"Since you know the wine so well." Jorges peered at Rodrigo over his glass. "Maybe you've heard news the King and Queen were sent off on a pilgrimage for trying to steal a man's wife. Odd country."

"Really?" Rodrigo raised an eyebrow. This story Harald never mentioned. "Are you sure it wasn't for trying to raid from the church's coffers? That's usually the reason for such a penance."

"The bishop and the King were like this." Jorges held up two fingers. "But you know how the church people are about..." he made a rude sign. Rodrigo took a sip of wine to hide the sneer. *Where did they find this guy?*

"Money, everything is about money." Rodrigo swirled the wine a bit and toasted Jorges before taking another sip. Jorges poured more into his glass and knocked it back. Rough drinking even for beer. Now someone who'd recently been on the steppes and forced to drink the fermented milk they brewed there, that's how they'd drink. Jorges was the Emperor's man, or at least someone connected to the Emperor.

"I've heard there are people here from all over the world," Rodrigo said. "I'll bet you could find someone selling macshka here." Jorges choked on his wine and Rodrigo reached around to thump him on the back. The newcomer by the door stiffened. Either incredibly tense, or one of the pack.

"I see you've tasted it." Rodrigo gave a theatrical shudder. "It's not for the faint of heart."

"If they offer it to you, it's an insult to say no."

"I wouldn't think they'd offer the Legions much macshka."

"They do when we're... damn." Jorges blew out his air and let go of his persona. He waved at the others and the three Rodrigo made got up and left the bar. Either the barkeep wasn't in on this or there were more layers to reveal.

"Word is you're traveling with the royal couple," Jorges swirled the wine and sniffed at it. "Too late," he said mournfully. "I've already ruined it."

"The sacrifices one makes for duty," Rodrigo sipped carefully at his wine. He felt fine, and the officer had poured from the same bottle. He'd gamble the wine wasn't drugged. Unless it had something in it to make him gamble, to increase his risk tolerance enough to put his neck in the noose. Aisa could probably tell him which herbs to use.

"Why would I travel with any royal couple?" Rodrigo said. "Unless you think I would rob them?"

"You did say it was always about the money." The guy whose name wasn't Jorges pushed his wine away.

"That was about church and state." Rodrigo tried to look offended. "Not a personal statement of value."

"You are wearing the clothes of the Black Heir," not-Jorges said. "I'd heard he was exiled for theft."

"It isn't quite that simple."

"So now we're even." Not-Jorges smiled.

"I suppose it depends on how you are keeping score." The wine called to him, but Rodrigo put the glass down and slid it away.

"I'm interested in their health," not-Jorges said. "It would be very unhealthy for them to return to their country."

"I suppose you think I can delay them?" Rodrigo pushed the wine further away.

"Take them down the wrong road, leave them in a bad corner of town. It isn't like they are your kind of people."

"And what would be the profit?"

"You would have the gratitude of a very powerful man."

"Powerful men are notoriously fickle."

Not-Jorges tossed his purse on the table. The fat one Rodrigo didn't steal. Not full of coins or pebbles, but gold nuggets, or something trying very hard to be. *Don't bet on it, he expects me to open it to check it out.* If he didn't check it out, he was dead.

"You don't buy a wrong road with gold."

"This is a down payment," not-Jorges leaned back and spread out his arms.

If he didn't pick up damned bag before the guy moved forward ... Rodrigo leaned back and rubbed at his face, then slid down under the table. Jorges shouted and a crossbow bolt blasted through the table. The customer. *Well played.* The guy flipped the table looking for Rodrigo, so Rodrigo stood and tossed the table toward the crossbow. He stayed low and kicked out at not-Jorges' ankles. The man fell on top of Rodrigo, still empty handed. A couple of short punches turned him into dead weight.

Rodrigo heaved to his feet pulling the limp man with him. Crossbow boyfriend didn't have a shot. The knife from the bar almost hummed through the air. Rodrigo caught it and sent it back. The barman ducked and the knife split a barrel top behind the bar. The deluge of cheap wine made a sufficient distraction to let Rodrigo step to the side and dive through the door. A bolt through the door told Rodrigo he'd over estimated the value of his hostage. He left the man on the floor and kicked one cook in the stomach, then caught and returned a thrown knife from the other. From there it was steps to the alley out back, which had to be watched. Rodrigo ran up the tiny steps leading to a room where the real owners of the bar lived. He hoped they were enjoying a bribe and not lying dead beneath the covers of the bed.

He opened a small door in the corner of the apartment and it let into an attic filled with dust and junk. He pulled himself out through a dormer window onto the roof and crawled to the end of the roof. It dropped a little to the next roof. Shapes in the shadows hinted at watchers waiting for him.

How many people to pull this off? Not too many or it would be blown. Ten was the usual special unit squad. Thieves and spies like him, but they practiced murder instead of poetry. Five in the bar, one front, one back, one on each roof going each way. Where would he put the tenth? What was the highest point? What looked like a tower stood two roofs down. A long shot, but possible. Rodrigo rolled hard to the side and the arrow skipped off the roofing tiles and over into the street.

Screams and shouts, the shadow moved toward him. Rodrigo lay on the roof sloped toward the street. What was on the other side? He ran up the roof and rolled over the ridgepole. This side was flatter. A good jump to the next roof. If he missed and hung, he'd be skewered for sure.

Rodrigo pushed himself up and sprinted to the edge. As he took off, the bells sounded. A wild laugh erupted out of him as he landed and rolled on the next roof. This house had a light well. He kept rolling across the roof and over the edge of the light well. He got his feet down to land on a balcony that gave a creak and started to tilt. Rodrigo dove through the door and landed in the midst of a gathering of women who shouted at him, grabbing sticks and brooms to hit him. He turned and went out the door, adjusting his jump at the last minute to miss the wreckage.

His roll this time took him under a bush. The women still yelled as they poured through the garden, past him and through the next house. He waited and let his breathing slow. The women came back and walked straight through the garden and into the house again. The streets were quiet. Rodrigo stayed in his spot. He wasn't dressed for sneaking around in the daytime. Night was his time.

Special units weren't known for giving up. As darkness fell, Rodrigo let the map of the area play out in his head. The tower was good for daytime, but not much use at night. He'd have a couple of people on each street, maybe someone on the roof.

He crawled out and slipped through the door the woman had used to chase to the street. Narrow, hardly wider than the alley he'd jumped; it had doors and gates up and down its length. Perfect for hiding and watching. So he hid and watched.

Few people used this street for all the doors, maybe it was another back alley. The people who did walk along it held up lanterns. Rodrigo didn't look at the light, but past it. His watcher, there, a leg briefly illuminated as the lantern swung. Rodrigo slid back until the walkers passed his door. He waited until he could see the hint of leg again. It moved.

Rodrigo groped around in the dark until he found something light enough to throw. Then he found another. Clay pots waiting to be used. The first one he threw in a high arcing throw as someone carrying a lantern walked between the positions. The lantern bearers turned to look at the noise and discovered the watcher looking as well. Rodrigo rolled from his doorway to one across the way. He didn't stop, but moved through the dim light to discover a hallway. The watcher had finished his discussion with the lantern bearers and returned to his spot. Sloppy, he should have changed places.

Footsteps echoed on the road. Boots rather than the soft slippers the people here wore.

He understood a few of the words they exchanged. Enough to know the watcher was being sent to report, and not happy about it either. Boots snuggled into the hidey hole and the watcher walked off. Rodrigo loped down the hall. Always soft soles in the city, even if they did get dirty faster. He jumped over a bed with a sleeping man and rolled out the window. Boots couldn't see this way because of the way he sat. Rodrigo followed the special unit legionnaire to where his squad hid. They were in a shed down near the docks. One of the few not reeking of fish. Rodrigo waited to spot the guards. Two, so if there were two people in the shed there were six people out looking for him.

The shed and the guards stood on a board walk above what? Rodrigo climbed down to investigate. He tied a cloth around his face to block the smell that hit him with physical force. His boots would never be the same after this. He crept along in the mud until he could hear the conversation in the shed.

"... we aren't paid to fail. We are expected to produce results. If our bosses don't get the bodies they are looking for, they'll start thinking about making us into corpses."

"Where's he going to go in this place? We'll pick him up in the daylight."

"No," the first voice said, "we're dealing with the waggoner Black Heir. This is who he is. Thieving and spying are in his blood, even more than the rest. We won't set eyes on him except for luck."

"So do we set up on the King?"

"Tanai reported he'd entered the Fevered City. That's the center of the sickness they have in this hell hole. People who live here, they steal something, or kill someone, they get sick, then they start attacking whoever is closest like they were beasts. But I'm not taking any chances the curse will land on us. The Holy Father isn't one of our friends. Tanai is watching, if he leaves we'll be on him."

"Too bad his woman went up to the Holy Father's palace. Grabbing her would have made life easier."

"She's part waggoner, raised in the haven of witches the Emperor wants to expunge from the earth. She'd curse you as soon as spit on you."

"She couldn't curse me if I--"

"Start thinking with this head." A slap made told Rodrigo what the commander meant.

Another soldier came in.

"Nothing at his house but more black clothes and a sword. We left everything. Ronlo is keeping watch."

"Good, I'd be surprised if he was foolish enough to return, but more than one man has died trying to retrieve a favourite sword.

If he hasn't returned by dark tomorrow, close it up and bring whatever is there here to me."

The soldiers left and soon snores floated down from the shed above. Rodrigo had to investigate the slight crack of light running against the grain of the board above him. He found a trapdoor opening down. Smugglers had built the shed then; Rodrigo understood smugglers. The bolts were not hard to pull. Someone kept them oiled. The snoring should have shaken the shed to pieces, but Rodrigo lowered the trapdoor slowly until it hung silent on its hinges.

He hoisted himself up with much care and took stock of the shed. The commander lay on a pallet along one side. A chair and a table stood on the other side. The man's sword belt hung on one of the chairs and a pair of boots stood under it. It took a matter of seconds for Rodrigo to get both in his hands. He lowered himself back down below the shed, then put the trapdoor back in place with barely enough of the bolt to hold it in place.

He would be far away when the commander fell through the trapdoor, and then realized Rodrigo had stolen his sword. Too bad, he'd like to have watched, but he needed to find Harald and Sarandia. Fevered City didn't sound like a place he wanted to go, so he headed up toward the Holy Father's house. He hated this city, but he remembered the short cuts.

Rodrigo didn't go to the front gate. There was a slim chance they had someone watching for him. He found a wall at the back, but before he climbed it, he stashed the sword safely away. He'd traded his stinking soft boots for the hard ones as soon as he climbed up to the road. This made it a challenge to get over the wall, but the Black Heir enjoyed a challenge.

The other side of the wall was too dark for even him to see. Scents assaulted his nose and in spite of everything he did to prevent it, Rodrigo sneezed. A lantern nearby lit up and an old man peered up at Rodrigo from where he sat on the grass.

"Join me." The old man pointed to the grass beside him. Rodrigo walked over and sat beside him.

"What do you intend climbing into my garden at night?"

"I had to find a priest immediately."

"Either you intend to marry before the girl's father finds you, or you have most grievously sinned."

"Bless me Father, for I think I have sinned, grievously."

"Our sacraments are not to be mocked, Rodrigo, any more than the balance between black and white is a laughing matter for you." The old man looked him in the eyes and Rodrigo was caught.

"If I meant mockery, Holy Father." Rodrigo lowered his eyes. "It is only of my own inability to take anything seriously."

"There is one thing you must take seriously, Black Heir. You know it; though you flee far away your responsibility will find you."

"So Grandmother says."

"You'd do well to listen." He turned the lantern down.

"I would like to hear the story causing the Black Heir to break into the Holy Father's residence in the middle of the night stinking of harbour mud—and wearing, if I'm not mistaken, boots belonging on a Legion Commander's feet."

Rodrigo started with meeting the man on the street and soon had the Holy Father laughing until he cried.

"Oh my," the Holy Father said at the end of the tale. "I haven't laughed like that in quite a while."

"I don't imagine you get much opportunity, being the representative of God on earth and all."

"I'm not quite that," the old man said. "Any more than Grandmother is the incarnation of the balance. Sadly, you are right, and most of what I do does not lead to laughter. Come," he stood up fluidly and waved to Rodrigo. "I'll show you where you can bathe and get clean clothes while yours are washed. You can see Sarandia tomorrow."

"I have this thing with clothes..." Rodrigo waved at his clothes.

"You invaded a priest's home." The Holy Father laughed. "I'll find you something black."

CHAPTER 21

The little girl didn't lead him to the food or the water. She took him to the gate and pointed at the tablet on his chest.

"It is time," she said.

"I didn't know you could talk."

"Warmth at night and company in the day." The girl smiled.

"Well, I'm glad you found me," Harald knelt in front of her. "I would have been lonely these days without you to guide me."

She smiled and put her finger on his forehead.

"Blessed brother."

"That's what they say."

"Believe them."

"I don't feel like a blessed brother."

"You see the humanity others don't."

Harald fell like he'd been hit by a thunderbolt. In his time as King, he'd never given much thought to the people outside of the palace and noble Houses. Marriette showed him his arrogance. This child showed him how blind he had been.

She sat down and held him until he stopped shaking. She touched a finger to his face. "Blessed brother, lesson learned." She put her finger on his chest. "Hope is real. Remember."

"Blessed brother!" a guard came to the gate. "Are you well?"

"I am better than when I came in," Harald said, "but it is time I rejoined the world." He stood and put his hand out to the girl. "Come with me. "

"She can't leave," The guard frowned. "She has no tablet."

Harald broke his tablet in half and gave half to her. She laughed and put the string over her head.

"It's OK," she said, "no trouble."

The guard backed up and bowed to the ground.

"Blessed brother, Successor," The man's voice shook. "I am honoured to serve." He opened the gate. Harald took his shirt, now mostly rags and put it on the girl. She laughed, but let the guard tie a bit of string around her waist to hold it on.

The guard led them away up the hill. People stopped and bowed to them as they passed.

"Why are they bowing?" Harald asked.

"It is welcome for your release from the city, and joy that you have brought this child out with you."

"Not many people leave the Fevered City?"

"Most call it the Fevered City or something like that," the guard said. "Its proper name is City of Death."

"One in a generation." The girl looked up at Harald. "They choose the Successor."

"I chose you?"

"You let me sleep and be warm. You chose." She shook his hand a little.

The arrived at a palatial building at the top of a hill. They walked toward the midpoint between two doors. On the right a tall, grandiose door, carved and covered with gold leaf. The other door was a good solid door, but it had no decoration. It was simply a door. The guard stopped at the point where the path divided.

"Which door do you like?" Harald asked the girl. She pointed to the door on the left, so they walked to the plain door and entered the Holy Father's home with no fanfare. The hall was as plain as the door. The craft work was exquisite, but most people wouldn't notice. They passed several doors, then a bend in the hallway let Harald see further. Sarandia stood waiting and Harald wanted to run to her, but the girl's hand gripped his tighter with each step. He stayed with her as she had stayed with him.

He reached Sarandia, and the priest beside her bowed low like the guard had.

"Sarandia," Harald spoke as if he hadn't been gone a week. "This is my friend..." he didn't know her name, so he looked down at her.

"Lydia," she said.

"This is going to be interesting." An old man who'd been standing behind Sarandia and the priest walked forward and knelt in front of Lydia. "Is it really you?" He looked deep into her eyes and she gazed back.

"Welcome." The old man had tears on his cheeks. "You are looked for."

She giggled and pirouetted.

Harald reached out with thinking and helped the old man up. Lydia took the old man's hand.

"Thank you." She tapped her temple. "Remember." The old man led her away down the hall.

The priest shook himself, then led them away through a nearby door. Harald claimed Sarandia's hand and held on. They came to a room with a bag and a club lying on the floor.

"I will leave you here for a while," the priest said. "No one will disturb you. When you are ready, there are those who would speak to you." He closed the door behind him.

Harald turned Sarandia to face him. He ran a finger down the side of Thuria's face. His daughter didn't wake.

"She sleeps a good while after she's eaten."

Something in her voice, the way she stood, reminded him of the first night they were married.

"When did she eat?" He caressed the sleeping infant's face again.

"Not long ago," Sarandia ran a finger down his side and he shivered. "This is a good look on you." She loosened his pants and let them drop to the floor. "But this is my favourite." She carefully took Thuria from the sling and laid her on a mat beside the mattress. Then she pulled Harald down beside her. "This is familiar," she said, "me still all dressed up and you...." she ran her fingers along his stomach. It didn't take long for her clothes to vanish too.

"Do you think we should?" Harald asked barely able to talk because of what Sarandia was doing.

"He practically ordered us."

Harald gave up talking and concentrated on getting reunited with his wife.

***

"So there is a special unit with orders to kill you," Rodrigo said. "Those guys take their orders seriously. The odd thing was at first they wanted me to delay you as if there were something they didn't want you to interrupt."

"Treachery," Harald clenched his jaw.

"You don't think your Regent would make a play for the throne?" Rodrigo asked. "You've been gone a while and absent Kings have been replaced before."

"I was all but ordered to make Marriette my Regent." Harald played with the club in his hands. "I would stake my life she is loyal."

"You might have to," Rodrigo looked sharply at him. "The only way to know what is going on is to get into the middle of it. Do you have a spy master you can communicate through?"

"He doesn't so much communicate as show up and hint at vague conspiracies. I don't know why I keep him around. He was my father's choice and I had no one to replace him."

"I'll bet he's all mysterious too."

"He loves secret passages. He never uses the hallways if he doesn't need to."

"So in essence he's useless." Rodrigo stood up and began pacing. "How are we going to get back as fast as we need to?"

"Maybe we take a ship," Harald said. "The council wanted me to take a ship in the first place, but the Archbishop wanted me to walk."

"You think the Archbishop is a player?" Rodrigo turned and looked ready to suggest they stop the conversation.

"No, he's not blind to politics, but he doesn't dabble. That's why he had authority to set my penance."

A knock at the door interrupted them. Harald's hand tightened on the club.

"Come in."

The Holy Father walked in and Harald put the club behind him.

"Come," the Holy Father said, "I must speak with you."

He led them to a garden and sat on a bench.

"Pardon an old man." He sighed and rubbed his knees. "I cannot walk and plot like I used to. I needed to let you know about some news I've heard from Belandria. The Archbishop died some months back. Apparently, he fell down some stairs. The acting Archbishop is one of those who've sold themselves to the Emperor in exchange for power. He could be behind some of the discord spreading in Bellopolis. I plan to act strongly to put him in his place, but it will be easier with you back on your throne with a firm hand on the country."

"I may not have much time to get home," Harald said, "I've heard there is a price on my head and Imperial soldiers looking for me. They have my signet ring, so they could announce my death. It would mean civil war. Only the possibility of my return will keep the council loyal. Torrance will be the sole man she can trust."

"I can arrange to get you home faster than walking or the usual ship, but it is no place for a young woman or a baby. I will follow in a more substantial vessel and bring your lovely wife with me. We will not be far behind you."

"I hate to say this." Rodrigo shifted his feet, "but your city is not secure. If we try to get to the docks, they will kill us."

"I may be able to help with that." The Holy Father pushed himself to his feet. "Let's go and find Sarandia and Lydia—they have made a deep bond—but do not speak of our plans. Even here there are ears for the Emperor."

***

Sarandia played with Lydia by one of the fountains in the gardens. A gaggle of priests stood and watched. Their faces showed they weren't sure what to make of this little girl in their midst. Harald thanked God he still had Sarandia at his side.

"What is so special about Lydia?" Harald asked, "All the people are nervous around her."

"She's the Successor," the Holy Father said, "when the time is right, she will replace me and become the Holy Mother. Many years ago, I walked out of the City of Death with only my name. I wandered the world learning what I could of God's people before I became a priest and began training to take this job.

"It has been a very long time since we had a Holy Mother, but there is something else interesting about her." The Holy Father nudged Rodrigo. "Wouldn't you agree she is Rehego?"

"She does have the look." Rodrigo studied the girl carefully. "But it is difficult to tell without certain tests I'm not prepared to administer here."

The Holy Father nodded and walked up to where Lydia played. She ran to the Holy Father and hugged him though she was soaking wet. He smiled and hugged her back.

"I would like to go with Sarandia when she returns home."

"If they will have you," the Holy Father said, "that would be an excellent place for you."

Sarandia nodded and stretched her hand to Lydia. She too got a wet hug, then Harald.

"I'm thinking we'll have a big mass to celebrate the safe arrival of Belandria's King in the Holy City and the completion of his pilgrimage." He stretched a hand to Sarandia and Lydia. "Let's see what we have for you to wear." The priests followed, still with frowns on their faces.

***

Harald woke as a hand shook his shoulder.

"It is time," the Holy Father said.

Harald woke Sarandia.

"I must go," he whispered. "I will see you, Thuria, and Lydia at home, but I need to make it safe for you."

"I will be OK," Sarandia kissed him. "God go with you."

Harald dressed then grabbed his club and hung it at his side. Rodrigo was up and dressed in the hallway. The Holy Father handed them long robes.

"These are for brothers who have taken a vow of silence. Do not speak while you wear them and keep the hoods pulled down, thus." He pulled the hoods down so Harald could hardly see past them.

A priest Harald hadn't met yet led them out of the buildings and through a tiny gate in the wall. They walked a direct route down toward the docks. The few people who were out and about walked past as if the three men were invisible. Their guide turned aside from the main docks and they walked almost out of the city. The sky was beginning to lighten as they reached a church, then walked past it down a path to the sea. The crunch of feet on the ground warned there were people behind them. A tiny low-slung ship bobbed at the end of the dock.

Harald and Rodrigo climbed aboard and were followed by four figures in the same robes as they wore. One pointed to a bench and the pair sat. In minutes, they'd set sail and skimmed across the water.

If they were travelling all the way to Belandria in this ship, Harald was glad Sarandia remained with the Holy Father. It had so little room they would probably spend the trip on the bench.

In spite of the wind, a mist formed and surrounded them. Rodrigo shrugged slightly.

Harald tapped a message on Rodrigo's arm.

Not traveling alone.

I'm always nervous when God shows up. Rodrigo replied. One of the brothers looked at them and shook his head slightly. Harald nodded.

Once they were away from land, a brother pointed them to a tiny berth at the front of the ship. There were two hammocks slung there. Harald fell into one and closed his eyes. As always, he was in God's hands.

CHAPTER 22

T he bar bustled tonight. Joan sat in the corner with Sam. She reassured Catrin nightly that he wasn't a suitor but his company was pleasant.

"What's wrong?" Joan waved a hand in front of his face. "You keep wandering away from our conversation."

"Work, sometimes it is tough." Sam took her hand for a moment. "Do you trust me?"

"I suppose I do now," Joan said. "What is going on?"

"It is going to look like I'm betraying you in a second." Sam took his hand away from hers. "It's OK if you hate me. It will look better."

Catrin walked into the bar and Joan waved her over. Sam stood up, but instead of helping her to sit, he gripped her arm tightly.

"Catrin," he said loudly enough to cut through the noise in the bar. "I'm arresting you on the charge of corruption and sedition. You will be held for trial in front of the King."

Joan wondered if it were possible to die from her heart breaking. Catrin looked at her with wide eyes, but Joan couldn't say anything.

Three men stood up and approached Sam.

"This is a church matter," they said, "we will take custody of this girl. She is an abomination."

"She is charged with the highest offense." Sam waved them back. "She stays in the King's custody."

"The King isn't here, fool. We insist."

"So do I." Six men stood and gathered around Sam and his prisoner. "When the King has dispensed justice, she will be released to you." He and his men walked out of the bar. The three church men walked toward Joan, but Suze stepped out of the shadows and stood between Joan and the men.

"No, you will not take her."

One of them looked at her in armour and holding her staff. He shook his head and they left.

"Pack your gear." Suze pointed up the stairs. "We're leaving. I've seen that look before. They'll be back with a bigger crowd."

Joan ran upstairs. She and Catrin had made themselves very comfortable. No way they'd be able to take it all safely. She put on her practice leathers and threw a loose skirt and blouse over them. Money went in an interior pocket, other necessities in a bag. She ran downstairs.

"Watch the rooms for me," she said to the innkeeper. "I will pay what I have been if you keep my goods safe. Don't fight over it though. If they show you steel, let them do what they will, and I will have an accounting later."

Suze led her out into the streets and they walked rapidly away from the inn. Two men peeled themselves away from the wall and followed them. They wove through the streets until they reached a section called the warren. Suze slipped away while Joan tried to sound like two people walking. There were a couple of smacks, then soft thuds. She walked back to where Suze stood over two unconscious men.

"What do we do with them?" Suze asked.

"Bring them with us." Joan frowned down at them. "If they want to arrest us, we might as well give them reason."

Suze found a cell of their staff cohorts and the men were carried away to be placed in a room until things sorted themselves out. Suze and Joan walked deeper into the warren before being welcomed into a home with a basement exit into the sewers.

"Put everyone on alert," Joan ordered her hosts. "It may be tomorrow, or it may be a month away, but trouble is coming."

***

"Trouble is coming whether we want it or not," reTaggin banged on the table. "We need a real King on the throne."

"I suppose you expect to be handed the throne," suDarche sneered. "Without an heir we all have equal claim."

"No, you don't." Marriette spoke coldly as she could. "I am the Regent and the King's heir. This falls to me." She picked up the signet ring lying on the table in front of her and put it on her finger. "We wait the length of mourning before we think of a coronation service."

"He's dead." Raspin almost sounded like he was trying to comfort her. "Harald wouldn't give up his Signet until his last breath."

"Yet Marshal stands hale behind me," Marriette pointed behind her. "He told me no matter what happened to the binding, he wouldn't survive the King's death."

"We don't know for sure," seGraine said. "It is grievous to need to talk about this but we must have a solid ruler on the throne."

"I will not consider it until the days of mourning have passed."

"If we declare mourning for the King, we will have panic in the streets," reTaggin scowled at her.

The others nodded their assent. Marriette looked at the empty seat where Torrance once sat. Their pretend split became a real one as they couldn't reasonably sleep together if they were fighting.

"When my babe is born. We will do what we need to do." Marriette stood, ending the meeting. She stretched to ease the tightness in her back, then Marshal walked her back to her rooms.

"You cannot hold them off much longer, and the long days are not good for you."

Marshal took his post outside her room while she met her maids. They undressed her and Illandria made her lie on the bed while she rubbed her back.

"You have a welcome visitor," Illandria whispered to Marriette before leaving the rooms.

"Hello, my love," Torrance grinned at her and brushed a cobweb from his hair. "If Tiron could use the passages then so could I. I have a much better purpose than he." He kissed her on the back of her neck. His warmth beside her reminded her of the early platonic days of their marriage. She slept better than she had in days.

She woke alone in the bed, but the memory of her company made her smile. The smile vanished when she tried to move.

"Uggh," she moaned, "is it always this awkward?"

"For some," Halonde said, "for others not."

"Helpful."

They dressed her in the tents called gowns. After she ate she swept out into the hall.

The apprentice stepped out behind her as she walked toward the Great Hall. Even in her extreme pregnancy, Marriette wanted to show up in the Hall. Courtiers were scarce, but the hall hummed with the conversations of the commoners who crowded the seats around the edge. Giving away toys had the unexpected result of making her a populist Regent. The Council eyed her suspiciously, but the people loved her unreservedly, making the Council more suspicious.

Sier Calighi strolled in with his guard. He sauntered toward her, but turned aside when Marshal stepped out onto the dais beside her.

"Expect trouble," Marshal spoke so his words wouldn't carry past her ears.

"What kind?" She worked to keep a face that looked like she was ordering tea instead of imagining assassination attempts.

"The church is roused," he said, "It appears one of your investigators arrested a person they were interested in. They want her back."

"It sounds like they never had her in the first place. Who is this dangerous individual?"

"Catrin, Joan's maid, and according to the Church she has led Lady Joan into a sin only the Church can cleanse."

"What did my investigator charge her with?"

"Corruption and sedition," Marshal said, "Capital offenses a ruling monarch must preside over."

"So until the King returns -"

"Or the crown sits on your head."

"So, she is safe, if uncomfortable." Marriette nodded slightly, still scanning the room

A few minor disputes came forward and Marriette disposed of them quickly. She had about decided she was done for the morning when the doors slammed open and acting Archbishop Velogoa stormed in with several priests at his side.

"Majesty," he said when he came close enough to speak without shouting. "You must release that woman to me immediately."

"No." Marriette cut off the one word answer. She would have laughed at the man's face if it weren't so serious.

"I am the Archbishop," he proclaimed loudly enough his words echoed through the Hall. His face turned red and blotchy as he spoke. "Disobey the Church and we will put your Kingdom under the ban." Panicked murmurs ran through the assembly. Marriette was sure the sword in the floor in front of her vibrated. Maybe it shared her anger.

"You can't." Marriette stared at him wishing her eyes held crossbows. "You are not the Archbishop, not until the Holy Father has confirmed your appointment, and only the Holy Father can place a country under the ban." She raised her voice to be heard in the furthest corners. "We will not allow a person under detention for such serious charges to be released under any circumstances."

"If I am not the Archbishop, you are not the Queen," the man shouted.

"Not yet." She leaned forward and spoke quietly to him. "If you do not calm yourself, we will have you removed. It is not pleasurable to us to see such venom in the representative of the church."

"If you remove me, you will never be Queen."

"Even so," she said, "tread lightly."

"We will find this Lady Joan, and then we will know the truth."

"Perhaps." Marriette sat up straighter. "Or you will put the words you'd have her speak into her mouth. Your anger causes us to mistrust your interest in this case. Even more reason to withhold our prisoner." She stood up and walked away. Marshal fell in beside her while the apprentice stood between her and Velogoa.

"Dangerous," Marshal murmured, "he didn't get placed here by accident."

"He wants to use Catrin to get to Joan, then he thinks he can use Joan to get to me. Place an extra guard on Catrin. Make sure he is loyal to me; I want no missing prisoners. Find this investigator and send him to me."

"Yes, your Majesty." He nodded at a couple of guards nearby and they ran off to do her bidding. Heady stuff having grown men run at her command. She pushed away temptation.

Marshal sat her in the chair in the sparring room. Minutes later a young man stepped in, still breathing hard from running. He knelt on the floor and breathed slowly.

"The investigator." Marshal nodded at him.

Marriette waited until he recovered before speaking.

"Explain yourself."

"Majesty." He kept his head down. "The Church may or may not have a case, but their aim is not the purity of the nobility, but the subjugation of Lady Joan."

"And how do you figure this?"

"There are many, many women like Lady Joan; the Church acts on this case for political gain."

"Clearly." Marriette tapped her leg. "We wish to know how you came to understand this truth and acted ahead of them."

"I have been investigating the Archbishop's death," the young man said. "It seemed altogether too convenient he should die just as Velogoa arrived on the scene. The convention to choose a successor was called in haste with many missing from its ranks. More concerning is he's been adding to the Church Guard."

"He has the right to the Church Guard."

"Why has it doubled or tripled since he took the seat of the Archbishop?"

"Do you know where Lady Joan may be?"

"No, your Majesty."

"If you hear of her whereabouts," Marriette said, "you are not to speak of it to me except in great need. I do not wish to lie to a man of the Church, even such a one as Bishop Velogoa."

"If she is with Suze, she will be safe enough. Suze as much as ran the estate before Joan came. She is a force to be reckoned with."

"We shall hope so," Marriette leaned back and bit off a groan. "What is your name, Investigator?"

"Sam, your Majesty."

"You have done well," she said. "When you leave this place put on a discontented face and grumble about people who do not understand the need for such a charge or the delay in its trial. Keep your ears open and obey Marshal in all things. You will report to him or whom he designates."

"Your Majesty," Sam bowed lower, even as he kneeled, then stood and walked backwards from the room.

"What do you think?" Marriette looked over at Marshal.

"Young and untried, yet he may do."

"We may spill the blood of the best of us before we're done." Marriette fidgeted trying to get comfortable. "The Bishop does not act alone in this. Did you observe Sier Calighi?"

"He seemed his usual self," Marshal said, "not quite rude enough to thrash."

"He didn't jump when the door banged, though all around him did. He is involved in this. The Empire is moving against us. I have nothing to strike at until I know who is involved in this treachery."

"The ring came to us by messenger from the Emperor." Marshal looking at the ring on her hand. "He gave his condolences and invited himself to the coronation."

"Whose, I wonder? If he travels only a little slower than this ring, we don't have much time. What have you learned from who approaches Torrance?"

"Not much," Marshal crossed his arms. "The usual jostling between houses, but nothing I can point at and say 'treason', nor has Torrance reported any attempt to recruit him."

"Which is to say their plans are complete enough to not need him. Keep watch," Marriette took a deep breath to calm herself. "There is treason in our Council. I would not like it to catch us unawares."

"We must make plans for your safety in event of violence."

"I fear violence is certain, and safety will be hard to find. I must be available to direct any action needed."

"With all due respect, Majesty, you are not a General. Once rebellion starts the defense will be in the hands of General Kouza."

"Are we sure General Kouza will side with the regency?"

"You won't find a man with a greater loyalty to Belandria and the throne. He worked his way up during Harald's father's reign, but Harald did well to post him at the Port. He has the garrison there in top notch shape, but he is hours away."

"What reason can we give to have him and some of his men come to the barracks here? I don't want to precipitate the very fight we are trying to prevent."

"I don't like the man we have in the barracks here. He is solid as a rock and about as smart."

"What if we promote him and send him to the Port? I'll ask the General to come and advise me on some issue and we'll have him in the city able to respond quickly."

"It could work."

***

Major Huntson wore his dress uniform though the city was buried in snow by a late winter storm. Marriette smiled at him and his honour guard as they stood at attention in front of the throne.

"Major," Marriette said, "We are pleased with the exceptional handling of the barracks in the city. Reports state the soldiers are well trained and content."

"A little too content, your Majesty." The Major bowed briefly. "We sent some squads out to help with clearing the streets and to check that the citizens have heat, so grumbling should return to healthy levels."

"Thank you, we are glad to know our people are well cared for."

He bowed and waited for her to speak again.

"With the reports of unrest in the Empire, and suDarche's gloomy predictions of invasion, we feel the need to seek our General's advice. We ask you and your staff to take command of the Garrison at the Port so the General may be given leave to offer his advice."

"It would be my pleasure." The Major bowed again, deeper this time.

"We would give you the acting rank of General," Marriette said, "to keep the lines of command clear. You will report to General Kouza or the throne."

A page stepped forward with a General's insignia and Marriette asked Marshal to fasten it on the Major's uniform. She should do it herself, but the throne trapped her and it wasn't dignified for the Regent to waddle across the Hall. The now General Huntson looked very pleased.

When he was done, Marshal handed the man his orders and a sealed letter with General Kouza's orders.

"I will not disappoint you, your Majesty." He bowed again and marched out with his honour guard behind him.

Marriette got up and left. Every day got harder. Her body ached in ways she'd never imagined before. Still she was pleased. She'd begun their counter plot. She hoped it would be enough.

The rest of the day she spent answering questions and justifying her actions. No more than she expected from a Council used to her doing nothing to upset the balance.

At the end of the next day's Court, Bishop Velogoa stepped forward and bowed.

"I offer my apologies, my zeal and concern for our people made me impertinent."

Marriette nodded, but she wasn't going to commit herself to anything until she knew what he planned.

"May I speak to you privately?"

"You may approach." Marshal stepped up beside her.

The Bishop didn't like Marshal's proximity, but Marriette didn't plan on walking anywhere except back to her rooms and a bath.

"It occurs to me if you were properly crowned as Queen, you could try the young woman, then turn her over to us.

"If she is guilty," Marriette met Velogoa's eyes. "she will be executed. If innocent, I would be troubled to immediately hand her over to be tried again. Assuming I am willing to take the throne simply in order to try one young woman, however dubious the Church may find her habits." She leaned back in the throne. *Damn, this chair is uncomfortable.* "You may go, Bishop Velogoa."

He went, but the sound of teeth grinding told her he wasn't happy.

"Is Catrin really so important?" she asked Marshal as they walked in the direction of her bath.

"If the Church got their hands on Joan, what would you do?"

"She's my friend, Marshal, but I know my power stops at the cathedral doors. They will not control me through threats to those I care about."

"It is easy to say now, when your friend is not in the stocks." Marshal said.

"Is it wrong to pray someone not be found by the Church?"

"With that Bishop, many people will be lifting such prayers to heaven." Marshal opened the door to her rooms to usher her in, but to her shock he staggered through the door and fell to his knees.

CHAPTER 23

"Go fetch the Doctor," Marriette ordered the apprentice.

"No," Marshal pushed himself to his feet. "I'm alright. It was the shock of the binding returning." He looked at Marriette and grinned. "He's back—whatever separated us is gone." He went still for a long moment. "King Harald has landed outside the Port and is making his way here. He warns of treachery."

"How long until he gets here?" the apprentice asked.

"He's traveling hard, but on foot." Marshall still looking inward.

"Go." Marriette pointed out the door. "Don't let anyone see you, make sure the King gets back here safely. Bring him in so no one sees. We don't want to force the rebellion."

"Your Majesty." Marshal bowed then ran through the secret door.

"Stay outside the door." Marriette said to the apprentice. "No one comes in or out."

"Yes, your Majesty," he stepped outside and exchanged some brief words with the guards. One took station beside him while the other headed off down the hall.

Marriette closed the door and dropped into her chair. Illandria came, put her tea on a table and took her slippers.

"Shall I run your bath, your Majesty?"

"No, Illandria." Marriette sighed. She'd love a bath. "The King will be here soon. I must be ready."

"Where is Marshal?" Illandria asked.

"He has gone to the King on my orders."

"You are vulnerable, your Majesty," Illandria's brow creased in thought. "If it is learned the King is returning the plotters will move now. I will be back momentarily." She ran into the room and through the door into the maids' quarters. Halonde and one of the other special maids, as Marriette thought of them, returned with her.

"I've sent for your husband, and such warnings as I thought wise to others. You are as safe here as anywhere else in the palace." Illandria knelt and rubbed Marriette's feet. "If we must move, we will move with speed. Rest now so you will be ready."

Marriette let her head lean back and closed her eyes. She tried to imagine life without the burden of the throne. She found it as hard to picture as life without the huge belly making her slow and awkward.

***

Marshal hated the secret passages, but he knew them well. They were part of his training. He ran through the walls of the palace as the binding gave him renewed strength. A small stable stood at the back of the palace; a very few people knew it existed. He readied a

202

horse and headed off through the city. His instinct was to gallop madly toward his King, but galloping men attracted attention. Unfortunately, General Kouza hadn't made it to the City yet. He would be the man to put a stop to this treachery.

Marshal spotted the tail as he left the city. At least one man. If there was one, there were probably a dozen. No one would send one man against Marshal. All too likely at least one of the others had a bow. Marshal couldn't lead them to the King. The only reason they hadn't taken him already was to find the King.

At least one of the guards at the Regent's door was a traitor. Marshal hoped his apprentice stayed sharp. Marshal left the city. He had an idea in mind of where he wanted to confront the traitorous scum who followed him.

The road ran long and straight to the southwest and Marshal gave the horse its head. He needed some space for what he planned. The cold air blew past and sucked heat from his body. Stupid not to have prepared better.

He reached the bend by a copse of trees he'd been aiming for. No side road split off within an hour's ride. The followers wouldn't be too close behind. Marshal stopped and jumped off the horse. He used a blanket from the saddle bags, sticks and leaves from the trees to make a dummy to set on the horse.

This horse was one of few extraordinarily trained horses. It looked like a mediocre horse, but Marshal had given it more than a few tricks. He used one now. His cloak and hat went on the dummy. It wouldn't look a lot like him, but it should be enough. Then he sent the horse along the road walking with a limp as if it had gone lame, explaining the slow pace and forcing the followers to bunch up.

He hid in the trees and waited.

***

The entire Garrison gathered in the center plaza to watch the transfer of command and to see their new General. Kouza introduced him to the people who knew the Garrison intimately, then the next day assembled a squad and marched off to the City.

Now, General Huntson sat in his office down the hall from General Kouza's office and tried to figure out what he should do next. Probably call a staff meeting. He would have called an aide to gather the staff, but they were all busy passing on word of the new command. He stood up and walked to his window to look out. Kouza's window faced into the Garrison, but Huntson wanted the view of the harbour.

The view didn't disappoint. He could see ships at the wharfs unloading and loading. Even in winter the commerce continued, but at a slower pace. Not all ship owners cared to risk their ships and cargo to the rare winter storms.

That made it strange when a flotilla of ships floated into the harbour. As they passed other ships, Huntson could see how large they were. Big enough to carry a few hundred men each. There were enough ships to hold at least a legion. Worse, the lead ship flew the Imperial flag.

"Hey," Huntson yelled into the hall. "I need someone now."

A sergeant appeared and looked out the window. He cursed, which made Huntson nervous.

"Rouse the troops," Huntson ordered. "Ships that big won't be able to land at just any dock. Find out where they'll land and meet them with whatever people you can put together in a hurry. Don't let them land, short of starting a war."

The sergeant vanished, yelling orders as he ran. As the aides returned, Huntson sent them out again. He wanted the Garrison armed and shut up. They blocked the road to the City and he wasn't about to let a legion march toward Bellopolis.

"I need a message to suDarche," he told one of the aides. "I want him to bring his new ships around to block the exit from the Port. We'll have to keep them busy until he gets here."

"Ready, sir." The sergeant returned faster than Huntson thought possible. He followed the man out of the Garrison at the head of two hundred men, some of whom were still fastening buckles as they marched. The walk warmed him up and gave him a chance to plan. The dock they were headed toward was owned by an Imperial shipping company, but was not diplomatic land. He could walk in and take over without worrying about a war, yet.

The people at the dock were as shocked by the arrival of the ships as Huntson. His soldiers rounded them up and protectively locked them in a warehouse for the moment. He lined the men up on the dock and waited. A boat separated from the huge lead ship and two sailors rowed a man to the dock.

"Welcome to Belandria," Huntson said when the man had climbed up to the dock. "May I ask your business here?"

"The Emperor wishes to visit and see his sister's coronation," the man said.

"There is no coronation planned. The Regent waits for her King to return." Huntson gave the man his best frown.

"King Harald is not returning," the man said. "We found his signet ring on the goods table of a known thief. We hung the thief and sent the ring to you with the Emperor's message of regret."

"I know nothing of this," Huntson stood straighter. "I have no orders to allow you to land."

"Orders?" The man looked shocked. "This is the Emperor himself. You don't get orders to let him land, you get out of his way."

"I have no orders to allow you to land," General Huntson said again. "So you will not land until I have orders."

The Imperial man started to bluster but General Huntson waved him away. The little boat rowed away again back to the enormous ship.

"Are you sure this is the only dock they can land at?" he asked the sergeant.

"It is the one part of the harbour with enough draft for them to tie up."

"What if they try to use boats to come ashore?"

"Can you imagine how long it would take to get a legion ashore on rowboats?"

"Good, but I want every able-bodied man in the Port with whatever they can carry guarding every possible place they could land so much as a dingy." Huntson pulled his cloak tighter against the cold wind. "Let's see who they send next."

***

The wind blew colder with his horse carrying away his cloak, but Marshal didn't expect he'd have long to wait. As the lead horse of the group rounded the bend, then pulled back, the others almost piled into the first soldier. In the moment of confusion Marshal attacked.

Rumours abounded of what Marshal training entailed. Some was weapons, but most of it involved training him to hold nothing back. Failure meant death, so failure could not be allowed without him dying first.

He unhorsed a soldier at the back of the group and snapped his neck before he hit the ground. The second and third to die took knives to the throat. A fourth man took a knife to the eye, but the fifth moved a little and instead of a silent blade to the throat it hit his cheek. The man shouted as he fell and the battle was on.

Marshal had a short blade sword in each hand. He stayed close in between the riders where it would be hard to attack him without hitting each other. He didn't worry about silence anymore and sliced into legs and backs.

It wasn't a fair fight. The rest of the soldiers lay cooling in the snow in seconds. One man galloped away toward the city. Marshal took a bow from a horse nearby and sent three arrows into the fleeing man. Since the horse beside him was as good as any, he mounted it and grabbed reins from another. It didn't take long to catch up to his decoy horse and retrieve his cloak and hat. He left the dummy for now. He didn't want to take the time to remove it.

The traitors were moving. Too late to worry he should have stayed with Marriette. The important thing was getting the King to the palace secretly and quickly. The binding tugged at him and he let the horses run to warm up. He was going to his King. It was what he was meant to do.

Marshal rode for a few hours until the binding pulled him away from the road toward the sea. Harald was close. There was someone with him, someone the King trusted, but not Sarandia. It was like he'd had hands over his ears all these months. He trotted along the trail until two figures appeared in the distance. King Harald pointed up the trail and waved. The other man shrugged.

"Marriette is well guarded?" King Harald asked as soon as Marshal arrived. He grabbed a horse and mounted. The other man jumped up on the horse without using the stirrups.

"Show off," Harald snorted. "Marshal, this is my companion, Rodrigo." *Trust* the scout language said on his arm, though Harald stood nowhere near him.

"I got your message," Marshal drank in the sight of his King. "But I was well on my way and she is surrounded by the Queen's maids."

"Let's get back and roust out some traitors then," Harald set his horse to walking back along the trail.

"Where is the Queen?"

"She is traveling in more comfortable circumstances," Harald said over his shoulder. "The Holy Father didn't think the ship we were on suitable for a mother and baby."

"It wasn't suitable for us," Rodrigo said.

"Baby? Congratulations, your Majesty."

"Yeah, we didn't realize until we were on the road or we'd have taken a different route."

"And likely died for it." Rodrigo shrugged. "Those special squad soldiers didn't know about any baby. They were set to hunt you early on."

"The Emperor?" Marshal asked.

"Or someone maneuvering close to him," Harald said. "Rodrigo didn't hear where the orders came from.'

"The ambassador and this new Bishop are almost certainly part of the plotting." Marshal tried to keep his dispassionate tone, but failed.

"The Holy Father doesn't like him; the man is in for an unpleasant surprise."

"The challenge your Majesty, is we haven't isolated the traitor yet. suDarche has new ships, seGraine is deep into selling goods to the Empire, reTaggin is massively in debt to Empire money lenders. Raspin is a competent manager, but he loathes the Regent. Torrance is the one House noble I trust, and even he is up to something. I get the impression Marriette is in on it. They've been playing at fighting to take some pressure off him and see who tries to recruit him. Nobody's taken the bait."

"The move is far enough along they don't need him," Harald frowned. "Let's hope we're not too late. If a whisper gets out I'm back, they'll move now or back off. I'm not happy with either option. I don't like the idea of a traitor in my Council."

"I'll get you into the City and the Palace. Then we'll see." Marshal led them off the trail and headed toward the city. When they arrived at the scene of the squad's destruction, Marshal frowned. He counted the bodies and cursed. "Majesty, in my rush to get to you, I got careless. One lived and headed toward the City. If he caught a horse, he'll be there by now."

"We'd best ride hard then." Harald leaned forward. "He will not know how close I am. We may beat them yet."

***

The soft thud woke Marriette. Master Tiron held a bloody knife and stood up from where he'd checked to see the woman on the floor was dead. Blood pooled beneath her.

"Foolish woman tried to stop me," Master Tiron said. "Women are good for one thing. They should not presume to rise above their place."

"Guards!" Marriette shouted. She couldn't see who had died for her. The lights were dimmed probably because she slept. "Guards!' She shouted again, but didn't think it would do any good.

"I own the guards." Master Tiron sneered at her. "They will be no help for you. I should be amazed at how oblivious you are to how many people want you dead, but you are a female."

"You're the traitor." Marriette tried to push herself to her feet

"Ha!" Master Tiron pointed the knife at her. "I'm one of a crowd. You are surrounded by traitors. Not one person wants you on the throne. Even your beloved husband consorts with that perverted Lady to supplant you. Marshal abandoned you without a second thought. You've served your purpose, now you're discarded as a pawn."

Marriette lunged to her feet. She wouldn't face death sitting down. The tiniest of motions caught her attention. The lever on the wall moved. She needed time.

"So what do you get from this?" She moved around behind the chair. "You're not noble, you have no hope of power."

"What do I need with the throne, when I have the King's ear?" Master Tiron waved his knife a little. "You don't understand. With a little push here, or tug there, I can make the King do anything."

"Torrance is right," she said, "you are a liar."

He moved to circle around the chair, but she moved back. He didn't move quickly. Torrance should have arrived by now.

"If you are wondering where you husband is," Master Tiron laughed at her. "I'm sure the guards have sent him off on a wild chase, maybe you went to the laundry again. You should have stayed there." He kept approaching, herding her into a corner.

Master Tiron must have heard something. He spun quickly to the open secret door, transferred his knife into his left hand and drew his sword. Torrance stepped out of the passage.

"Treachery!' Marriette screamed and threw the closest thing at hand at Master Tiron. The man dodged it until he saw the hideous stuffed toy. Marriette kept throwing things until Torrance got his sword out and ready. He didn't look as comfortable with the weapon as Tiron. His motions were awkward and barely parried Tiron's blows. Tiron didn't bother with dodging the animals. Marriette reached for the tea service.

The tea pot hit Tiron square on the side of the head. He staggered slightly, but still parried Torrance's thrust. Torrance jumped back as Tiron counter attacked. Tiron threw his knife at Marriette, but she already held the tray and the knife clanged off it. She threw the tray at Tiron. He stepped to the side and put his foot on the frog/knight toy and lost his balance for a second, long enough for Torrance to step in and run him through the heart. Master Tiron dropped the sword and fell to the floor as Torrance pulled the sword out. Marriette bent down and picked up the knife. Torrance ran over and helped her back up.

"We must go," Torrance took her hand. "The palace is in an uproar. There are rumours the King is back, that you are claiming the throne, that you have the army ready to stop the King."

"So if I call up the army," Marriette snarled, "it will be evidence of my treachery."

"We go through the secret passages," Torrance pulled her toward the door. "The guards on your door were not the usual ones.

"They are Tiron's men."

"Where are your maids?"

"One is dead," Marriette went over to the woman. Not one of the maids Marriette knew well. "This isn't Illandria or Halonde, but she is one of their group."

"We can't wait. I'm sure someone will come looking for you soon." Torrance took Marriette's arm and led her to the passage. "It is narrow, but you will be fine. We don't have far to go."

Scuffling noises came from the passage and Torrance pulled Marriete back and put her behind him. Illandria and Halonde came out of the passage.

"The exits are being watched," Illandria reported as Halonde examined the other maid and Tiron. "We barely got away without being caught. The passages are a trap."

"We can't stay here," Torrance looked around.

"The sparring room," Marriette said. "There are no passages there and it is defensible."

"We'll need to go through the halls." Illandria looked at her steadily. "There is fighting in the palace and it is hard to know who is fighting for which side."

"The guards on the door have been bought." Marriette pointed to them. "We must deal with them."

"Let me." Halonde said.

She opened the door and murmured something Marriette couldn't hear. The guards laughed coarsely and followed her back into the room. They saw Marriette and looked puzzled for a second, but then Halonde's knife went up through one's armpit, while Illandria's knife struck the second guard in the eye. The woman recovered their weapons then led Marriette and Torrance into the hall.

Screams of anger and pain echoed through the palace. Swearing and clashing weapons sounded behind them. Illandria and Halonde prowled on either side of Marriette. Torrance led her with one arm while he held his sword with the other.

A group of guards saw her and shouted, but another group attacked and the fight moved away from them. Marriette saw the door of the sparring room. It wasn't guarded, but right now that was a good thing. They'd have no idea where the guard stood.

Another shout came from behind them and running feet.

"Hurry, in the room and lock the door."

Illandria pushed Marriette through the door into the sparring room. The apprentice stood in the center of the room.

"I'm glad you're safe," he said. "I was lured away on a pretext. Forgive me, I should have been at your side."

"You're here now," Marriette said. "How about you go help Torrance fight the traitor guards."

"You mistake me, Majesty. I'm not glad you're alive. I'm glad I get to kill you." He lunged at her with a feral grin. His knife hit the leather armor and punched through. The pain impaled Marriette as he pushed her against the wall. "Now you die, and a real King will take the throne."

The white-hot pain in her belly pushed further in as he leaned on the knife. His face contorted with hate. How had so many come to hate her? The baby kicked and Marriette shared the pain as the knife cut her child. She slammed the knife she still carried into his throat and twisted it.

The apprentice tried to say something more, but blood poured from his mouth and throat. The door opened behind him and Torrance came through the door.

"Marriette, it is--' His face went white and he rushed to her side.

"Leave the knife." Marriette whispered. "You may hurt the babe."

Illandria followed Torrance into the room. Halonde leaned against the door with her hand on a bloody wound on her arm.

212

Marriette grabbed Torrance's shirt.

"Rouse the city," she said, "We must stop the violence. I will not die knowing I've failed so utterly. Tell them the King returns and they must be prepared to fight for him."

"How do I get out?" Torrance asked, his face crying out how much he wanted to stay at her side. "All the doors are watched."

"The cells," Marriette squeezed his arm. "There is an exit there. Easier going down than up. Go."

"I'll stay with her," Halonde made a sign to her partner. "Illandria, go with him. He'll need your help to get out."

Torrance and Illandria ran out the door. Marriette touched the knife sticking out of her and let tears run down her face.

"Sorry, little one," she whispered. "I'm so sorry."

CHAPTER 24

Torrance dashed down the hall with Illandria. His leg ached with the effort. The angel had healed his fatal wound and at the same time reduced much of the weakness in his bad leg. It still hurt and made him awkward, although not as much so as Marriette with a knife in her.

No one guarded the door to the cells.

"If we can go out through the cells, someone can come in," Torrance said.

"Nothing we can do about it now." Illandria dragged him along.

The two guards from the other side of the door lay in a bloody heap.

"Invaders," one said with a groan. "Dressed as palace guards. Accents."

"The Legionnaires in the city." Torrance cursed and Illandria glanced at him.

"If there were five hundred soldiers in here, we would be dead already."

"Some of them then, and we've got to stop the rest."

They ran down the stairs. Torrance expected to meet soldiers coming up, but they didn't see anything until they got to the cells. The investigator, Sam stood in the hall with a drawn sword.

"I can't let you go. There is treachery in the palace. I heard them pass while I questioned the prisoner."

"The question is whether you are part of the treachery or not," Torrance lifted his sword.

"He's just confused," a girl's voice came from one of the cells.

"Quiet, Catrin." Sam didn't look away from Torrance.

"Sam," the girl said, "you arrested me to protect me and Lady Joan. Don't you think it would be a good idea to listen to what I have to say?"

"Lady Joan is involved in this." He scowled. "Why else would she hide out in the City?"

"She's hiding because there are people trying to arrest her to use her against the Regent."

"But what has she been doing? Not inspecting schools. None of them remember seeing her, only Torrance. You've been arguing with the Regent." He lifted his sword to point it at Torrance. "What is going on?"

"The Regent asked Lady Joan and her friend Suze to train a citizen militia," Torrance lowered his sword, Illandria stood ready at his side. "She suspected rebellion and wanted a loyal force."

Sam lowered his sword.

"Training a militia is treason."

"Not if they all take oaths of loyalty to the throne. The men who came through here were provocateurs. There is the better part of a Legion out there waiting to join the fight."

"You think you can stop the Legion?" Sam asked.

"Not me," Torrance smiled coldly, "but twenty thousand citizens can."

"Go." Sam waved to the exit. "Quickly, before I change my mind."

Torrance ran down the hall to the gate where prisoners were brought in or out of the palace. He saw no one on guard so he darted across the street and ran to a house Joan told him housed one of their people.

"It's time," Torrance closed the kitchen door behind him. "We need to rouse the city. I want to surround the palace so no one gets in or out. We are going to lock down the city. I don't want to kill anyone, but if they try to get past us, we'll have no choice." The man and the woman looked at each other and nodded at Torrance. They grabbed the staves leaning against the wall and ran into the street. Torrance followed them as they banged the staves on the cobbles. The clatter echoed through the streets. Citizens poured out their doors with their own staves and added to the sound. Young men ran out to rouse other parts of the city.

The sound of the staves on the cobbles made Torrance's heart pound. It was a primitive noise that roused his anger. He gripped his sword, almost wishing for a foe to fight and kill. He put his sword in its scabbard.

A girl ran back to him.

"There are soldiers coming toward us." She pointed behind her. "They'll be here any minute and they have armour and swords and everything."

"There's a square ahead," one of the men said, "we can trap them there." He ran through the crowd giving orders. The hammering on the cobbles stopped and others dashed off to spread the plan. The man waved Torrance forward. "Let's go see who is marching through our city."

   ***

The admiral sputtering in rage at General Huntson was better dressed than the General. He'd been rowed to the dock in a large boat with a dozen sailors and at least as many soldiers. The General had his archers cover the boat and allowed only the admiral up on the dock.

"That is the Emperor of all the world," the Admiral waved at the fleet behind him, "and you are defying him."

"He can't be the Emperor of the whole world," General Huntson responded politely. "He's not my Emperor and he doesn't give me orders. I've sent a messenger to the palace to request orders. Until I get those orders, you and your Emperor will stay on your ships."

"We will raze this mud-hole you call a city, then we will hang every tenth citizen, and make the rest..."

Huntson didn't give the man time to finish. He waved a hand. The sergeant, along with another big soldier, picked the admiral up and tossed him off the wharf.

"I expect his boat will pick him up." Huntson shook his head. "But his clothes will never be the same."

"Look," the sergeant pointed out past the sea wall. Huntson saw a flotilla of vessels led by four ships of similar design, though smaller than the Emperor's fleet.

"Now we'll see," General Huntson refrained from rubbing his hands. "They won't be able to get out of the harbour, and they can't land."

The boat picked up the admiral and they rowed back to the Emperor's ship. Huntson could hear the words the admiral shouted, carried on the wind; the man had an extensive vocabulary. They were taken back up onto the ship. A small boat was let down and a single man climbed into it and rowed toward the dock.

Huntson signaled to let the man climb up on the dock. He looked to be as old as Huntson and dressed in a very simple white uniform.

"I had to see the man who dared hold up the Emperor of Vandelusia because he didn't have orders." He walked around General Huntson while the men on the dock kept their hands on their swords.

"To be perfectly honest," the man said, "I needed to get off that damned boat. There is a reason I don't travel by ship. It does terrible things for discipline when one's Emperor is puking over the side of the ship."

"What do you want here?" General Huntson stood at attention. "No one comes for a friendly visit with ten ships and a Legion on them."

The man laughed and shook his head.

"This is a small part of my navy, and the men who are on board are my personal guard. If we were invading, you would see ships from here to the horizon." He pointed out and stopped and glared at Huntson. "What are those ships doing out there?"

"I asked them to come. I don't want you getting around my back and flanking me."

"We'd crush them and hardly notice."

"I've been watching how difficult it is for your ships to maneuver in the harbour," General Huntson allowed himself to smile slightly. "I wonder how well you would do if the harbour was blocked."

"We can land and burn this town down around your ears. The Legion on those ships are the finest fighting force in the world."

"Which is why they are going to stay on the boats. If you try to land, we will fight."

"Then you will die," the Emperor glared at him.

"Everybody dies," the General said, "even Emperors."

"You have four hours."

The Emperor turned and stomped back to his boat and rowed toward the ships.

"Evacuate the Port," General Huntson ordered his men. "All women and children in the Garrison or in the country past it. Men of fighting age will stay in the Garrison to aid in the defense. All soldiers not visible on the dock will retreat to the Garrison and secure it for defense. If we make it back, I will command. Otherwise, you know the chain of command in this place better than I do. Tell them they are in charge."

His aides carried his orders to the men. Huntson didn't turn as boots clomped on wood, then stone, as the men he'd brought left him behind with perhaps twenty other soldiers.

He'd never fought a real war. In battles against bandits and some skirmishes with the people to the south, he thought he'd done well. Yet he was better at administration than fighting. There was a flurry of activity on the ships.

"They're coming soon," the sergeant said, "forget the four hours. Should we hold here or retreat to the Garrison?"

"There are still people in the Port who need to get to safety," Huntson checked his sword. "We stay and draw the fight."

"Sir," the sergeant saluted. "You've impressed the hell out of me today. An honour to serve you."

"Thank you, Sergeant," General Huntson returned the salute. "If we get through this, remind me to buy you a drink."

"Yes, sir."

The wind picked up and the General's face ached, but he faced into it and waited for death to come.

***

Joan heard the commotion in the streets and ran out with Suze.

"We're called to protect the palace," the young girl shouted, hardly out of breath even after running across the city. "The King is coming home."

"Block the streets," Joan ordered, "No fighting unless you're given no choice. Give people a chance to surrender, but don't take any chances. Anyone who's not carrying a staff stays in their homes. I will have no riots and no looting."

"We've got the palace covered." Suze put a hand on her shoulder. "We need to find the King if he's close enough to get here. He may be the one chance to stop a civil war."

"Father didn't cart much to suDarches's estates," Joan said, "but when he did send wagons, he used a small road going south before turning east."

"You think the King will come up that way?"

"If he's coming in secret, he won't come in through the Port. He had to have landed in one of the small harbours south of the city. The fastest way from there to here is on that road."

They walked rapidly through the city. Joan ordered the people as she went. Mostly she told them to block the streets and not let anyone pass. Some people wanted to find a fight while others looked at their staff like they couldn't understand how it got into their hand. Joan kept waiting to reach the part of the city where the training hadn't reached yet. They didn't find it. Well-to-do or poverty stricken, every neighbourhood crowded with people holding staves and ready to defend their country.

"What have I done?" Joan asked after she'd given orders to a group of merchants, a street sweeper and handful of young women. They were commanded by a fearsome woman who ran a school for young children. "These people will never let themselves be pushed around again."

"Good."

"But there will be fights and it is illegal to arm a non-noble."

"We didn't arm them. We taught them. They found their own staves. This could make Belandria the strongest kingdom on earth. If every single person knows how to fight, and when not to fight, no army can beat us."

"I hope we don't need to put it to the test." Joan sighed and pointed to the next road. "There's the road." She slowed to a walk as a man on a horse galloped toward them.

Suze hit Joan so she stumbled to one side. She caught her balance and turned back. The horseman had a sword in his hand now and rode straight at Suze, Joan wanted to yell something, advice, a warning, but everything happened too fast.

The soldier leaned out from his horse to get a better angle to attack, but Suze flipped her staff in a tight circle, then ducked under the sword, but slid the staff up so it crossed his chest. A couple of quick steps and Suze let the force of the staff hitting the horseman carry her up. She grabbed the neck of his shirt and pulled him off the horse. Suze landed on her feet, the man landed on his back. His sword spun across the cobbles as his horse continued without him.

"Now," Joan pointed her staff at his face, "you will tell us what you are doing."

"The Marshal murdered us," the man said, "I'm after getting some justice when the Emperor gets here." He coughed, and then couldn't stop coughing. Seconds later he lay dead on the street.

"Look," Suze nudged him with her toe. "Knife wound. That's tough against a man on horse."

"He said *murdered us*."

"If anyone was meant for mayhem, it is your Marshal."

Joan found a spot where she could watch the road leading to the sea.

"So we know he's coming this way." Joan pointed at the road. "But we don't know if he'll be here in time."

They settled into corners to get out of the wind and waited. Joan decided to give up several times, but never moved. Partly because she was so stiff, and partly because Suze looked like she could wait forever.

Three horses appeared on the road and Joan pushed herself to walk to the middle of the road. As soon as she recognized the King, she went to one knee and waited with her head down.

"A welcoming committee," the man who was neither the King or Marshal said, "how quaint."

"Quiet, Rodrigo," the King held his hand up. "Loyalty is to be honoured wherever we find it."

"You are right," Rodrigo said. There was no sound of him dismounting, but a warm cloak wrapped around her shoulders. Her stomach stopped fluttering.

"Rise, Lady Joan, and give an account."

"Your Majesty." Joan spoke after Rodrigo helped her get to her feet. "The palace is in confusion. Armed men disguised as your guards are fighting with your loyal guard and staff. We have roused the city in your defense, but it may be difficult for you to move through the crowds. It only takes one man and we are without a King again."

"I am most interested in how you roused the city," the King said, "but we have no time to talk. I must get to the palace."

"The palace is closed and guarded." Joan pushed back the despair.

"If you get us to a certain building close to the palace," Marshal said, "I can take it from there."

"I hope you don't have sensitive noses." Joan sighed and waved to Suze. "The best way to travel quickly now is through the sewer."

"Lead on," the King said. "Time grows short."

Joan led them into the city until they got to one of the houses with the trapdoors to the sewers. She and Suze had spent a lot of time exploring. The horses were left in the back and the five of them climbed down into the sewer. Joan picked up a lantern and led them away.

"I would never have imagined complaining about a source of warmth," Rodrigo put his hand up to his face.

"Bundle your cloaks up and we'll carry them in the packs," Joan said, "If we need to go out into the streets, you'll want them."

The sewers were brick lined and tall enough for Joan to walk comfortably. Marshal had to bend over constantly. Rodrigo didn't need to, but he crouched anyway. Harald ducked under the low spots. Joan followed the marks left by generations of people paid to clean the sewers and took them straight toward the palace.

They reached a space with four sewers coming in one from each direction. The Marshal nodded and ducked into one tunnel without pausing. The King and Rodrigo followed with Joan and Suze after them. Marshal set a harder pace than Joan and she had to work to keep up. She almost ran into Rodrigo.

"We climb up here," Marshal whispered, "and we'll come up in the cells. It is going to get dangerous from here on."

"We're with you." Joan set her face. "Everything we've done has been to assure the King's safe return. We're not turning back now."

"Your staffs are appreciated. I will signal when it is safe." Marshal climbed up the ladder and pushed the rock up on hinges. He jumped up and through the hole before it the trapdoor crashed to the floor. Words floated down, then the clanging of swords. A second later a man fell through the hole and crunched on the floor. He wore the uniform of the palace guard.

"Some signal." Rodrigo climbed up the ladder. "I like this guy."

They gathered in the cells. Men in uniform were sprawled about the hallway.

All the cells were empty.

"The staircase is probably held against us," Marshal said. "We will need to take the other way in. I need oaths you will never speak of what you see. This route can only be opened by the Bound in aid of the King." He put his hand over a stone in the wall and a faint glow answered from the stone. Marshal pushed the wall and it swung away like it was weightless. He lifted a lantern from a shelf and led them into the passage. The wall closed behind them.

CHAPTER 25

"**Q**ueen's woman," Grandmother said from the cell, "I must go to the Regent."

"She is beyond even your skill." Illandria pushed the sadness away. "She may even now be dead."

"Will you argue, or will you take me to her?" Grandmother pushed her cell door open. Illandria laughed at Sam's expression.

"No door will hold the Rehego Grandmother if she doesn't will it." Grandmother walked out. "Bring the girl and come. This will not be safe much longer."

Sam opened Catrin's cell and brought her out. Grandmother led them up the stairs to the hallway. Illandria slipped forward and put her ear to the door.

"Nothing, let's go." She opened the door and scanned the hallway as Grandmother, Sam and Catrin joined her. "This way."

Sounds of violence came through doors or from around corners, but no one came near them. The door to the sparring room was closed. Illandria knocked on it and Halonde opened it for them. The Regent's face was dead white and the slightest movement betrayed her breath. The gown she wore dripped red and a pool of blood lay on the floor.

Grandmother walked in and pointed at a table.

"I need that, here." She pointed to a spot on the floor. "Push the junk off."

Sam swept the swords to the floor, and Illandria helped him move it to where Grandmother indicated.

"Put her on the table." The old woman ordered them. Illandria tried not to see the glow of the woman's hands. Magic made her itchy, one of the main reasons she followed the Queen here years ago.

"Queen's woman," Grandmother said. "Go fetch some clothes for the Regent." She looked at Illandria and the itch of magic made her scratch her scalp.

She left them there with the Regent while she ran to rooms. Stalea's body lay crumpled in the corner. The poor girl had been the youngest of them, recruited here in Belandria. The traitor lay sprawled with a shocked look still on his face. Illandria covered the young girl, then the magic forced her to the wardrobe with Marriette's dresses. Illandria didn't think about what she took, trusting to the magic to choose rightly. She ran back to the sparring room. No one moved in the palace. Either the invaders had been pushed back or they had taken over and the servants fled.

Marriette lay on the table with her clothes cut away. Catrin sponged blood from the woman. While Grandmother hummed over her, Sam knelt beside Halonde and bound up her arm.

"I need your strength, Queen's woman," Grandmother said. Illandria put the clothing where it would stay clean and walked over to Grandmother. She put her hand on the old woman's shoulder and almost fainted.

"Halonde, I need our sisters, whoever you can round up." Halonde nodded and ran out the door. Illandria set herself to stand. Her hand and arm itched unmercifully. She balled her hand into a fist and refused to scratch.

A short time later one of the Queen's maids arrived. She put her hand on Illandria's. Another one came and another until four of them gathered around the old woman. Halonde returned and took her place.

"It is enough to hold her here," Grandmother said, "but I need more to do what I need to do. We must wait." Footsteps ran past the door. People shouted in anger or fear. Swords clashed. None of it mattered. only holding on.

One of the maids gave a sigh and fell to the floor. Sam rushed over and pulled her to the side. Illiandria could barely spare a glance to see whether her chest rose and fell yet.

A while later another fell and Sam pulled her away too, her face grey.

A third fell soon after. Grandmother's humming made Illandria itch worse. Her whole body screamed at her, but she held on. Halonde fell next. The tramp of feet came through the door and harsh voices yelled orders.

The fourth fell without a sound. She lay boneless and unmoving as Sam pulled her aside. Illandria knew she would be next. There wasn't much left in her.

A small hand lay on top of hers and Catrin looked at Illandria with fear and determination.

    ***

Torrance walked out into the square and waited. The street behind him was packed with citizens holding staves. Other streets meeting the square were also full.

"Let's run a double line around the outside of the square." Torrance pointed. "Everyone stand at ready. We need them to know we are serious." The sounds of marching got louder until the head of the column marched into the square.

Sier Calaghi walked behind the first few rows of soldiers. It was a large square, but with five hundred Legion soldiers and at least twice that many citizens it felt crowded.

"Halt," came the order from the Legion. Sier Calaghi sauntered forward.

"We have been called to put down a riot." he said. "If you do not move, I will decide you are the riot."

Torrance made a hand signal and the man beside him spun his staff and planted it on the cobbles. Immediately a thousand other staves spun and crashed against the cobbles. Sier Calaghi stepped back into the column.

"I have been called by the proper ruler of this Kingdom to quell a riot." He yelled again.

"The proper ruler of this kingdom lies dying by treachery," Torrance called back. "There is one aside from her who could be titled ruler, and he is not here."

"He is dead!" Sier Calaghi's face turned pink. "He died in Lucia like a beggar while being robbed of everything he owned."

"He is on his way," Torrance shouted so everyone could hear, "alive despite your treachery. Marshal went to meet him at the Regent's order." A rustle ran through the people.

"Lies!" Sier Calaghi was red now. "From the husband of the woman who would seize the throne as her own. We will pass. If you force us we will march on your corpses."

"I've heard it said the Legion soldiers are each worth four other soldiers." Torrance signaled and the staves crashed again. "But are they worth ten others, or twenty?" With each number the staves crashed. The noise rolled like thunder as people lining the streets of the City spun and slammed their staves against the cobbles. The Legion didn't move, but Sier Calaghi winced with each clash.

"Reinforcements are on their way." A voice in the column yelled an order and the column became a square. "We will wait, and then you will all die."

"I'm not sure the Emperor will be impressed with being given control over a wasteland," Torrance said. "I am sure every man, woman and child in this city and throughout the land will fight to their last breath against invasion by the Empire." The staves roared one more time then the city fell silent.

Torrance stepped back into the crowd and stayed warm. He almost wished the Legion had attacked. Then he'd have died and this pain would be done. Marriette's last wish was for him to rouse the city to protect their home. He wouldn't die until his work was complete.

He hated what the Regency had done to his beloved Marriette, even as he admired the woman forged in the flames. He let the tears flow down his face. Someone else would have to pick up the pieces, his life had broken beyond repair.

Shadows crept across the square. The Legion never moved. The men may as well have been carved from stone. How did a few ragtag people with sticks hold these men in place? They'd conquered every land they set their eyes on—all except for the Queen's country. How could Belandria hold out?

A new wave of sound approached. Torrance tried to figure it out, but the wind tore it apart and he heard fragments. As it slowly got closer he made out cheering and clashing staves. It didn't sound like battle, but as it got closer he heard the tramp of feet. Maybe what he took for cheers were screams and the noise of death.

The people in the street behind the Legion moved into the square and started banging their staves together. The others in the square did the same thing until the square was the centre of a maelstrom of noise.

Torrance saw the man at the head of the column and laughed despite his heartache. He lifted a hand and the noise stopped. He wondered if he'd gone deaf.

"The reinforcements have arrived," Torrance spoke into the quiet, "but I doubt they are who you were looking for."

General Kouza stood at the front of a column of soldiers. Movement on the roofs suggested archers were taking their positions.

"Surrender." The General's voice echoed like grinding stone. "Or die and your death will be the embarrassment of your Empire as long as it stands. You were brought here by lies and treachery and will die at the hands of righteous anger."

"We will never surrender." Sier Calaghi screamed, his face now purple. "We'll kill you--"

His shout cut off as the Legion's commander punched him in the gut.

"Drop weapons." The commander shouted. "We will surrender. This is not our fight to die for." He unfastened his sword belt and dropped it to the ground. Immediately five hundred other swords fell to the cobbles and the Legion put their hands on their heads.

"If you gentlemen will follow me," the General said. "We have a comfortable place for you to wait for your return to the Empire." Members of his troop surrounded the Legion and they marched away into the city.

"Secure the streets," Torrance told the men around him. "No one leaves or enters the palace until I say so. We still have traitors about and I don't know who they are."

"Trust us, Lord Torrance." The men saluted with their staves.

Torrance followed the General. He had nothing else to do.

They locked the Legion in the parade ground of the barracks. General Kouza had men go through the Legion taking their oaths they wouldn't attack, before distributing tents, food and drink for the prisoners.

Torrance followed the General up to an office where two men dropped the moaning Sier Calaghi on the floor. They took up positions against the wall.

"You can't treat me this way," Sier Calaghi shouted as soon as the men had stepped away. One man stepped forward, but the General waved him back. "I am the Emperor's own ambassador."

"As far as I am concerned you are an agent of revolution. The Emperor tolerates the work of agents who are successful. I don't believe he is kind to failures."

"I haven't failed." The man pushed himself to his feet. "There will be a new King on the throne and he will deal with you quick enough."

Torrance stepped forward and punched the man in the face sending him to the floor again.

"Now, Lord Torrance," the General said, "don't be hurting your sword hand on rubbish like this." He nodded to the men who picked up Sier Calaghi and held him against the wall. The General handed Torrance a sword.

"He's a spy and deserves death. I don't care if it is your hand or another's that deals it."

Sier Calaghi straightened and glared at Torrance.

"Do your worst," he said, "but it isn't bringing back your precious wife, is it?"

Torrance brought the sword up and examined it closely.

"This is a fine blade. One of your own?"

"I have to admit it is," the General said. "There is a blacksmith in reTaggin's estates who I swear is a wizard with metal."

Torrance moved the sword through the air until it whistled.

"What do the old folks say?" he asked. "A blade sharp enough to cut the North Wind." The sword stopped a finger's width away from Sier Calaghi's eye. The man tried to push himself back into the wall. Torrance pulled it away and handed it back to the General. "I wouldn't gut fish with it, nor will I kill a traitor." He walked up to Sier Calaghi. "I suggest we wrap him in chains and send him back to his Emperor as the first person to lose a Legion in battle in centuries. I'm sure the Emperor will be understanding."

"I can tell you who the traitor is," Sier Calaghi shouted. "I can help you."

"I am going to walk into the palace." Torrance stared into the man's eyes and watched him wilt. "If the person sitting on the throne is neither the rightful King of this land, nor my wife, I will cut them down on the spot, though I may die doing it. I don't need your help."

"Bind him and gag him," General Kouza ordered the men. "I want him alive to give back to the Emperor."

They hauled the prisoner away, when a man ran up to the General.

"Begging your pardon, Sir. I could not gain access to the palace. I need orders. The Emperor wishes to land at the port with his Legion in attendance. General Huntson has forbidden him to land while he awaits command from the palace."

"He's holding back the Emperor?" General Kouza raised his eyebrows. He looked over at Torrance. "How many of your staff waving lunatics are there?"

"Most of the people in the city," Torrance said.

"Good, I want people to line the road between here and the Port. They are to salute the Emperor in whatever impressive, noisy fashion you concoct. Let him march his Legion along a road with tens of thousands of people ready to take them apart. Not even an Emperor messes with my country and gets away with it."

"I'll spread the word," Torrance wrapped his cloak around him and left to go out into the city again. He'd barely gone a hundred steps when a man on a horse thundered past him on the way to the Port. As Torrance spoke to people they followed the horse. Soon people streamed past him as he walked. He waved, but kept walking the direction he started. He would get to the palace, find the man who dared put himself on the throne, then die killing him.

CHAPTER 26

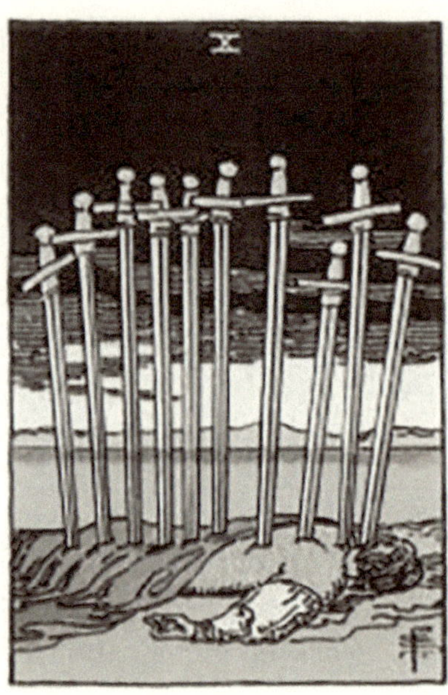

Harald watched Marshal climb up to the trapdoor and unbolt it. It swung down and caught against the wall. Marshal pulled himself up into the room.

"You'd better get up here," he called. "You aren't going to believe this."

Harald climbed up next with Rodrigo on his heels. Joan and Suze were behind him. They were in the sparring room. Marriette lay on the table with an old woman praying over her and another woman leaning against the wall. Marriette had a knife in her swollen belly. Harald let himself be consumed by rage. It might easily have been Sarandia. He pushed the emotions away and walked over to the old woman.

"What may I do to help?" he asked.

"I need your strength if you are willing to give it." The old woman didn't turn around.

Harald put his hand on her shoulder and the two women staggered away and crumpled to the floor. A force gripped him with harder hands than the binding.

"Marshal," Harald reached out his hand. The huge man who served him with his life didn't question, but put his hand in Harald's. The old woman's eyes went wide for a second. Then Rodrigo climbed out of the hole followed by Joan and Suze.

"Son," the old woman said. "I need your help."

"It is forbidden," Rodrigo's voice trembled.

"She lives yet as does the babe, but I can't hold them much longer."

"Very well," Rodrigo walked around to the other side of the table and joined his hands with the old woman's. Their hands glowed until Harald had to look away. The force still pulled at him and the binding sent energy through him from Marshal, but there was more than him and Marshal. Something else was happening, power flowing through him faster and harder. His hands shook but he refused to let go.

The glow filled the room now and pushed against him like rising water. A baby cried and the glow vanished with a snap that brought him to his knees. The women who'd been lying near death on the floor got up and surrounded Marriette before he got to his knees.

"Gentlemen, let's give them some privacy for a moment." Harald climbed down the ladder and leaned against the wall. Rodrigo followed, then Marshal and a man Harald didn't know.

"Who might you be?"

"Sam." The man went to his knees. "Your Majesty."

"Get up, Sam." Harald squeezed his shoulder. "If you are in this company, you have no need of kneeling."

They climbed back up when the old woman called them.

Marriette sat with the babe against her breast in a chair with a cloak thrown over her.

"Sire, forgive me for not rising."

Harald knelt in front of her.

"I must beg your forgiveness; my carelessness has almost cost your death." He looked, still kneeling at the old woman, "Grandmother, you are Rehego, are you not?"

The woman nodded.

"From this moment, the Rehego have the freedom of Belandria. They may wander at will and though they will be held to the law, they will also be held to be honoured guests of our Kingdom."

"I thank you," the old woman said, "but you have work to do before you may offer that welcome."

"She is the Rehego Grandmother," Marriette smiled. "A little like the Emperor and a little like the Holy Father."

"Not much like either," Grandmother said, but she smiled at Marriette.

"So," Harald looked around the room. "We need to take back my kingdom and rid it of traitors."

"They planned the invasion of the palace," Marriette said, "so they might ask the Emperor for aid in quelling the confusion. I am sure they are promised rule over Belandria as a province of the Empire for their efforts."

"So they need to be on the throne to make it work." Harald said. "That is where we will find them, as they wait for their Legion to arrive." He winked at Joan. "I hear it may take longer than they expect for help to come. We'll arm ourselves as we can from this room and go take the throne room."

"They'll have archers in the bays," Marshal said. "I can deal with one or two, but not all eight of them."

"We'll help." Illandria picked up a sword.

"As will we." Joan hoisted her staff, Suze and Catrin nodded, then chose their own staves.

"I'm coming with you," Marriette stood. "I didn't go through this to stand apart at the end." She settled the baby in her arm.

"Let's go," Rodrigo said. "Pity anyone who takes on Grandmother."

"Behave," Grandmother pointed at Rodrigo, but she smiled. Harald could see how an entire people would follow this person to the end.

"Majesty." Marshal turned to him. "I suggest you take the passages to the main entrance of the Hall. We'll clear the bays of archers."

"Hmm," Harald said. "Tap on your hand."

Marshal tapped his fingers on the back of his hand.

"Harder."

"Try using the point of a knife." Rodrigo rolled his eyes. "He can be a bit dense."

Harald felt the point of a knife through the binding.

"Signal when we are clear," Harald said.

"Yes, your Majesty." Marshal loped out of the room, his helpers following. Someone in the hall squeaked and ran the other way.

Marriette swept through the hall heading to her rooms where she could enter the passages. Jeremiah ran out and threw himself at her feet.

"They told me you were dead, Your Majesty, both of you." He looked over at Harald. "They forced me to give them the location for the coronation jewels."

"Thank you." Marriette raised him up. The poor man's face was covered with bruises. "My brave secretary, come with us and see justice done." Harald tried to get her into the passages, but at every step someone from the staff would prostrate themselves in front of Marriette. She seemed to know them all and soon a sizable crowd walked through the halls. They bowed to Harald, but worshipped Marriette. Several men in palace guard uniforms stood outside the door. They moved to block her way and were swarmed by dozens of staff people. Other guards saw, but instead of helping they ran and the mob ran after them shouting and jeering.

Harald didn't think the invaders stood much of a chance. Four knife pricks stung the back of his hand.

He and Rodrigo threw the doors open with as much force as they could muster and Marriette walked into the Hall. People scrambled away from the door. Those gathered around the throne turned and stared.

Marriette walked with as little concern as if she were strolling in a garden. Harald and Rodrigo flanked her, but he didn't think anyone recognized him.

"Kill them!" one of the people around the throne yelled. Harald thought it was seGraine. No arrows flew. A body fell from one of the bays, and landed with a thud. More people screamed and ran for the doors.

"Stay," Marriette's command echoed off the walls and the people froze in place. "We need witnesses for this day." Marriette had reached the space always kept open in front of the throne. The Councillors looked at her like they'd seen a ghost. "Release him," she ordered the men holding Raspin between them. He would have fallen to the floor if Rodrigo hadn't caught him.

"They need a majority of the Council." Raspin gasped, "I would rather you than either of them. I gave my oath."

"And paid dearly in the keeping of it." Marriette touched his face and the swelling faded as he stood a little taller. "My gratitude for your loyalty." She climbed the steps to the throne and sat herself in it. After a smile at her baby, she leveled a glare out into the hall.

"Bishop, you look foolish with that crown in your hand. Put it down, your touch sullies it. SeGraine," she crooked her finger like she would for a naughty child. He walked to her and knelt before her. She slapped him with a crack that resounded through the hall. "You have broken your oath. You are stripped of your House. Any in your House who conspired with you will be exiled. I would have mercy on you, but you tried to kill my child. You will hang as a traitor."

He backed away and would have run, only Rodrigo tripped him and banged his head against the floor.

"ReTaggin," Marriette crooked her finger again.

"I don't know how you're alive, you witch, but I'll never bow to you." He drew his sword and rushed the throne. Harald had his sword out and stood between Marriette and the noble. ReTaggin impaled himself on the sword before he recognized Harald.

Harald cleaned his sword on reTaggin's cloak.

"Orders, Regent?"

"The palace will be cleansed. The invaders will surrender or die. Then we will account for our dead."

Harald took up position behind the throne and stood with his drawn sword. Rodrigo stood on the other.

Raspin put the crown and the coronation jewels back in their box and carried it to Marriette.

Reports came in from different parts of the palace as the invaders were found and either surrendered or died. Men who did well in a surprise attack fell easily to the fury of the mob roaming the palace.

Harald stood and waited and guarded Marriette. He snuck a peek at the baby and thought of Thuria.

***

Torrance walked through the doors of the palace unchallenged. Bodies lay in the halls, some in palace uniform and some dressed as servants. Running feet and slamming doors echoed, but no one stopped him.

He walked to the Hall. One of the doors hung crooked on a broken hinge. The other was open. Tears blurred his vision. That his beloved country should come to this. He would revenge it and his Marriette. He walked through the hall aware of dying whispers and a swell of conversation.

Torrance stopped and wiped the tears from his face. He would need to see clearly for what he needed to do.

"Husband." He heard Marriette's voice. "Come and meet your son."

His head snapped up and he looked at the throne, then ran the rest of the way to bury his face in her lap. He cared little for the buzz of conversation from people whose sole purpose was gossip. His chest ached with the agony of his relief.

I thought you dead," he said when she lifted his face and dried his tears.

"By the grace of God and skill of the Rehego Grandmother, I live and our son too. I would not have my husband kneel to me." She patted the arm of the throne. Torrance sat himself and peered in bemusement at the perfect little being sleeping in Marriette's arms.

"I should tell you." Torrance said after he'd properly inspected his heir. "The Emperor, with his Legion, is on his way."

"Fine, we'll deal with him when he gets here." Marriette flipped her hand. "What shall we name our boy?"

CHAPTER 27

Huntson couldn't tell if his hand was still there or if his face would still move. He'd expected men to pour over the sides of the ships and run across the water at him. Plenty of activity on the ships, but no boats let down or anchors weighed.

Even though he looked to freeze to death, Huntson celebrated each moment nothing happened. It meant that much more time for the Regent to decide how to protect their country. Maybe they'd get four hours after all.

Men were finally lowering the boats when a runner came to Huntson.

"Orders, sir." He saluted. "We are to allow them to land and continue to the City."

Huntson tried very hard to speak, but he couldn't get the words out. The sergeant nodded to him and spoke to the other men.

One ran and fetched a stick with a white cloth on it. They waved it until they saw someone on the ships respond.

Huntson looked to the sea and saw a new ship approaching. This one flew a simple gold circle on a black background for a flag. It sailed up to the wharf and sailors jumped out to make it fast.

An old man walked down the gangplank and nodded at General Huntson.

"The Church thanks you for your welcome," he said.

"My pleasure," Huntson forced the words past his frozen face.

"Come now, you must be freezing. Join me on my ship with your good sergeant and warm up."

"Thank you," General Huntson followed the old man onto the ship with the sergeant at his back.

The heat in the cabin almost put him to sleep. The girl with the baby looked familiar, but he had to concentrate on not embarrassing himself.

"Holy Father," the girl said, "this man needs some warmth in him."

"We have tea." The old man went out for a moment. He came back with a tray with a pot and some chipped mugs. "We used to have better, but we hit some rough weather and all the china got broken."

"I don't mind it rough. The girl is right, I need warmth in me." She laughed and he looked at her again, still feeling he should know who she was. She carried a babe in arms and a young girl sat at her feet. The sergeant accepted a cup and sipped at it, so the General did the same.

"Not to be rude," General Huntson asked when he started feeling warm inside, "but why is the Holy Father here in this weather?"

"I promised your King Harald to return his wife and child."

"Your Majesty!" General Huntson tried to get up to bow. She waved him back into his seat.

"No harm, General Huntson. I hardly recognize myself these days."

A sailor knocked on the door.

"Pardon me, but the Emperor would like a word."

"Certainly," the Holy Father said. "We're having tea. Ask the Emperor to join us."

Minutes later the door opened and the Emperor walked in and sat down across from the Holy Father.

"Hello, Jules," the Holy Father waved at the newcomer. "Cream and no honey, right?"

"Why do you persist in calling me Jules?" The Emperor picked up his cup and sipped at it.

"It is your name," the Holy Father said, "and while you might be the Emperor of Vandelusia, you are not my Emperor."

"What should I call you?" The Emperor looked daggers at the old man.

"Holy Father is a little cumbersome, but it works." The old man smiled at the Emperor over his tea cup.

"Why should I call you Holy Father?" the Emperor asked.

"Am I not? You may corrupt some of those who serve the Church, but you cannot deny my authority."

General Huntson drank his tea, fiercely willing his warming hands not to shake. The tiny cabin trembled with the energy of a storm before a lightning strike.

"I never could win an argument with you." The Emperor leaned back and the danger subsided. He pointed at General Huntson. "What do you call me?"

"As long as my orders permit," General Huntson said, "I will call you Emperor out of courtesy due a visiting ruler."

"And if your orders didn't permit?"

"I would call you enemy."

The thunder in the room focused on him and the General apprehended for a second the immensity of the battle between these men.

"He's got you there, Jules." The Holy Father smiled at General Hunston.

"I would much rather call you friend," General Huntson said.

"Do you have no thought beyond your orders?" The Emperor sipped at his tea.

"Her Majesty, the Regent promoted me because of the way I follow orders," General Huntson replied. "A small delay is preferable to acting incorrectly."

"Hmmmph," the Emperor took another sip. "You kept me *hours* on that ship."

"Admit it, Jules," the Holy Father said. "You are jealous because he is not one of yours."

"If you ever find yourself in need of work," the Emperor turned his gaze away from the General. "I can find you something to do."

***

The incomparable sergeant had organized moving the Holy Father's ship to one side and allowing each Empire ship to land and disgorge its cargo of soldiers. When General Huntson climbed back up to the dock, a large wagon waited for them with seats added for the dignitaries to ride. Blankets were piled in a heap for extra warmth.

"Let's get on our way," the Holy Father said.

"I think I should have my own wagon." The Emperor looked around as if one would appear from thin air.

"Now, now, we'll share the wagon and you can accept all the adulation for yourself." The Holy Father climbed up on the wagon and wrapped a blanket around his shoulders. The young woman with the baby and the girl climbed up beside him with the help of a couple of soldiers. The Emperor stomped his foot and climbed up to sit beside the Holy Father.

"Take a blanket, Jules," the Holy Father held one out. "It will be a cold ride."

"Emperors don't wrap themselves up in blankets."

"I am doubly glad I am no Emperor."

General Huntson clambered up and sat behind the Emperor and the Holy Father, waving for the sergeant to climb up with him.

"Whenever you are ready, Sergeant," Huntson said, "give the order to march."

"I anticipated you wanting an escort for the Emperor and the Holy Father," the sergeant said. "We will pick up half the complement of the Garrison as we march through."

"You are a genius."

A century walked ahead, five abreast. The wagon followed, and the rest of the Legion marched after the wagon. A few faces peered from behind curtains.

"Sergeant," Huntson said, "please pass the word it is safe for the people to return to the Port as we pass the Garrison."

"Yes, Sir."

They stopped at the gates of the Garrison and one of General Huntson's staff did a fine job of ordering the escort out to march with the column of the Legion. They would march on the outside of the column. General Huntson gave the man command of the Garrison while he was gone.

The gates opened and the column marched through. An odd noise came through the gate. When the wagon got under way the cause of the noise became clear.

People lined the road holding staves. As the soldiers passed the sticks were twirled in a complex pattern including taps against the neighbour's staff. When the wagon passed, the staves were grounded with a bang on the cobbles.

"How delightfully martial." The Holy Father grinned and waved at the people.

"I wish they could be a little less forceful." The Emperor rubbed his temples. "I'm getting a headache."

"Sergeant?" General Huntson looked at the man next to him. How had he managed without someone like this?

The sergeant hopped off the wagon and went to speak with someone in the crowd. A ripple traveled from there along the road as far as Huntson could see. Afterwards the staves froze in vertical position a finger's breadth from the cobbles.

The Emperor nodded and pasted a smile on his face.

"How many people do you think are here, General Huntson?" the Holy Father asked.

"It looks like a large part of the city," the General said. "Ten or twenty thousand people?"

The Emperor shuddered while the Holy Father grinned and waved. The people grinned back, but stayed in time. Many of them weren't as proficient as their neighbours, but they all worked hard.

The Legions bragged that one of their soldiers was worth four soldiers of other countries. It would take ten or twenty legions to defeat the people who lined this road. General Huntson stifled the giggles threatening to erupt. His Queen sitting beside the Holy Father turned and winked at him.

Halfway to the city, General Huntson wrapped his cloak around the shoulders of the Emperor and grabbed a blanket for himself. He too was glad he wasn't an emperor.

The people lined the road all the way into the city, then crowded the sides of the streets in the city too. The Legion and the escort had to adjust the order of their march to fit the narrower streets. The last march up to the palace followed a wide boulevard, meaning another change. The Legion shifted flawlessly, and the Emperor's escort kept their pace and their place in the march.

A single man stood waiting for them in the plaza in front of the palace. Huntson recognized Marshal. He knew no one else that big who communicated lethal grace with the simplest movement.

"Welcome, guests," Marshal said.

General Huntson climbed down off the wagon and marched over to Marshal.

"May I present for audience with Her Majesty, the Regent, the Emperor of Vandelusia and the Holy Father with his entourage."

"The Emperor didn't bring any entourage?" Marshal asked quietly.

"He brought a Legion," General Huntson said, "That will have to do."

Marshal's mouth twitched in what might have been a smile. The two old men had been helped off the wagon.

"I need to bring my men with me," the Emperor said as they reached Marshal and General Huntson.

"You bring ten men." Marshal stood like stone. "The others may take their rest out here."

Apparently even Emperors didn't argue with Marshal. General Huntson followed them through the palace.

"My apologies for the state of the Palace," Marshal spoke matter of factly. "We were invaded by disguised soldiers earlier and the staff are still hunting them down. The servants enjoy the exercise, but it does mean little things like removing bodies get left undone."

There were plenty of bodies. Many wore servant's uniforms or palace guard uniforms. Some of those in guard uniforms had the hard edge of a battle tested soldier even in death. In fact, they looked a great deal like the Legion soldiers outside in the plaza.

The General desperately wanted a glimpse of the Emperor's face. They reached the large doors to the Hall. Marshal waved them through as if the doors weren't hanging on broken hinges. The usual hangers on crowded the Hall. The Regent sat on the throne. Was she holding a baby? General Huntson almost stopped to stare. The young woman with the Holy Father smiled broadly as she held the little girl's hand. She bent to point things out to the youngster.

"Greetings, Brother," the Regent said, "you find us a little out of sorts today. We are in the midst of dealing with treachery and a most cowardly attack in our palace. However, some good has come from this day. We have located and will be able to return to you the better part of a Legion which somehow found themselves in our City. They are housed comfortably in the Barracks until you decide to transport them home.

"There is also the small matter of your ambassador who conspired with traitors to claim the throne. We can't imagine he operated under your orders, but you must understand we do not wish him to stay in our Kingdom. I would offer you the sorry excuses for nobles who conspired with him, but it is our custom to deal with traitors quickly. They will hang at sundown."

General Huntson edged his way around the crowd until he could see the Emperor's face. The man was not used to defeat, but Belandria had soundly defeated him. The sergeant's hand on his arm and the tiny shake of his head kept him from dancing in delight.

"I must apologize for the zeal of my people." The Emperor bent his head. "You know how it is when people get carried away."

"We do," the Regent said. "Yet this getting carried away has upset my kingdom, causing the death of many of her loyal subjects. On the other hand, it has revealed weakness in the debt our nobles have. We are afraid we shall have to severely limit the amount of imperial debt any citizen is allowed to incur. It seems the threat of bankruptcy is sufficient cause for some to break their oaths. We must protect our people against temptation."

"If we are to do business," the Emperor looked up at her. "A certain amount of debt is inescapable."

"We are creating a Bank to hold all the debt on behalf of our citizens."

"I am sure the Empire will be delighted to work with your bank." The Emperor shrank a little with each exchange. Huntson was sure the man had expected to march triumphantly into the City and take charge of a new province. "As long as it is clear you have the gold to back your claims."

"Yes, gold." The Regent leaned forward. "What is a fair weregild for the death of my people by treachery? I'm thinking twenty gold coins for each."

"Twenty?" the Emperor shouted. "Are you crazy, woman?"

The growl in the Hall came as much through the pavement as the air. The huge room was more crowded now. People in bloody and torn uniforms stood around the outside and fixed their eyes on the Emperor. It wouldn't take much for them to surge forward and tear the Emperor apart, then destroy the Legion. The cost in lives would be immense, but Huntson didn't doubt the Emperor and the Legion would vanish without a trace.

"I can't allow a lesser amount than twenty-five gold coins." The Emperor's face was white and the men in his honour guard looked worried.

"Your generosity is legendary." The Regent smiled sweetly. A page ran forward with a chair for the Emperor. The page's arm was bandaged, but he moved like he'd never been hurt.

The Emperor fell into the chair.

"Holy Father." The Regent nodded her head. "We welcome your visit, not the least because we find ourselves displeased with the service of Bishop Velogoa who was elected acting Archbishop."

"Ah, my child," the Holy Father said, "it grieves me to see one of the servants of the Church wander so far from their work."

"We still need an Archbishop. We would be pleased to welcome whomever you send."

"You are gracious." The Holy Father nodded his head. "Is there anything else I may aid you in?"

"Curiously," the Regent said, "our laws require an Archbishop to confirm a King in his duties. Perhaps we could create an exception and ask the Holy Father to perform the service?"

"I would be delighted." The Holy Father looked a little shocked when the crown and the other jewels were produced on the spot.

"My people," the Regent handed her baby to her husband who stood at her side. "I was made Regent over you while King Harald fulfilled his penance. It is time for my Regency to end."

One of the guards behind the Regent stepped forward and the General's knees almost buckled, then he deliberately went to his knees.

"Hail, King Harald!" The rustle of people dropping to their knees was drowned out by the shouts of acclamation.

CHAPTER 28

"I am very glad to be Marriette leBraun again." Marriette put her hand to her temples. "The crown fit very uncomfortably on this head."

"It is supposed to be uncomfortable." Harald said. "I must get used to it again, but not too used. I learned much on my travels."

"So, where do we go from here? We can't go back: two Houses giving in to treachery, peasants being sold into slavery to pay their debt."

"Not to mention the people are no longer cowed by the Houses," Torrance leaned back. "Once they realized they had defeated a Legion, our small forces hold no fear for them."

"People shouldn't be ruled by fear." Sarandia put her hand in Harald's. "Fear can become hate very quickly."

"The poor Emperor." Marriette shook her head and grinned. "I almost felt sorry for him."

"We can't let up," Harald said. "He will be a terrible enemy when he decides his defeat was our fault. Taking Belandria will be a point of pride for him."

"General Huntson had some suggestions about making the port more secure," Marriette sipped at her wine and rocked the cradle with her foot. Nikay slept peacefully. The scar on his arm from the apprentice's knife was visible only to the most discerning eye. Thuria sat on the floor and burbled at Harald's crown.

"General Huntson?" Harald raised his eyebrows. "The man who ran the Barracks with an iron rule book for years?"

"The General Huntson who held back a Legion long enough for us to prepare a proper welcome. He has this big sergeant on his staff now. General Kouza released him. It appears General Huntson has taken on the habit of thinking."

"I would be most delighted to hear the thoughts of General Huntson," King Harald rolled the crown for Thuria, who gurgled with delight. "I am going to need to re-meet all my people. Maybe that's good. If we are going to change, we need all the help we can get."

"Joan told me, before she returned north, that she gets a lot of help and advice from a holder's council who meet on the estate you gave her."

"Interesting," Harald looked at Sarandia thoughfully. "We could broaden the Council, add some new voices."

"You need a spy in the Empire," Rodrigo said from the corner. "You can't ignore the Empire any more. If they can get ten ships here, they can get a hundred."

"Are you volunteering?" Harald asked.

"It would give me something to do." Rodrigo shrugged, then grinned wickedly.

"And you could watch your sister," Sarandia said.

"There's that, too," Rodrigo frowned. "I'm not sure whether she or the Emperor is more dangerous."

"There's more activity to the south, too." Harald rubbed his jaw. "We should send some people down there."

"Let Jeremiah keep track of them," Marriette said. "He's proven himself, and perhaps a clerk as a spymaster won't give into temptation as Tiron did."

"I'm willing to give it a try," Harald nodded at her. "But alas, I hear my bed calling me."

Sarandia picked up Thuria and put the crown over her arm while she carried her.

"I will put Thuria to bed with Lydia and the nurse." She pointed a finger at Harald. "Don't you dare fall asleep without me."

"Come." Torrance stood and offered his hand to Marriette. "We have a carriage ride home. Perhaps Nikay will sleep the whole way and we can pull the blinds down." They left hand in hand with Marriette carrying her babe.

***

Rodrigo sat alone and twirled the glass in his hand. It was nice to be in a place where people weren't trying to kill him as a matter of course. He lifted the glass to admire the light through the rich red wine.

He didn't pay any attention to the smash of glass on the floor. His shirt was bright red with blue embroidery. He knew without looking his pants would be a darker blue and a yellow sash wrapped his waist.

He was no longer the Black Heir. Either his sister had died, or his people had decided to follow her. The wine looked like blood on the floor and he shuddered.

ACKNOWLEDGEMENTS

If it takes a village to raise a child, it also takes a community to bring a book into being. The Devil Reversed took almost twenty years to come to print, I never planned to write a sequel, but one day the plot jumped into my head and refused to leave. That's the beginning of the work. After I'd written and rewritten I sent the book out to beta-readers - Jessica Martinez, Anna Boon, Katrina Thiessen-Beasse. Katrina also helped me with the tarot cards to head each chapter, making my life a lot easier.

Krista Burdine is my go to for light edit and proofreading. She's quick, efficient and it helps that she's enthusiastic about books.

The cover designer is Jian Guo from China. A great artist to work with.

OTHER BOOKS BY ALEX

Calliope and the Sea Serpent
Wendigo Whispers
The Devil Reversed
Generation Gap
The Gods Above
Tales of Light and Dark
Like Mushrooms (poetry and photography)
The Heronmaster
Blood and Sparkles, and other stories
Princess of Boring
By the Book
Sarcasm is My Superpower
Playing on Yggdrasil
The Unenchanted Princess

Alex also has stories in:

Song of the Axe
Words on the Rocks
Beyond the Wail
Collidor Stream Collection 2016

Read short stories and excerpts from his novels at alexmcgilvery.com

Alex McGilvery